SHE FELL INTO MY ARMS...

DO I GET TO KEEP HER?

I'm Rowdy Lawrence, the captain of the St. David Devils. We're the worst team of misfits in pro hockey and the most fun you'll have on ice. We thrive on chaos.

Lately though, being the town's favorite son has become a burden. I'm restless and bored. I want more and a job offer at another team is tempting. But I can't imagine ever leaving my hometown.

Until Tressy stumbles into our local bar, dressed in a Cinderella gown and carrying her sweet little girl. She falls into my arms, looks into my eyes and steals my heart. She needs help, but she's not used to asking for it. She's beautiful, fiercely independent and hiding something.

Luckily for her, St. David is the perfect place to lay low. And now I have the time to prove she can trust me. And to prove that the heat between us is real. I just have to convince Tressy to embrace the crazy...

ROWDY HEARTS

ROWDY HEARTS

STEPHANIE JULIAN

MOONLIT NIGHT PUBLISHING

Don't miss Stephanie Julian's other hockey romances:

FAST ICE

Bylines & Blue Lines

Hard Lines & Goal Lines

Deadlines & Red Lines

REDTAILS HOCKEY

The Brick Wall

The Grinder

The Enforcer

The Instigator

The Playboy

The D-Man

The Machine

The Ghost

Join Stephanie Julian's newsletter at her website at

www.stephaniejulian.com.

CHAPTER ONE

owdy

"Listen up, ST-Double-Ds! Season starts tomorrow so what are we gonna do?"

"We're gonna kick some ass!"

"And whose ass are we going to kick?"

"Deer Run Stags ass!"

The cheer went up from the other twenty-two members of the St. David Devils, loud enough to be heard over the blaring jukebox, the old-fashioned kind that played actual vinyl records.

Right now, it blasted Ozzy Osbourne's "Crazy Train," which had been the Double-Ds theme song since the first Devil skated onto the ice fifteen years ago.

"You bet your asses we are!" I shouted over Ozzy's maniacal laughter and the deep bass pumping out of the speakers mounted in all four corners of the Tea Room, which did serve tea but sold a hell of a lot more beer on any given day. Especially the night before the Devils opening game of the season.

Like almost everything in St. David, first impressions were usually deceiving. Or just flat-out wrong.

Raising my glass over my head, I saluted my teammates then downed the rest of my soda, having reached my one-beer limit an hour ago. Around me, a motley crew of players, fans, and support staff filled the bar with raucous laughter and enough f-bombs to get us thrown out of our own game. Tonight was the night to let it all hang out and blow off some steam.

Tomorrow, the show started, and the real work began.

"Hey, old man. We keeping you up past your bedtime?"

Rebel smacked me on the shoulder hard enough to make my muscles groan. Not that I would ever admit it, especially not to my younger brother.

"Watch your back tomorrow night, Jedi." My brother's team nickname was both an insult and a compliment. "I'm just saying, it might not be the other team running you into the boards."

Rebel laughed so hard I thought he might shoot beer out of his nose. "You know you can't do that. Mama still knows how to use her wooden spoon."

I couldn't argue that, so I smacked my younger brother on the back of the head, just hard enough to sting. Rebel was just the slightest bit taller than me, which meant I could hit him just a little harder than I should. Because that was the unwritten rule of brothers.

In retaliation, Rebel elbowed me in the side, taking care not to hit me anywhere that could do damage. Fucking hell, I wasn't that old.

"Boys. Save it for the game tomorrow."

Colonel Reston Lawrence didn't need to raise his voice to be heard over the jukebox. The old man's normal speaking voice was just below a bellow. My spine snapped straight, an automatic response to my pop's voice, which I immediately countered by shoving my hands in my pockets and slouching forward. Goddammit, I was thirty-fucking-years old, and he wasn't my commanding officer. Or anyone's commanding officer, since he'd retired nearly twenty years ago.

Rebel smirked at me before he grinned down at our dad.

"He started it, Pop."

Pop and I exchanged a look before he put an arm around our shoulders and bear-hugged us. And damn, the man was still strong enough at seventy-two to make my bones creak.

"Save it for your mom, boys. She buys all your bullshit. I know better."

Since it was true, I shrugged as he released us, watching with a grin as our dad purposely messed Rebel's dark hair.

"There," Pop said, "Now you look like a real hockey player."

Rebel rolled his eyes, running his fingers through his perfectly cut hair, which annoyingly fell right back into place. The guy looked like he'd just stepped off a photo shoot for some fancy magazine. Hell, even tonight, at a bar in the middle-of-nowhere Pennsylvania, he stood out in black slacks and a perfect white button down amid a sea of henleys and flannel shirts and cargo pants.

"I'm going for Lundquist, not Burns, Pop. Rowdy's got that one covered."

Couldn't argue with that. My own brown hair brushed my shoulders and looked like it hadn't been cut in months. Which it had. I just didn't like it short. I hated having to get it cut every couple of weeks. Besides, women loved to run their fingers through it.

Yeah, and when was the last time that had happened?

Ignoring that smartass inner voice, I watched Rebel grab a bottle of the family's whiskey off the bar, lift it over his head and turn to the rest of the team.

"I think we're gonna have a good year, Pop." I shouted over the cry of "Shots! Shots! Shots!" as Rebel took the bottle to the nearest table and started pouring.

"I think so, too, son." Pop nodded, his gaze skimming over the crowd. "Good group of boys. If we can keep them together." Then his voice dropped until I could barely hear him. "Be a nice way to go out."

I'd heard my dad talk about retiring before, but I didn't believe the old man would ever do it. He loved the game too much. Hell, my entire family loved hockey, even more than we loved the multi-million-dollar whiskey business that enabled us to play hockey.

Decades ago, my granddad had created a craft distillery in central Pennsylvania and, through hard work, determination and a shit-ton of luck, had created a multimillion-dollar business. And when dad had resigned from the Marines and married my mom, he'd made that distillery work for him, until he'd been able to create a hockey league from the ground. The league that kept me, Rebel and our sister Rain gainfully employed.

While Rebel and the team downed their shots, I leaned closer to my dad.

"Fuck that, Pop. You can't leave. What would we do without you?"

My dad's laugh held an edge. "The same thing you've been doing. This is what we've been working toward, son. We've got good people where we need them. And you and Rebel and Rain know what needs to be done. You'll all be fine when I decide to step back."

Guilt slammed into my gut, the phone call I'd gotten a couple days ago weighing on my mind. I hadn't said anything to anyone about that call. Hell, I knew I wasn't going to take the offer, but I still hadn't called my old friend back to turn it down.

My future was here. In St. David. With the Devils. That had always been the plan. For as long as I could remember. I'd play until I couldn't or didn't want to. Then I'd take over so Pop could retire. Maybe I'd coach. Maybe I'd be the general manager.

Maybe you don't want that anymore?

"Shots! Shots! Shots!"

Bullshit. Of course, I wanted it. Just not yet.

I leaned closer to my dad. "Your team needs you, Pop."

My dad glanced at me, shaking his head with a smirk. "They certainly don't need me to give them an excuse to drink."

No, this crew definitely *did not* need an excuse to drink. Or party. Or raise hell.

That's what we were paid to do. To raise hell on the ice. To give our fans the show they'd come to expect. But some of these guys were here because they owed the Colonel their lives. Literally. And they showed him their appreciation in the only way they knew how.

"Shots! Shots! Shots!"

The Colonel gave a wide grin to his team and reached for the nearest shot glass.

"Alright, you mangy lot." Then he turned and bowed to the women of the dance squad, gathered in a group at the end of the bar. "And lovely ladies. Here's to a successful year."

Everyone raised their glasses of whatever they were drinking and called out "Hear, hear." Or "Fuck yeah," depending on who was saying it.

I raised my glass along with everyone else, though mine was empty.

Kinda sad commentary on your life lately.

Goddammit, I needed to shut my brain off and just enjoy the night.

"Rowdy, honey, you look like someone kicked your puppy. What's wrong, babe?"

I turned with a smile for the gorgeous blonde behind me. Sunny Yeakley's smile could light an entire sports arena, and her body gave men of all ages the will to live another day.

"Hey, Sunshine." I curved an arm around her waist and drew her close enough to lay one on her hair. Didn't want to be a dick and muss up her perfect makeup. "Just my resting grump face. Everything's fine."

Her perfectly arched brows rose. "Yeah, not buying that. You can fool a lot of people, but I know you better than most."

Couldn't argue that one. We'd been high school sweethearts. Prom Queen and King. She'd been voted Most Likely to Succeed, and she definitely had. We'd broken up before going to different colleges, but we'd remained friends. Even after she'd married John Yeakley, who ran the distillery for my dad. Smart guy all around and a good friend.

"It's nothing. Just season-opening nerves."

"You don't do nerves." Now she frowned. "What's going on with you?"

Since I couldn't tell her, at least not until I'd turned down that offer, I gave her a grin most women couldn't ignore. Sunny wasn't most women. Her frown deepened.

"You did not just try to use the heart-breaker smile on me. You know that hasn't worked for years."

Yeah, I did. "Honestly, Sunny, there's nothing wrong, Just pre-season jitters."

For a second, I thought she wasn't going to let me off the hook. But there was a reason Sunny had put up with me longer than any other woman. She knew how to handle me.

"Uh huh. I've never known you to have jitters before, but I guess it could be your age. It does creep up on you."

Her grin made heat pool in my gut, but it was a phantom sensation, a ghost of what we'd been to each other years ago.

"That's a low blow, but I know you mean it with love."

Sunny's laughter caught the attention of a couple of the new guys, who looked at her with naked lust. I couldn't blame them, but I pitied them. She adored her nerdy husband and would never give anyone else a second look.

"Absolutely." Then she lowered her voice and leaned in a little closer. "You know if you need anything, I'm here."

"I know, and I appreciate it. But…I'm fine."

Out of the corner of my eye, I saw the front door open. Since the regulars all used the side door to enter, curiosity got the better of me. But someone shifted in front of me just as the door swung inward so all I saw was a flash of bright hair before it disappeared again.

Something made me say, "Hey, be right back," to Sunny as I headed for the door.

With everyone else's attention focused on the team chanting for my dad to do another shot, I was the only one who saw the woman as she stumbled inside, clutching a pile of blankets. I weaved through the crowd but was still only halfway to her before my brain registered the strange way she was moving. Jerky, like there was something wrong with her legs.

I reached her just as she stumbled forward, my arms outstretched to catch her. She cried out hoarsely as she fell, her arms clutching the blankets tighter and her body twisting as if those blankets were precious cargo, and she didn't want to fall on them.

I realized why the second she collided with me.

"Whoa. Hey, I got you," I said as I caught the child she was carrying with one arm and the woman in the other.

A split second later, the woman blinked up at me with big blue eyes, took a deep breath and said, "Oh, thank god," before sagging into my arms in complete exhaustion.

Stunned, my brain went blank for a second before it kicked into high gear. Apart from the show I gave the crowd, I was a damn good hockey player. Though not a great one, as evidenced by my lack of an NHL contract. But I could think fast on my feet, and I was good with my hands.

I swept up the woman and the kid and carried them to the nearest booth. Maneuvering the woman onto the bench, I unwrapped the blanket from the kid in my arms. Dark curly hair, dusky skin and wide green eyes stared back at me.

"Hey there, darling. How are you doing?" I smiled at her, but she just stared back at me with unblinking eyes. "Wow. Tough crowd."

Then the cold of the blanket seeped into my arms. Fuck, I'd forgotten how low the temperature had dropped tonight. They had to be freezing.

"Hang on, sweetheart. Gonna get you warmed up in a sec. Just let me check your momma."

Her gaze slid to the woman slumped over the table with her eyes closed and her chest heaving. I couldn't see her face, but I realized now her blonde hair was swept up in some kind of complicated style on top of her head and studded with diamonds. At least they looked like diamonds. She also wore what looked like diamonds around her neck and a long blue dress with a slit up the side and sequined like she was going to the Oscars.

"What the hell happened to you?"

I didn't really expect her to hear me, so I was shocked when she answered.

"A wr-wrong turn and a fl-flat tire. And my general b-bad l-luck."

Her hoarse voice reminded me she and the girl were freezing.

"Damn, let me get some help."

Finally, she lifted her head, and I blinked. Holy shit. She was fucking gorgeous. A goddess with sapphire-blue eyes, cheek-bones high and sharp, and full lips painted a bright pink.

"I would appreciate that." The woman's voice held a hint of an accent I couldn't place. "Here, I'll take her."

Leaning down, I intended to put the girl next to her mom on the bench, but thin little arms wound around my neck and clung.

I let out an amused huff as my arms tightened. "Guess I'll just take her with me."

"Rowdy, what the— Well, hell. What happened to you, honey?"

Bar owner Mitzi Naugle elbowed me out of the way so she could get to the woman in the booth. And since you didn't get between Mitzi and, well, anything, I moved aside, realizing I'd been replaced by the person who would get shit done.

The blonde opened her mouth to speak, but a shiver wracked her body, and Mitzi switched into mother mode. She'd had a hell of a lot of practice at it, having birthed six of her own kids and mothered most of the town's population of teenagers at one time or another.

"Rowdy, tell the girls to get blankets out of the back room. Then get the doc to come over here. Last I saw, he was striking out with Bets. Again. What's your name, hon?"

I waited until I heard her answer.

"Tressy. Tressy Meyers. My daughter—"

"Is perfectly safe with Rowdy. He's just going to find the doctor to give you a look." Mitzi threw a glance over her shoulder at me, and I got my ass in gear because Mitzi didn't say things twice.

"Okay, pretty girl." I smiled at the kid. "Let's go find that doctor to take a look at you and your mom."

"I'm not just pretty. I'm smart, too."

The girl's voice took me by surprise, and I looked to find her scowling up at me. I started to grin at that absolutely adorable face, surrounded by a mass of dark curls, then pulled it back when I realized she was deadly serious.

"I bet you are. What's your name, sweetheart?"

"I'm not supposed to tell strangers, and you're a stranger."

"Sounds fair. Hold that thought. Hey, Doc. I need you."

I'd made my way to the team doctor, who was talking to a few members of the team. Four large men turned to face me, and the little girl huddled closer, turning her face into my chest.

"Dude, I didn't know you had a kid."

That was from the newest member of the Devils, rookie Reid Wellar, a nineteen-year-old from a farm in northern Ontario. He wasn't the brightest bulb in the string, but the kid could skate. He'd had some trouble in the OHL, and his former coach had thought he'd be a good fit for the Devils since no other professional team would touch him.

Of course, the Colonel had said yes.

"Dude. It's not my kid." I rolled my eyes at Dr. Nelson Morelli, who just sighed and shook his head. "Doc. We need you over here."

Sonny Morelli knew in a glance he'd never seen the kid before. Our town was small enough that he was the only general practitioner in a fifty-mile radius. You had to know where you were going to get to St. David. Or you had to be really fucking lost.

I was guessing on the latter for the woman and kid.

When I nodded toward the door, Sonny tilted his head and looked over my shoulder, zeroing in on the woman in the booth. His eyes widened and, without another word, he walked away. Sonny was a man of few words at the best of times, which was fine because Iro had enough for both of them. Usually.

Good thing they were friends.

"Well, hello, sweetheart. What's your name? Rowdy, where did you steal this child?"

With a sigh and gritted teeth, I turned to address my annoyingly perfect younger sister, Rain.

"He didn't steal me," the kid said, sounding offended. "My mom said I could go with him."

Rain's pretty face lit up with a smile. "Well, that's good to know. You should always listen to your mom."

"Says the woman who never listens to hers."

Rain glared at me with a smile sharp enough to slice off my face. So I stuck my tongue out at her. Her expression softened into an actual grin, even as she rolled her eyes. She never could stay mad at me. I was still her hero. At least, I liked to think so.

"Just ignore old grumpface," My sister waived a hand in my direction. "I'm Rain."

"I'm Krista."

"Well, Krista," Rain smiled. "Welcome to St. David. We're happy to have you here."

Krista looked around the room, bright green eyes taking in everything before looking back at Rain.

"Do all these people live here?"

"Not here in this building, no, but we all live in town."

The little girl's head turned to the side, like she was trying to figure something out. "What's town?"

Rain's smile deepened. "The place where we live. Where do you live?"

"In the city."

She said that as if there was no other place in the world. And maybe to a five- or six-year-old there wasn't.

"How old are you, Krista?" Rain asked.

"A lady never reveals her age."

This little baby said it with so much prim old-maid energy, I had to choke back a laugh. Rain's smile widened until her eyes nearly closed.

"Well, however old you are, you seem pretty smart for your age."

A yawn interrupted Krista's smile, reminding me that she and her mom had been through an ordeal tonight. And didn't need a cross examination.

"My mommy says I'm too smart for my own good."

She said it with so much pride, I could tell she'd heard it more than a few times.

Rain leaned closer, as if to share a secret. "My mom tells me that too. And it's a good thing. Never let anyone tell you you're not. If they do, they're just jealous. Or stupid."

"I like you."

Rain nodded. "I like you too. Now, this big hairy guy is Rowdy."

Her little face screwed up in a frown as she looked up at me. "Why do you have so much hair?"

"Because he's too lazy to cut it."

"Hey, not true." I leaned in close to Krista's ear, making her giggle when my hair brushed her cheek. "She's just jealous because she doesn't have curls like ours."

Rain's hair was stick straight, like our dad's. My brothers and I took after our mom, with her wavy brown hair, courtesy of her Italian parents.

"Your curls are gorgeous, Krista. Rowdy's are just messy." Before I could get another word in, Rain continued. "I bet you're cold, aren't you? Why don't we get you a blanket? Would you like that?"

Damn, I'd forgotten the second part of Mitzi's marching orders.

"Mitzi told me to get the girls to round up blankets."

"You don't have to worry about that. They already know."

I looked over my shoulder and saw the St. David Angels already doing what they did best. Working as a team.

They'd surrounded Krista's mom, an Angel wrapping a blanket around her shoulders while another set a plate full of food in front of her on the table. Still another Angel placed a steaming mug next to the plate and another was rummaging through the depths of the suitcase she called a purse. After a few seconds, Emme let out a whoop and pulled a packet out of the depths.

"Rowdy, bring that baby over here so we can warm her up."

The Angel's captain Caity Lopez, a redhead with the personality to match, waved me over to the table.

I got there just in time to hear Krista's mom say, "...cheerleaders?"

"Technically, we're a dance squad. We've won more championships than any other squad in our class. In fact—"

"Don't you dare finish that thought, Caity. Because I swear you will regret it."

The look Caity gave me was laced with enough sass to fuel a

teenage drama queen as she draped a blanket around Krista, who snuggled even deeper into me.

"Can't say it's not true, now can you, Rowdy?"

No, I couldn't. But I didn't have to like it.

So, instead of letting Caity have the last word, I turned to the bedraggled blonde in the booth. "I think I heard you say you got a flat. You wanna tell me where your car is? Me and a few of the guys can go get it for you."

Once again, the woman trained her gaze on me. And once again, I was struck dumb by the intense blue of her eyes. They were so damn striking, I felt like I'd seen them before. I just didn't have a clue where.

"Have we met before?"

Without hesitation, she shook her head. "No, we've never been here before."

Not exactly what I'd asked, but she was clearly exhausted, so I let it go.

"Rowdy," Mitzi barked. "You and a few of the boys go out and get Tressy's car. And give me that baby. You've been hogging her long enough."

Without waiting for an answer, Mitzi held out her hands to Krista, who jumped ship like I'd suddenly grown another head. Then again, when Mitzi said do something, you didn't argue.

Mitzi turned her attention to the little girl, cutting off anything I would've said by addressing Krista.

"Okay, little miss, what would you like to eat?"

Krista and Mitzi disappeared into the mass of perfectly perfumed women surrounding the booth, leaving me standing there trying to get a glimpse of the most gorgeous woman I'd ever met.

"Hey man, you look like someone stole your beer money."

Rebel elbowed me hard enough to make me wince. I returned the favor, enjoying Rebel's muted "oof" in response.

"Come on, I need a ride."

"Where're we going?"

"To pick up the lady's car."

Just then the sea of beautiful women parted and there she was. Damn, she was even prettier than I'd first thought. I was pretty sure my mouth dropped open and my libido chose that second to remind me that it'd been several months since I'd gotten laid.

"That lady, huh? Now I see why you look like you've been smacked on the ass."

Snapping my mouth closed, I shot Rebel a look. "Let's go, dickwad. Shit to do."

"Rowdy, mouth!" Mitzi yelled. "Children."

I lowered my voice to a whisper. "I swear that woman can hear a pin drop from a mile away."

"And she has eyes in the back of her head."

"Boys! Car!"

"Yes, ma'am."

We didn't exactly fall over each other to get to the door, but we didn't waste any more time. And we grabbed reinforcement on the way out.

"Kane! Let's go."

Kane "The Fed" Ness's head snapped up, away from the two women he'd been sweet talking for the past half hour. The town was small enough that I knew the women, knew their families and the year they graduated from high school. Which was probably many more years ago than Kane probably knew. Or cared. Kane loved women. All ages, shapes, sizes and personalities.

"Uh…Huh?"

But he definitely did *not* have a way with words. How the hell the guy got laid as much as he did was a mystery. Then again, Kane was six feet of sleek muscle, a panty-stealing grin and a face that shouldn't draw women like flies. But did.

Which is how he'd landed with the Devils.

"Ladies, he'll be back in half an hour." I slapped Kane on the back and steered him toward the door. "Well before last call."

The women shared a look that didn't bode well for Kane's chances, but I didn't care. I'd brought Rebel because we might need the muscle. But Kane was the only one of the guys who hadn't been drinking at all.

Kane waited until we were outside to smack me on the head.

"Jesus, Rowdy. I've been trying to convince Bethann and Crystal to give me a go for two fucking years, man. Why you gotta cock-block me?"

A solid two-hundred-ten pounds, Kane had some serious strength. Luckily, he'd pulled his punch, or I'd be on the floor.

"Fuck me, Kane. We open tomorrow night. You wanna give me a concussion already?"

"Aw, that was just a love tap, you wimp. But seriously, what the hell? I was about to get laid."

"Only in your dreams."

I rolled my eyes at Reb's snarky comment. He never did know when to keep his mouth shut.

"Reb, when, exactly, was the last time you got laid, huh?" Kane shot back. "All the women around here know you can't give them a good time."

Rebel had smartly taken himself out of reach. But he couldn't let Kane have the last word.

"Because I've already given them a great time, and now they're left with you."

"Jesus. Children." I shook my head. "Stop your fucking bickering. Thank god we don't have to be in the car for long. Tressy said her car's only a mile away."

That got their attention.

"Who the hell's Tressy?" Kane said. "And why do we need to get her car?"

"Christ, Kane. How can you be so damn oblivious? Didn't you see the woman stumble into the bar, like, twenty minutes ago?"

"Huh?"

I couldn't roll my eyes hard enough. "Oh, for fuck's sake. Just get in the goddamn car. How the fuck are you two my best options?"

"Just lucky." Rebel said. "You're the one who wants to be the knight in shining armor. We're just the red shirts along for the ride."

CHAPTER TWO

I'D BEEN LISTENING with half an ear to the commotion around me, still trying to figure out why I felt like I'd stepped onto a movie set.

The women surrounding the booth all looked like models. Perfect hair and makeup, silk blouses and jeans that looked like they'd been painted on. But tastefully. And some of these women wore Louboutins. Maybe my bias was showing, but I didn't realize that women in middle-of-nowhere Pennsylvania dressed in designer clothes to go to a roadside bar.

Then again, maybe I just felt like a half-dead cat left by the side of the road, even if I was wearing my own designer gown and Louboutin heels.

Just thinking about my feet made them throb even more than they already were. I didn't know how far I'd had to walk carrying Krista, but I wouldn't have stopped until I got her out of the cold.

I couldn't believe my car had blown a tire. It was like the most stupid plot twist of a bad horror movie. And I should know because I'd been in a few pretty damn bad horror movies in another life.

But, of course, it had to be so damn cold I could see my breath. Why the hell was it so cold? It was mid-October. It wasn't supposed to be freezing. At least, it hadn't been in New York when I'd buckled Krista into her booster seat, and we'd driven out of the city as fast as I could, headed for...wherever we'd ended up.

I hadn't been thinking of anything more than getting away. From my mom, my sister, my ex. From everyone who wanted something from me.

Damn my mom for guilting me into doing that damn concert. I never would've agreed to it if I'd known what she'd been planning.

And now I was stuck in…

I focused my attention on the nearest woman, a blonde who looked like she'd just stepped off a film set. Maybe there were hidden cameras somewhere. Or maybe I'd just lived in New York City too long because when I'd first seen this place, I'd figured everyone here would be wearing overalls and shitkickers.

Well, the joke was on me, in more ways than one tonight.

"Excuse me. I'm sorry, but where exactly are we?"

The blonde, whose name was Romy or Ronny or something that started with an R. "Well, we're not quite within the city limits, but we consider anything within twenty miles part of St. David."

"Is this...Pennsylvania?"

The look the woman gave me made me think I'd guessed wrong. "Honey, how long were you driving?"

"I honestly don't know."

The women went quiet, and I felt the gaze of every single one of them in the semicircle around me. I wanted to squirm but forced myself to be still. I wasn't used to being in the spotlight anymore. I'd spent most of my teenage years in it and the last eight trying to avoid it at all costs. It'd kept me and Krista safe from prying eyes. Sure, every now and then some member of the press would want to do one of those "Where are they now" interviews, but I always turned them down. I didn't want to talk about my past.

The brunette in the booth across from me—I thought her name was Crystal—reached across the table and put her hand over mine.

"Is someone chasing you? Someone you don't want to find you? Trust me, some of us have been there. We know what to do. We can help. If you want."

I blinked, pretty sure Crystal had just asked if I wanted to disappear. First of all, no one had ever offered to help me before. I'd always been the one people came to for help. Well, for money, anyway.

These women were offering to help with seemingly no ulterior motive. But everyone had an ulterior motive. No one offered anything for free. There was always a catch.

"No, no one's chasing me." At least, I hoped that was true. I didn't think my mom would actually send someone after me. Even with this much money on the line, Bebe Meyers wouldn't want a public scandal. Unless it earned her more money, then she'd be all for it.

Crystal didn't look convinced, but she didn't push.

"Okay. Then how can we help you tonight?"

Reflexively, I looked around the room, but I didn't see the man who'd caught me in his arms. I did see Krista smiling at Mitzi, who held Krista's hand as she talked an older couple.

"Oh, don't worry about your daughter." Crystal's voice soothed. "She's perfectly safe. You're with the Devils now. They may look like a bunch of heathens, but they won't let anyone hurt you."

I blinked up at Crystal. "Devils?"

Crystal grinned and nodded toward the other side of the room, where the "heathens" were gathered. "The St. David Devils. Otherwise known as the ST Double-Ds."

I could not have heard that correctly. "Excuse me."

Crystal's grin widened. "The Devils are the worst team in the Northeast Professional Hockey League and the most fun you'll ever have at an ice rink."

Should those words mean something? My brain must've been addled by the cold, because nothing was making sense.

"Don't sweat it, sweetie." Crystal waved it off. "You don't look like you're from around here. When you live in the middle of nowhere, you take your entertainment where you can get it. So, why don't we find you a place to stay tonight?"

"Oh, that would wonderful. If you'd give Krista and me a ride to the nearest hotel that would—"

"Yeah, I'm afraid that's going to be a problem." Crystal's grin finally disappeared. "We're a one-hotel town, and it's totally booked. The season starts tomorrow, and we're playing the Stags and…" She drew the last word out to about five syllables, "you don't have a clue what I'm talking about."

"There's only one hotel?"

I couldn't wrap my head around that. How could there only be one hotel? I had definitely passed several before I'd gotten off the turnpike. But there'd been an accident and the GPS had suggested another route, and I'd followed it blindly. Until somehow, I must've taken a wrong turn that left us stranded here…in the middle of fucking *nowhere*.

And now we had nowhere to sleep tonight?

"Oh yeah, but don't worry," Crystal continued. "You'll have a place to stay. Pretty sure it'll be better than the hotel."

"Wha—"

"Tressy? Hi, I'm Raffi Lawrence. I understand you're going to need a place to stay tonight."

I turned to see an older woman smiling at me, holding out her hand. I took it without thought, something I never would've done in New York or LA. You never let a stranger touch you. Unless you were on the red carpet or in a public space filled with rich people where lots of people were watching.

Yes, I lived in a fucked-up world.

But this woman had a friendly smile on her pretty face, dark hair shot through with silver. She was probably mid-fifties, laugh lines around her dark eyes and carrying a few more pounds than any fifty-year-old I knew, because all of the fifty-year-olds I knew were more worried about what they looked like than if they smiled or weighed more than they had when they were a teenager.

And she exuded an air of kindness that couldn't be faked.

"I guess we do. Crystal told me there're no hotel rooms available?"

Raffi waved that away. "You don't have to worry about that. We have plenty of room at our house for you and Krista."

I blinked. This woman wanted to take me and my daughter home with her? She had no idea who we were. We could be grifters. Or worse. "Oh, no, we couldn't—"

"Yes, you absolutely can." Raffi's voice made it clear she wasn't going to take no for an answer. "Trust me, it's not an imposition. We have people stay with us all the time. Since our youngest left for college, that house is way too big for just the Colonel and me."

Did she say Colonel? "Oh, but—"

"The boys and Rain have their own places now," Raffi just kept talking, patting my hand, "and honestly, I miss the company. We see them almost every day, but I miss the chaos. Though I would never tell them that. So, I don't want you to worry about not having a place to stay. Now, I know you don't know me from Adam, but anyone in this bar can vouch for me and the Colonel. You'll be perfectly safe with us."

Crystal touched my shoulder, drawing my dazed attention. "Miss Raffi's absolutely right. This is the best solution. You and

Krista need somewhere to sleep tonight. And honestly, hon, you look like you're about to fall over."

Crystal wasn't wrong. I felt like I could just close my eyes and fall asleep right here. But I couldn't because I had to make sure Krista was taken care of. My daughter needed me, and we certainly couldn't sleep on a park bench. If this place even had a park.

We needed help, and I couldn't be picky about it because, apparently, I'd blown a tire in the literal middle of *fucking* nowhere.

Where the hell had I gone wrong?

About twenty years ago, sweetheart.

Ugh, why did my inner sarcastic bitch sound like Carrie from Sex in the City? Seriously, it was annoying as fuck. And Sarah Jessica Parker was the absolute sweetest person in the world.

Which didn't mean a damn thing right now when I was about to fall flat on my face on the table in exhaustion. But...I didn't know these people. I didn't know any of these people. I couldn't just leave with this woman. I had Krista to consider.

As if she'd read my mind, Crystal laid her hand on my shoulder and leaned in closer. Was she going to tell me to run? We had nowhere to go—

"Tressy, I know you don't know any of us, but Miss Raffi and the Colonel are two of the best people in the world. You can ask anyone in this place. They'll all give you the same answer. Mitzi," Crystal glanced up at the woman currently holding my daughter, "back me up."

Mitzi nodded, her expression serious. "Absolutely. You're dead on your feet and the little one here needs to get some sleep. You will be fine."

I looked back at Crystal to see if she was trying to signal me to run. Instead, she nodded, her lips curved in an understanding smile.

"You'll be fine with Raffi and the Colonel. Honest."

It wasn't like I had that many options. I'd given my car keys to a man I didn't know. The cold must have addled my brain. And now I was about to leave with a woman I'd just met.

I forced a smile. "Thank you so much. I really appreciate the offer."

Miss Raffi—where the hell did these people think they lived? Stars Hollow?—nodded, her smile softening the faintest bit. As if she knew exactly what I was thinking. Maybe she did. People in small towns were like that. They were gossips and busybodies, and they knew everything about everyone. At least, they had in every show and movie I'd ever been in. But that had been a long time ago. Things changed.

I'd changed. I was no longer a gullible child whose mother ruled her life.

No, you're a mother who ran when shit got too much to handle.

Shit.

"Tressy?"

My attention snapped back to Miss Raffi, and I realized she must have said something.

"Yes, sorry. I…" Drifted off? Ignored her? Went into a coma? "Sorry."

Miss Raffi's smile returned, lighting her dark eyes. "I asked if you're ready to leave."

For a brief second, I thought about the man who'd caught me when I'd stepped through the door. For some reason, I wanted him to tell me everything would be okay. Which was ridiculous. I didn't need a man to tell me what to do.

"Yes. Thank you so much. I really appreciate it."

Miss Raffi held out her hand. "Then let's get you and that adorable little girl out of here."

Oh god, I really hoped I wasn't going to regret this.

I took a breath and took the other woman's hand.

"Let me introduce you to my husband then we can get going."

"Get a good night's sleep," Crystal said as I slid out of the booth. "I'll check in with you tomorrow. Just have Miss Raffi give you my number. You can contact me at any time. You want to talk at two a.m., I'm your girl."

I nodded, my brain not really processing complete thoughts at the moment. As if she'd read my mind, Raffi took another look at me as I stood.

"On second thought," she said, "let's just get you home so you can get some rest."

I glanced at Mitzi, still holding Krista, who'd fallen asleep, her face slack, little lips parted. Raffi and Mitzi waited for me to stand, Raffi looking as if she wanted to reach for me but unsure I'd take the help.

God damn my feet hurt. I wasn't sure I'd make it far without help. So I took her hand and let her lead me outside to an aqua-blue Mercedes SUV parked just to the left of the entrance. Raffi opened the back driver's side door. The thought that the color was custom floated through my foggy brain.

"Don't have a booster seat because my slacker kids haven't provided me with grandchildren yet," Raffi gave Mitzi the side eye at the other woman's snort, "but I figure you can hold her in the backseat. We're not going far."

Too tired to ask any questions, I just nodded and slid into the backseat, reaching for Krista. Mitzi put her in my arms then closed the door as Raffi got into the driver's seat. The car started with barely a hum, and Raffi put the car in drive. I wrapped my arms tightly around Krista, resting my cheek against her soft curls and—

"We're here."

My eyes flew open to see Raffi smiling at me from outside the open car door. Jesus, I must've fallen asleep. How long had I been out? We could be anywhere. Even as tired as I was, I could feel anxiety rush back in.

"Oh, hon." Raffi's mouth curved in a slight grimace. "I can tell you're scared. But honestly, you're perfectly safe here. Come on in and let's find you a bed."

Raffi reached for Krista, and, after a split second, I handed her over, knowing I was too tired to carry her safely. My baby was getting big. And no longer a baby.

Swinging my legs out of the car, I stood...and my mouth dropped open.

Okay, was I still sleeping? Dreaming? I didn't know what I'd been expecting when Raffi had invited me to her home, but it hadn't been a freaking mansion. Like a literal mansion with huge double wooden doors and columns and about twenty windows. It reminded me of a lodge I'd stayed at years ago in Colorado.

"Don't let the outside fool you." Raffi beckoned to me from the wide wraparound porch, wooden rocking chairs and benches, decorated with pumpkins, hay bales and mums. "It may still look like an inn from the outside, but it hasn't been for almost a hundred years."

Raffi opened the front door, and warm light spilled out, practically calling out to me. I released an unconscious sigh. I was so damn tired. I just wanted to shut off my brain.

"Come on, sweetheart. You're about to fall asleep on your feet. Everything'll seem better in the morning."

I didn't think that was true. But right now, I didn't want to think about the mess I'd left behind. I didn't want to think about anything. I just wanted to get my daughter into a bed, curl up around her, then maybe this heart-pounding anxiety would ease just a little.

CHAPTER THREE

 owdy

"DUDE, what's wrong with your face?"

I glanced over at my brother, riding shotgun. Rebel stared at me like he was looking at a pile of dogshit on the floor.

"What the fuck are you talking about?"

"Your face looks like you took a hit from Big Tony."

As I rolled my eyes, Kane barked out a laugh from the backseat.

I glared at him in the rearview. "What the fuck, Kane? Whose side are you on?"

Kane continued to laugh until he could barely catch his breath. Of course, that didn't mean he couldn't talk.

"Because he's not wrong." Kane managed to wheeze out. "You look like you got t-bagged."

Now I rolled my eyes, because… "Fuck you, asshole. You both suck."

"Nah." Rebel snarked. "But we know you do."

Jesus Christ, why the hell did my brother still act like a fucking twelve-year-old? I punched Reb in the shoulder, hard enough to make him flinch.

"Bitch."

"Jerk," Rebel shot back at me. "At least, I'm not lusting after some strange woman who stumbled into the bar and conveniently dropped into your arms." He paused. "She is damn pretty, though."

"I'm not lusting after her." Okay, maybe I was a little, but I certainly wasn't going to admit it. "And you don't need to worry about how pretty she is. The woman was practically dead on her feet. She would've fallen if I hadn't caught her."

"Uh huh. Sure."

I swear, my brother deserved whatever I decided to dish out the second we got out of the damn car. I didn't care if Reb tattled to our mom. Christ, we were fucking adults. I should be able to smack my younger brother for his asshole-ishness without our mom getting in the middle.

But Reb wasn't wrong. The woman was damn pretty.

For now, I decided to ignore Rebel and concentrate on finding the woman's car. She'd been fairly specific about where her car had died, so it shouldn't be hard to find.

"Hey," Kane pointed out the front window. "That must be it."

I checked the mileage readout on my Bronco and realized we'd driven almost three miles out of town. No wonder she'd nearly passed out.

"Damn, I can't believe she walked all that way." Rebel shook his head. "And in those shoes, too."

Pulling my Bronco onto the shoulder, I stopped it in front of the high-end Acura.

"Nice car." Kane leaned forward between the two front seats, gaze narrowed as he stared out the windshield. "Really nice."

Yeah, it was. And the latest model, too.

"I think the lady's above your station, dude." Rebel's tone held no trace of snark. I couldn't really argue with him, and that really pissed me off.

"Let's just change the damn tire and get back."

I shoved my door open and got out before my best friend and my brother could continue to piss me off. Their razzing was getting on my nerves, but what pissed me off more than anything was the fact that they were probably right. The beautiful blonde who'd fallen into my arms tonight looked like she had places to be, and those places definitely didn't include St. David.

And this was where I belonged.

I tuned out Kane and Rebel, who continued to talk shit as I got the spare and the jack from the trunk, and we jacked up the car to change the tire.

"I don't know, man," Rebel said to Kane. "He kinda looks like he got struck by the stupid bus."

"I guess you'd look like that, too," Kane grunted as he worked on the lug nuts, "if a woman who looked like her fell into your arms."

"Fuck that shit." Rebel huffed. "I don't need a woman falling anywhere around me right now. I got too much shit going on as it is."

"Good thing none of the women around here want anything to do with you, then because you're a moody SOB. And what shit do you have going on anyway?"

Kane and Rebel kept up a steady banter, but I tuned them out as we changed the tire. The damaged one was going to need a new rim, and she probably didn't want to drive back to wherever she'd come from on the donut. Which meant she needed a mechanic. And the only mechanic in town didn't work on the weekend.

Maybe she'd be sticking around a little longer than expected.

Once we got the donut on, I threw the jack and the flat in the trunk then headed for the driver's side door. I was just about to open the door when Rebel planted his ass on the door, arms crossed over his chest.

"All right, asshole." Reb glared at me. "What the *fuck* is wrong with you?"

I blew out a hard sigh, shaking my head.

"Move your ass, Reb. I don't have time for this shit with you."

He didn't move, eyes narrowing as he stared at me like he could read my mind. "You haven't had time for anyone lately. And now some random woman drops into your lap, and you're ready to take my head off. What gives? I know you haven't been happy lately, but damn, man, you're not acting like yourself."

I didn't have the slightest clue what to say to that because, one, my brother rarely discussed anything serious unless he was talking about hockey. And two... well, Reb wasn't wrong. And when my brother noticed something was off, everyone already knew. Because Reb wasn't known for being intuitive.

Turning to Kane, I got the same look. Except Kane looked much more relaxed about the whole thing. Rebel never looked relaxed about anything. Kane always looked like he was idling in neutral. Until he got on the ice and then he kicked some serious ass. Some players had been known to skate the other way when they saw Kane headed for them.

I shrugged. "Nothing's wrong."

"Yeah, that's bullshit." Kane spoke before Reb could open his mouth and say something that would truly piss me off. "We all know something's been eating at you for weeks."

"Hell, even Dad's noticed." Reb snorted. "So you know it's gotta be bad."

Shit. Our dad was pretty fucking oblivious most of the time unless it had to do with the team or the business. Not that he ignored his kids. Or his wife. Reston and Raffi Lawrence had had a legendary love affair. From their almost twenty-year age gap to their late-night elopement and her parents' attempt to get their marriage annulled, even though she'd been twenty-four at the time.

"Has everyone been talking behind my back?"

Rebel shrugged. "Pretty much, yeah."

Well, fuck. Just what I didn't need. The entire town all up in my business. Not that they weren't most of the rest of the time, but usually I could shrug it off because it was all surface shit. Who I was dating, how bad the team was playing and why it was my fault. I was the team captain, after all. And this team was woven into the town's DNA, so everyone had an opinion and the feeling that they had a right to it.

And right now, I had something on my mind I really didn't want anyone to know about.

Shaking my head, I used the key fob to open the door. "We don't need to talk about this now."

"No," Kane nodded, "we don't. But we will later."

Fuck that shit. I had nothing to talk about. That phone call I'd gotten last week didn't mean anything to anyone but me. It wasn't like I was going to take the job I'd been offered. I couldn't. I belonged here.

"Let's get back to the bar."

"So you can see your new girlfriend?"

Kane snorted as I rolled my eyes and consciously unclenched my hands.

"Rebel, you are going to lose your fucking teeth. Get in the damn car with Kane. I'll see you back there."

Climbing in, I shut the door in Reb's face. It took me a couple seconds to realize the damn car started with the push of a button, which for some reason just pissed me off. Why the fuck didn't cars have keys anymore? Why did people have to fuck with everything?

Shit.

Maybe Rebel and Kane had picked up on more than they

should have. Which just meant I needed to be sure I kept my mouth shut. Or maybe I just needed the fucking season to start so I felt like I had a purpose.

Because I had more trouble keeping a smile on my face lately. Probably best to keep that thought from getting out there. My parents and siblings would be all over me. And I definitely didn't need that on my shoulders, too.

The car purred and dinged after I pushed the button, engine noise nonexistant. Nice *expensive* car. Shaking my head, I got the car back on the road and was halfway back to the bar when I got a text from my mom.

MOM

Heading back to our place with Tressy and Krista. Bring the car here.

YEP. That's what I'd figured would happen. Not only because there were no open hotel rooms anywhere near St. David because the season opened tomorrow, but because that was the kind of person my mom was. Raffi Lawrence gathered people like they were stray cats, and she was the Humane Society. My dad grumbled, but he rarely ever said no to his wife, and he wasn't quite the hard ass he pretended to be. Actually, no one ever said no to Raffi. She was just as much a force of nature as her husband. She just didn't do it as loudly.

But when she had an opinion, she let you know. I loved my mom, but she sometimes got a little too invested in her children's lives. And if I told her about the phone call I couldn't stop thinking about, she'd tell me exactly what I needed to do.

And I wasn't sure I wanted her to be right.

Coward.

Maybe. Or maybe I was a thirty-year-old who didn't need my mom to solve my problems and didn't need any more shit floating around my head before the game tomorrow.

A game that doesn't mean shit. It's not like you're playing for the Stanley Cup.

Hell, it wasn't like we were playing for any cup. Our league was barely professional and made up of the same teams every damn year. Sometimes a start-up joined, but they usually failed in a few years or moved up to the ECHL if they brought in enough money.

There were always new players every year, and some of them stuck around long enough to get their nicknames in their second season.

But, for the most part, if you started in this league, you stayed in this league. The guys who came to us from other leagues, like the ECHL and the WHL, usually went back after they got their shit together. That's what Pop was good at. Helping these guys get their shit together.

And you're gonna turn down a legit offer to advance? Maybe the only one you'll ever get? Why is that?

Jesus, I needed my brain to just shut the fuck up.

I cut through Main Street, the one traffic light blinking yellow, only a couple of cars on the road. If you were out driving now, you were late for your third-shift job at one of the two factories in the county or you were heading home from the bar.

No lights shone through any of the businesses' windows at this hour. Gerhart's Hardware. Maggie Mae's Beans and Leaves. Levengood's Funeral Home. Steinbeck's Flowers.

St. David also boasted a CPA, a tiny bookstore, a thrift store, a Subway and a couple of diners, one on either end of the main drag, which consisted of about five blocks.

If you blinked, you'd miss half the town. Most people traveling through never knew they were in St. David. Not that a lot of people ever drove through.

At the end of the last block, I pulled into the half-circle driveway in front of my parents' home, parked the car by the front steps and ran up the flight of stairs to the wide front porch. I walked through the door and into the entrance hall that'd been a lobby when this place had been a bed and breakfast. Turning left, I headed for the great room, where the family typically hung out. When I didn't find anyone there, I headed for the kitchen at the back of the house.

I couldn't get over how quiet the house was. How empty it felt with my parents living here alone. No wonder my mom wanted us to visit so much. I made a mental note to remember this when she asked me to stop by the next time.

No one in the dining room or kitchen, either.

Which left the bedrooms. Knowing my mom, she already had her guests tucked into the suite on the first floor. My parents' home had been built by an iron magnate in the 1910s who had promised the local farming community that his factory would provide for them for the rest of their lives. And it had, until the early '60s when his last remaining descendent sold the plant to some huge corporation, which had kept it running for a few years then shut it down, putting a third of the town's adults out of work and crippling most of the other businesses in town.

Some enterprising young couple had turned the house into an inn in the '70s, but by then, the town had had one foot in the grave, with little to attract visitors. My parents had moved here after getting married. Pop had just resigned his commission from the Army and my mom had recently graduated from college. Between my parents' almost twenty-year age gap, their purchase of the biggest house in town, my dad's ownership of a multimillion-dollar business, and his crazy dream of building a hockey dynasty from scratch, the residents of St. David had thought they were either insane or arrogant, or both, and maybe delusional, as well.

Probably a little bit of all that. But my parents had won over almost every single person in town. There were a few holdouts who thought the Lawrences were too damn uppity, but those people had a stick up their ass. My family did a hell of a lot for this town and for those who lived here.

And they collected people like a beach collected driftwood.

Heading for the guest wing, I began to hear voices, so I was on the right track. Seconds later, as I rounded the corner to the guest wing hall, I stopped short when I nearly ran into Tressy. She let out a little shriek and put her hand on her chest. Without thinking, I put my hands on her shoulders to steady her. Then immediately took them back when I felt the heat of her skin seep into mine. And sink straight into my gut.

"Oh, hey. I didn't mean to scare you. You okay?"

The t-shirt she wore was at least two sizes too big for her, falling off her shoulder, and had my face splashed across the front of it, a promotional giveaway from a few seasons ago. I had my arms in the air and a stick over my head, and I looked like a fucking mountain man. She probably hadn't even recognized me. Which was a good thing. At least tonight I looked somewhat civilized.

And damn, I'd been staring at her bare shoulder.

You're not a fucking perv. Knock it off.

No, but I was a red-blooded male, and she was a stunningly beautiful woman I wanted to strip naked and fuck against the wall.

Shit.

"Tressy? Everything okay?"

But not with my mom sticking her head out of the doorway down the hall.

Fuck.

Tressy turned her head, her mouth already curving in a smile that made me wish I was wearing pants that didn't make it perfectly clear I was getting a hard on.

"It's fine. Rowdy just startled me."

My mom turned to me with a wry grin. "Yeah, he was a way of doing that."

I couldn't let my mom get away with that. "I still don't think I was born a month early, Mom."

Mom didn't even bite on the old joke. "Rowdy, what are you doing here?"

Rolling my eyes, I smiled at Tressy, making sure I poured on the charm. "Ma, you told me to bring the car here."

Tressy's smile was a punch to the gut, making me feel a little drunk. What the hell was going on?

Maybe you're just horny.

Yeah, probably, and it absolutely sucked that she was just passing through. It wasn't like we'd get the chance to flirt. Or fuck.

Double fuck.

"Rowdy?"

Crap. I'd been staring at her, smiling like an idiot.

Because you are an idiot.

I dragged my gaze away from Tressy, trying not to notice my hands on the t-shirt were positioned directly over her nipples. Yep, not the place I wanted to be looking now, because my mom was staring at me, and her expression said she knew what I was thinking.

"Anyway, so the car's out front. I left the key-fob on the table downstairs."

"Thank you. For everything." Tressy's soft voice drew my attention back to her like a fly to honey. "I appreciate it."

When she spoke, I swore my blood heated and fizzed.

"No problem. Didn't take much to change the tire."

Her wry smile fired heat in my gut. "I obviously couldn't do it, so..."

Her gaze dropped and mine followed. I'd never considered

bare feet sexy before, but her toes, nails polished with black paint, made me think about having her rub them against the back of my bare legs while I—

My gaze snapped back up, finding a point over her shoulder to look at.

"Yeah, anyway, I think the rim's bent so you're gonna need to see Donny. He's the local mechanic. I should probably get going. Season starts tomorrow."

Even though she looked exhausted, I still saw interest in her eyes.

"You're a hockey player, right? Your mom told me you have a game."

"Yeah." And then because I couldn't help myself, I said, "You should come to the game tomorrow night. I'm not sure Donny's going to be able to fix your tire right away so you could be stuck here for a few days. You should come."

She didn't say no right away, and my pulse kicked up.

"I guarantee you'll have an amazing time."

"Guarantee, huh?"

Her smile spread, and I had to lock my jaw so my mouth didn't hang open.

Gorgeous. So fucking pretty.

"Absolutely."

We stood there staring at each other for several seconds until she blinked, and her slight smile disappeared in a flash. I felt like I'd been robbed.

"I wasn't planning on being here tomorrow." She shook her head. "I'm sorry, I'm just so tired. I'm not thinking straight. I can't thank you enough for everything, but—"

"Rowdy, why don't you say goodnight, sweetheart?" My mom's voice knocked me back to reality. "Tressy's about to fall asleep on her feet."

Tressy was studying her feet at the moment, blonde hair

falling around her face. And I was an asshole because she was clearly exhausted, and I didn't want to leave.

"Yeah, of course. Goodnight, Tressy."

She looked up but didn't meet my gaze directly. "Goodnight, Rowdy. Thank you again for all your help."

"No problem. I'll see you tomorrow, Tressy."

That was a promise.

CHAPTER FOUR

*ressy*

I woke up to absolute silence.

Which was a dead giveaway that I wasn't at home. When you lived in a city—any city, really—the first thing you noticed when you weren't there was the absence of sound. No bus engines, no honking horns, no sirens, no traffic sounds at all.

It was kind of freaky, actually.

Opening my eyes, I looked past the foot of the queen bed I'd slept in to the empty twin on the other side of the room. With a gasp, I sat straight up.

Where was Krista? She'd always been an early riser, but I can't believe she didn't wake me up when she got out of bed. I hoped she hadn't gotten herself into any trouble. I checked the bedside table for a clock and caught sight of the note set on top of my phone.

I hope you don't mind I set up Krista with some breakfast and cartoons so you could sleep.
We're in the small room just off the kitchen. Join us whenever you're ready.
Raffi

I TOOK a breath and then another, trying to get my heart rate back to normal.

Krista was fine. No one had taken her. We were safe here.

Wherever here was exactly. I really should drag my ass out of bed and find out.

And oh my god, was it really almost eleven-thirty? I had no idea what time I'd gone to bed last night, but I hadn't slept this late in… Well, I couldn't actually remember when I'd slept this late. Not even as a teenager, because I'd always had somewhere to be. On set. A press event. Rehearsals. Classes.

I really must've been out of it last night. With a sigh, I let myself fall back on the bed again, careful not to close my eyes, because I was afraid the next time I opened them, it'd be closer to five.

Instead, I stared at the ceiling. The plaster design riveled anything I'd seen in an exclusive New York brownstone and the chandelier was crystal.

Who *were* these people who lived in the middle of nowhere in a freaking mansion and had taken in a couple of strangers and let them sleep in their home?

I needed to find Krista, thank Raffi for her hospitality and get back on the road to…

Where are you going exactly?

Hell if I knew. What I did know was that I needed to get my shit together, but after the night I'd had, maybe I could give myself a little slack. Sighing, I let my head sink a little deeper into the mattress.

Last night had been a shit show. The stunt my mom had pulled… Ugh. I didn't even want to think about it. But now that I had, I couldn't stop. And the anxiety and panic began to eat at me.

Stop that. You're safe here.

I really hoped that was true. But it still needed to find Krista. I couldn't just let a woman I'd just met care for my child. What kind of parent was I to let a woman I'd just met take her—

To breakfast.

Get a grip.

I pushed myself back to sitting, then read the note again, the anxiety easing just a little.

Krista was fine. She was safe with Raffi. I don't know how I knew that so completely, but I did. We were safe here. Raffi would make sure nothing happened to my daughter.

But what kind of mother are you if you don't check?

Tired. That's what I was. I was so fucking tired. Anxiety. Stress. Fear. Anger. They all combined to make me exhausted. My business partners had been telling me I needed a break for months, but I'd brushed aside their worries and continued on like nothing was wrong.

And then last night had happened.

Maybe we can stay here for a while. Like a mini-vacation. Away from…everything else.

I remember Rowdy… with those dark eyes and scruffy beard and the hair I wanted to sink her fingers into… he'd told me something about the tire and needing a mechanic. Maybe we would have to stay for a few days.

Would that be such a bad thing? I couldn't remember the last time I'd taken time away from work. Maybe last year? This past summer, I'd made sure Krista had stayed busy with classes and camps and everything New York City had to offer. But the agency Jen, Leon and I had taken over three years ago was still growing. It needed my attention.

But Jen and Leon were more than capable of holding down the fort on their own for a few days. Maybe…

Except I'd left a mess behind that I'd have to clean up eventually, because that's what I did. I didn't make messes, but I'd have to clean this one up because my mom would never admit she'd done something wrong, and this situation would all be my fault.

Shit.

My head started to throb, and my stomach chose that moment to growl.

Time to get up and start dealing with the shit show that my life had become.

Rolling out of bed, I headed to the en suite Raffi had shown me last night, when I'd barely been able to hold my eyes open. In the bright light of day, I noticed how lush it was. Marble shower and sink, a soaker tub, bamboo floors, gorgeous cabinetry. The room gave four-star hotels a run for their money.

Really, who are *these people?*

I really wanted to know the answer to that question. Pulling the t-shirt I'd slept in over my head, I almost tossed it on the bed before I realized there was a face on it. I hadn't really noticed last night, but that was Rowdy's face staring back at me. Beautiful dark eyes and long lashes that couldn't possibly be real. Cheekbones to die for. And a panty-dropping grin.

It took me way too long to lay that shirt on the bed and head for the bathroom. And some sense.

After a quick shower, I walked back into the bedroom and looked for my clothes from last night. My dress was laid over a chair, and my luggage sat next to it. On top of the dresser was an unopened pack of underwear in my size, a pair of cream lounge pants with a matching top, and a bralette in my size with the tags still attached. A pair of fluffy slippers sat on the floor.

I just shook my head. If this was a dream, maybe I didn't want to wake up.

By the time I was dressed, my stomach had become an angry monster and, when I opened the door, I caught a whiff of something delicious. Following my nose, I walked down the hall, taking note of the original artwork on the wall and the Persian wool rug on the floor.

Maybe this place was actually a bed and breakfast, and I just hadn't noticed last night.

The hall dropped me back into the entrance foyer I remembered from last night. I looked for a reception desk or a sign to the dining room, but of course, there were none.

Did Rowdy live here? Not that I cared. Of course I didn't. I was just curious. At least I wasn't wearing the guy's face on my chest anymore.

I really hoped I didn't see him first thing in the morning. Okay, late morning.

Liar.

Yeah, maybe I'd just go back to bed and stick my head under the pillows.

From farther back in the house, I heard Krista's laughter. The sound immediately lifted my mood. I hadn't realized how low I'd been feeling until everything seemed just a little brighter at my daughter's joy.

How long had it been since I'd heard Krista laugh like that? Months, maybe. A little of the brightness dimmed. I was a totally sucky mother if my daughter hadn't been laughing and I hadn't noticed.

Cut yourself a little slack. The last couple of weeks haven't exactly been normal.

I snorted. That was a bit of an understatement.

My daughter's laughter rang out again, a carefree giggle this time. I followed the sound through another couple of amazingly decorated rooms, including a library, before I turned a corner and entered an open-concept kitchen.

This place was freaking huge. It'd probably fit four of our apartment.

"Ah, Tressy. You're up." Raffi smiled at me across the huge island. "How did you sleep?"

"Mommy, Rowdy made me pancakes, and Miss Raffi gave me pineapple juice. I didn't know pineapple's had juice."

Krista held her arms out to me, so I walked over and gave her a hug, just like I did every morning. But this morning, Krista was sitting in someone else's kitchen, and I was wearing someone else's clothes.

"Do you want something to eat?" Raffi smiled as she opened the built-in refrigerator that looked big enough to feed an army. "I can whip up an omelette or a sandwich or—"

"I can make you pancakes."

My gaze tripped over to Rowdy, who leaned against the counter on the opposite side of the huge island. And my mouth dropped open for a split second before I snapped it shut.

Had he been this hot last night?

Tight, worn jeans showed off bulging thighs. Tight, worn t-shirt stretched across a broad chest. My fingers curled with the desire to pet him. Like *actually* pet him. Dark stubble on a strong square jaw. Dark messy hair with a wave that made me want to run my fingers through it.

It only took seconds for my gaze to reach his eyes, which were so dark, I felt like I could fall into them and drown. I got caught in those eyes and only realized I was staring when Krista said, "Mommy, you should try Rowdy's pancakes. They're really good."

I blinked, breaking the connection as I turned to smile at my daughter.

"Oh, I'm sure he doesn't have the time—"

"Actually, I do have time." His voice sent a shiver down my spine. "I don't have anywhere to be for another couple of hours."

"Rowdy's gonna play hockey, Mommy. He has a whole team."

"Yes, I know. That's why I don't want to bother—"

"It's no bother." Rowdy shifted against the counter, recrossing his feet, which I now realized were bare. "You like blueberries?"

"Um, yeah?"

His smile made my breath stutter, damn him. That was not good. I needed to watch that. No, I needed to make sure it didn't happen again. Taking a breath, I shoved all those wayward feelings into a little ball that I then slam-dunked into a wastebasket in my brain. My therapist had taught me that one.

Rowdy's gaze narrowed as he pushed away from the counter and headed to the refrigerator. As if he knew exactly what he was doing.

"Chocolate chips?" he asked.

Oh, he was good. Tempting me with chocolate and worn jeans and a tight t-shirt.

After he caught you in his arms like the hero of some ridiculous movie.

Did this small-town Romeo have some kind of weird mojo? Or was I simply so messed up in the head that any tiny bit of attention from a man made me crazy?

"Blueberries are fine."

"Yeah, but you've never had my blueberry and chocolate chip pancakes. Trust me, they'll change your life."

Something warm began to unfurl in my stomach, something I hadn't felt in years.

Nope, not happening. Not now. Not here. Not this guy.

At twenty-seven, you'd think I'd be better able to control this shit. And it was shit. Because there was no way in hell I could even think about falling for this guy.

My practiced smile came easier this time. "Well, then I guess I have to, don't I?"

The smile he gave me was a shot across the bow. He knew. Somehow, he knew that I was walling him off, shutting him down.

Smarter than the average bear.

But it didn't matter, did it? Because Krista and I were leaving as soon as we could. Well, as soon as my car was ready. Damn it.

Raffi and Krista watched me from the other side of the island, my daughter's eyes wide and interested, Raffi's expression carefully neutral.

"Tomorrow morning, we'll have a proper spread."

My brain stuttered. *Tomorrow.* We wouldn't be here tomorrow.

Won't we?

"What's a proper spread?" Krista asked.

"Well, I don't know where you're from, but around here, a proper spread includes all the food groups." Rowdy held up one hand and started to count off fingers. "Meat. Cheese. Carbs. Sugar." He shrugged. "Maybe some fruit. Definitely no vegetables."

This man thought he was irresistible. And maybe he was, but I wasn't going to give him any more ammunition.

"Mommy likes vegetables." Krista chimed in. "She eats them all the time."

"Then she's missing out on the finer things in life."

He winked at Krista, whose smile widened. So did his. Rowdy honestly seemed enchanted with my daughter and not just playing up to Krista to get on her mom's good side. He was either a damn good actor or a decent guy. And I hadn't met many of the latter.

"Krista, honey, I have a few errands to run." Raffi filled the short silence that fell. "Would you like to come with me? If it's okay with your mom, of course."

Krista turned to me, her eyes wide. "Can I? Miss Raffi said we could see the hockey rink where Rowdy plays."

"Why—"

I stopped before I asked Krista why she cared about seeing some small-town hockey arena and insulted the family who'd been so good to us. I'd taken Krista to a couple of Rangers games at Madison Square Garden, which had to be a palace compared to whatever was going on in St. David. Krista hadn't cared about the game. She'd been more interested in whatever snacks were available in the private suite we sat in that night.

"I don't know, honey. I need to get in touch with the mechanic about the car and I don't know when we're going to leave."

Krista's mouth tightened into a little pout. "Miss Raffi said we could stay as long as we want."

"I know she did and that's very nice of her, but we can't just stay—"

"Actually, you *can* just stay." Raffi's smile never faltered, never showed any sign that she didn't mean exactly what she said. "For as long as you like. As you can see, our house is big enough to get lost in, and it'd be nice to have company for a while. The Colonel and the kids are going to be wrapped up with games all this weekend, and I'd love to have some girls to talk to. And you still need to check with Donny about your tire."

"Donny?"

"He's the only mechanic in town at the moment."

This town had one mechanic? Where the hell had we gotten stranded?

My brain whirred and clicked, like a broken computer trying to boot.

What can it hurt? If you're just gone for a few days?

We had nowhere to be. We had nowhere to go. Except home. And home wasn't where I wanted to be right now.

No one knew who we were here. And no one, especially my mom and sister, would ever think to look for us here.

"Mommy, I wanna go to the hockey game tonight."

Krista looked at me with that face, the one that usually got her whatever she wanted.

What could it hurt to stay another night? Krista didn't have to be back at school until Tuesday. And it wasn't like the private school I paid so damn much money to would kick her out if she didn't show up for a day or two. Attendance wasn't required for children in kindergarten. If we decided to stay a few more days—

We'd be home by Tuesday, at the latest. We couldn't hide forever.

We're not hiding. We're just taking a well-deserved break.

Jesus, I couldn't even convince myself of that.

"I guess…" I carefully didn't look at Rowdy, "we could stay to see the game. We could leave tomorrow."

"There's another game tomorrow," Raffi said. "We always have two home games opening weekend. Keeps people in town to spend money. If you maybe wanted to stay another day."

That meant we wouldn't leave until Sunday. But of course, traffic back into the city would be awful. So it wouldn't hurt to wait until Monday.

"I really don't want to impose."

Raffi's smile widened. "Oh, hon, you are *not* imposing. I love to have company. Especially this time of the year when Reston and the kids are so busy with the start of the season."

So, we'd be doing Raffi a favor if we stayed?

Sure, you can justify it like that.

"If you're sure we're not imposing…"

"I'm very sure." Raffi's tone was decisive. "Now that that's settled, do you mind if I take Krista with me on my errands?"

Krista's smile was infectious, and I found my lips curving to match my daughter's.

Still… "I really don't want to intrude on your home, though. There has to be somewhere for us to—"

Raffi waved a hand through the air. "Honestly, you'll be doing me a favor if you stay here. This house gets really empty around here on game days and, since my youngest left for college, I have to admit, it gets lonely. My grown children don't exactly visit as much as I'd like."

"Don't let her fool you with the 'woe is me' routine." Rowdy's voice made a shiver snake up my spine. And not a creepy shiver. No, this shiver was definitely *not* creepy. "When Rocky left, I'm pretty sure she and my dad drank a bottle of wine and danced all night."

Raffi gave her son the side eye. "When you drop your last baby at college, then you can tell me how to act. Until then, your mother gets to have her feelings, and you don't get to comment on them. Of course, that may never happen, since you don't seem in any way ready to settle down and give me grandchildren."

Rowdy laughed under his breath, but the look he gave his mom was filled with so much love, it made my heart ache. This was the relationship I wanted to have with Krista. Loving, teasing, understanding. Functional. I wanted so badly to give my daughter one functional parent. She'd never had a father, probably never would if my track record with men was any indication.

And I'd never actually had decent role models growing up, except for the fake ones.

That's pretty damn pitiful.

"You can stay in the same room you stayed in last night," Raffi continued. "It has its own private entrance and two bedrooms. We renovated it for my mom, but she lives in Florida now and won't even think about coming back up here to stay for more than a few months. Especially not during hockey season. You and Krista can have your privacy, for as long as you like."

Were these people for real? They were opening their home to complete strangers. Krista and I could be grifters or serial killers or … or just awful people. Or maybe the Lawrences took people in off the streets all the time and those people just disappeared. Happened all the time in the city.

But I knew that wasn't what was happening here. Raffi was just a decent person.

It's the perfect place to lay low. Just for a few days.

"Mommy, please?"

Krista stared at me with so much anticipation, I was answering before I realized I was going to.

"If you're sure we're not intruding—"

"Not at all." Raffi's smile widened, eyes twinkling with the same light I'd seen in Rowdy's. Not that I'd been looking. Nope. Not looking.

"Does that mean I can go with Miss Raffi to do the errands?"

Leaving me alone with Rowdy.

I swallowed hard and smiled at Krista. "Sure. If Miss Raffi really doesn't mind—"

"I absolutely don't mind." Raffi looked thrilled, actually. "I've got a lot to do today, so would it be okay if we had lunch while we're out?"

"Sure, but she's kind of a picky eater…"

Which was putting it mildly. My daughter was used to living in a city where she'd acquired a taste for authentic Thai and Indian food. Krista had become a real food snob.

"Is there anything she can't have?" Raffi asked. "Any allergies?"

"No, no. Nothing like that." This woman was almost too good to be true. "Thank you again for… everything. I'm so grateful—"

"Oh, now, none of that." Raffi waved her hand like she could make worry and distrust disappear just by willing it so. And who knows, maybe she could. "Come on, Krista, let's get you dressed and then we'll get started our errands."

Krista hopped off her chair like she'd had a fire lit under her butt. I wondered if I should be worried about how fast my daughter wanted to get away from me. Then again, maybe I should just be happy she didn't seem to be traumatized by last night's shitshow.

"We'll be back by four. Rowdy, don't burn Tressy's breakfast."

Behind me, I heard Rowdy mutter, "Shit," and when I turned around, he was sliding perfectly browned pancakes off the griddle and onto a plate.

Setting the plate on the island, he added a fork and knife and a napkin, then got a bowl of fruit out of the fridge. Strawberries, grapes, melon.

"OJ or coffee?"

It took my brain a second to process his question, because I was still a little shocked by the sight of this big man with the long wavy hair and the muscles in his arms on full display, who looked like he'd just come in from a hard day of building houses or maybe wrestling cows or something stupidly masculine like that.

He didn't look like he should be asking me whether I wanted coffee or juice after he'd just made me breakfast.

"Um, orange juice, please. I'm not a big coffee drinker."

Sliding into a chair at the island, because I couldn't think of anything else to do and I was starving, I picked up my fork and started eating. After the first bite, my eyes widened and my gaze shot up to Rowdy, who was staring at me over his mug.

"Oh my god. These are amazing. What did you put in them?"

He sipped his coffee before answering, lips curving in a smile that made me think of warm summer nights and stolen kisses. Then he winked, and my stomach did a flip-flop that was not at all related to intestinal distress of any kind. No, this was the butterflies-flapping and thigh-clenching kind of flip-flop.

The kind I hadn't experienced in years. Mainly because I wouldn't let myself feel those feelings. Attraction, love, lust, whatever. Not in my plan for the next few years, at least. Been there. Done that. Had my heart broken for the trouble. And when he'd exited stage right, I realized I'd won the lottery, because he'd been all kinds of wrong for me.

Maybe I was still tired from last night and these feelings would pass.

My inner bad girl snarked out a laugh.

"Little bit of this. Little bit of that."

I gave him a look designed to let him know he wasn't as cute as he thought he was. Even if he actually was.

His expression shifted into playful hurt. "What? Can't give away all my secrets on the first day."

"Do you have a lot of secrets?"

Now, why had I asked that? It sounded like flirting. I wasn't flirting. Hell, no. Not even a little bit.

Bad Girl laughed louder this time.

Rowdy's gaze narrowed, as if he knew exactly what I was thinking.

"Not really." He opened his arms like he was inviting me in for a hug. "What you see is generally what you get. What about you, Tressy? You have secrets?"

Way too many.

"So you're a hockey player."

The left corner of his mouth twitched, as if he wanted to smile but wouldn't give me the satisfaction. He let my words hang in the air for long seconds, while I forced myself to continue eating. When what I really wanted was to take a bite out of his perfect chin.

Bet he'd taste yummy.

Nope. Not happening.

Finally, when I thought for sure he wouldn't let me get away with the change in conversation, he pushed away from the island and turned to pour more coffee.

"Yep, since the first moment I could skate. I can't remember a time when I didn't have skates on my feet and a stick in my hand." He took another swig of coffee and my gaze slipped from his lips to the strong column of his throat. "What about you?"

Uh oh. "What about me?"

He waited until I looked up at him. "What do you do?"

"I own my own business." Which was true, just not the whole truth.

I went quiet, and I thought maybe he would let it go. I should've known better.

"You don't like to talk about yourself, do you?" His voice sounded wry. "Just a warning, but gossip is even more popular than hockey in this town. And you made a hell of an entrance last night."

I held his gaze but wasn't sure what I should say, or if I should say anything at all. I felt like I owed him an explanation. I'd fallen into his arms last night like the heroine in a romcom. His mom had given me and Krista a place to stay with no questions asked. And the women in the bar last night had been ready to rip the limbs off whatever man had done me wrong.

"I'm not in any kind of trouble. And I want you to know there's no one dangerous following me."

I just couldn't stomach returning to the shit show I'd left behind. My mom was going to be pissed as hell and my sister...

"I guess that's good to know."

His voice had an amused edge that tweaked at my conscience.

"Look, I know I owe you more—"

"You don't owe me anything."

Yes, I did. And I hated that. I hated owing anyone anything. I'd spent so much of my life being told I owed my family everything.

"I do. I owe you my thanks."

"You've already thanked me."

"Well, let me say it again. Thank you."

"You're welcome."

I wished I felt better for saying it. And I wished I didn't feel like I wanted to tell him more. Something about him made me want to keep talking.

He's definitely going to be a hazard to my well-being.

Dropping my gaze to my plate, I continued to eat, breathing a sigh of relief when he let the subject drop. When he turned to the sink and started to wash the dishes, I thought I'd be able to catch my breath. For some reason, though, I couldn't. Probably because my gaze got stuck on him.

Jesus, when did backs become sexy.

Maybe because it's his.

His t-shirt was tight enough that I could see the play of muscles beneath. The man had a body I wanted to touch. And that was something new and different for me. I hadn't dated in a really long time, mainly because I hadn't met anyone I remotely wanted to date. That didn't mean I didn't notice men. Especially nice-looking ones. In my world, those men were either married and out of bounds or they knew just how good looking they were and used it to their advantage.

I'd never met a man with a body like Rowdy's. When I did date, those men usually wore expensive suits, kept their bodies in shape with cycling classes, and loved a good brunch.

I wasn't sure Rowdy had ever been to brunch. Or a cycling class. And he probably didn't own a suit. But, damn, the man could cook. The last bite of pancake was on its way to my stomach when he turned from the sink. Since I had nothing more to eat, I couldn't ignore him. And honestly, I wasn't sure I wanted to. He was hard to look away from, making my blood tingle and my stomach flutter.

The feelings made me short of breath, as well, and that was—

"So, what do you want to do today? After we drop your car off at Donny's."

I wanted to forget that last night had happened. I wanted to forget I'd run away from my problems like a child. Wanted to forget that my mom had ambushed me and that my sister had once again nearly gotten her way without any thought for anyone else.

"I think I'd like to sit in a corner and breathe."

The way he looked at me made me feel like he could see straight into my soul. It was weird and oddly comforting.

No, no. It was just weird.

"I can arrange that," he said, "if you don't mind sitting in the corner of a cold ice rink and watching a bunch of guys be idiots."

Without trying to be, I was curious. And amused.

"Aren't you being a little harsh on your teammates?"

"You wouldn't think that if you knew them."

"Do you count yourself among the idiots?"

I hadn't meant to sound catty, and I immediately opened my mouth to apologize, but he started to laugh. The sound curled down into my core and made it clench.

What a god-awful time for my body to decide to be attracted to a man, which meant I really shouldn't go with him.

"Yeah, actually I do." He didn't look at all offended. "But I'm the captain of the idiots, so…" He shrugged, his smile widening.

And I saw how Rowdy made all the women around him smile whenever they said his name. The guy was a charmer. Not slick, at least not in the ways I was accustomed to. Rowdy was…different. I liked him. Which was kind of shocking.

"So what do you do the day before a game?"

"Well, we all get together at the rink to give offerings for a good season."

I blinked. "I'm sorry, did you say…offerings?

He nodded. "I know. You're speechless at our amazing ingenuity. Or struck dumb with wonder at our incredible stupidity. It's a toss-up, I admit."

My smile escaped, even though I tried hard to suppress it, and I watched his gaze dip to my mouth. That heat in my core spread through the rest of my body like a flash bomb. My cheeks flushed bright red, but luckily his attention was completely focused on my lips.

I swallowed hard and drew in much needed air. But his gaze narrowed when my lips parted, and now that air got stuck in my throat.

Tell him you can't go. Tell him you're exhausted. Tell him you're sick. Tell him you're allergic to ice. Do not go anywhere with this man.

"When are we leaving?"

My inner, reasonable self smacked the Bad Girl's forehead and called me an idiot. Yep, totally agreed.

"Whenever you're ready."

I looked down at my borrowed clothing. I tried to remember what I'd packed in my suitcase. Did I have something appropriate for a hockey rink? Had I packed any practical clothes?

"I'm not sure I have the right clothing."

I caught a flash of his bemused expression before it evened out into a grin. "If you've got jeans, I think I can come up with something that'll fit you on top. Just give me a sec."

He walked away and disappeared through the door, leaving me sitting there, wondering what I'd agreed to and second-guessing everything.

I'd almost talked myself out of going when he walked back into the room.

"I guessed on the sizes but if they don't fit, we've got a whole damn room full of them."

He held out his hand, and I took the plastic-wrapped packages. A t-shirt and sweatshirt, both black, with red lettering. It took me a second, but finally, I remembered my manners.

"Thank you."

"Welcome."

Then I was staring at him again, struck by the dark beauty of his eyes.

Damn it.

"I guess I'll go change."

Then I left before I could do something even more stupid than agreeing to go anywhere with this man.

CHAPTER FIVE

I DEFINITELY WANTED to kiss her.

I wasn't sure why exactly, except for the fact that she was beautiful and had all the hallmarks of a damsel in distress. Yeah, yeah, I had a hero complex. I'd been told that enough times to make me think it was actually true.

And you know what? I didn't give a shit what anyone else thought. I liked to take care of people. It was practically imprinted in my DNA. That's what you got for having parents who'd told me practically since birth to look after my younger sister and brothers.

But when Tressy had fallen into my arms last night, that protective instinct flared into immediate life, along with the need to kiss her. Now I just had to figure out how to make her want to kiss me back. She definitely had the look of a woman who'd been hurt and built hundred-foot walls around her heart. Apparently talking about what she was running from wasn't the way through those walls.

And she was running from something. I wanted to lock her and her daughter in my house and make sure no one could get to them. But that was called false imprisonment, and I should steer clear of that. At least for the first half of the season, anyway.

My dad would appreciate if I didn't land in jail again this season, although the Devils' attendance had jumped last year after me and a few of the guys had been caught—

"It's a little big, but I think it'll be okay. I guess."

Tressy walked back into the kitchen, head down as she examined the clothing I'd given her. I guessed she wore the t-shirt under the sweatshirt, which meant my name and number were plastered all over her back like a brand. I liked that a little too much. And she definitely didn't need to know that.

I'd purposely chosen the most sedate Devils sweatshirt ever made just so she wouldn't balk at wearing it. It had the STDD logo of the devil with a leer and across the back it said, "Let mayhem reign."

Not their best slogan ever but still one of the most accurate.

Don't know why you're getting yourself all worked up. She's not going to stay. This is a bad idea, dude.

Nah. I never had *bad* ideas. Maybe they weren't all exactly the best ideas, but spending time with this woman was not a bad idea. Besides, this is what my mom wanted. Raffi didn't have to speak to get her point across most of the time. She just had to look at you a certain way. Hell, the goddamn president would do my mom's bidding if she stared at him long enough. I was sure of it.

"Looks pretty good from where I'm standing." And before she could take that exactly how I'd meant it, I added, "You ready to go?"

She hesitated for a second, and I geared up to go full charm on her. Full-charm mode was usually a last resort. Then she lifted her head and smiled at me. Not even a full-blown, happy-to-see-you smile. Just a little hesitant grin that made her full pink lips curve and her blue eyes crinkle at the corners.

And holy hell, my gut clenched, and my blood sizzled like she'd lit a fire under my balls. The hair actually rose on my arms.

I couldn't remember the last time a woman had made me feel like this. Like I'd been awakened after a long sleep. Damn, did I really just compare myself to Sleeping Beauty? That was kinda weird.

Then she took a deep breath and nodded, like she was going into battle, or at least headed out to take on a seriously pissy elementary school principal.

"Sure."

"Then your chariot awaits."

I thought about holding out my hand and waiting for her to take it, but I didn't want to push my luck. I waved her toward the mudroom at the back of the kitchen that connected to the garage and to the driveway where I'd parked my truck.

It'd been years since my brothers and sister and I had made that mudroom our first stop after practices, so it didn't smell like rancid teenage sweat and disgusting hockey equipment anymore. Must've taken my mom years to get rid of that odor.

My mom was a freaking saint. I knew that now.

"What about my car?" she asked when I opened the passenger door of my truck for her.

"We'll run by garage, tell Donny what happened." I did offer my hand now, because the Bronco was jacked up enough to make it hard for her climb in. When she stopped for a second to assess the situation, I realized she only just came up to my shoulder. Probably weighed half of what I did. She looked a little underfed, like a model. Or an actress.

She was certainly pretty enough to be one, with her shiny blond hair and bright blue eyes, the sharp angles of her high cheekbones and the lushness of her lips. The woman was stunning. Hell, she looked even better without all the makeup she'd been wearing last night. Not that she'd looked bad. She just looked amazing now.

Or maybe that was my little head doing the talking.

Didn't matter. I was already halfway to being gone for her. I didn't know her middle name or her favorite food. But she didn't take my shit and she loved her daughter with the ferocity of a mama lion.

When she took my hand to let me help her into the seat, heat seeped into every nook and cranny of my body. Even my scalp tingled with it. But yeah, I felt it mostly in my cock. Christ, I hoped she couldn't tell. She'd probably run like hell in the opposite direction. Frankly, I'd been shocked as shit that she'd agreed to come with me.

She released my hand as soon as she slid onto the bench. Shutting her door, I hustled over to the driver's side and hopped behind the wheel.

I saw her glance at me out of the corner of my eye, but I got us on the road instead of getting lost in her eyes again. I turned down the radio before Springsteen, singing about a barefoot girl, spilled out of the speakers at a deafening volume. I patted myself on the back for not forgetting my gear in the back. If I had, the stench could be sickening. My stuff was already at the arena waiting for tonight.

The first game of the season.

For the first time in forever, that thought didn't bring the buzz of excitement it usually did. And I couldn't figure out why that was. I couldn't blame it on Tressy. I'd realized something was different with me at the end of last season. And now…

"So these offerings… You're not going to, like, sacrifice a chicken or anything like that. Are you?"

Since I couldn't tell if she was joking or not, I answered honestly. "Nah." I paused. "But it can get kinda strange."

"Strange how?"

Putting the truck in gear, I stomped on the gas and tore out of driveway before I realized I had a lady in the car and should probably drive like a normal human. I dropped the speed back to only ten miles over the limit. Of course, it felt like I was crawling, but when I looked over to see how Tressy was handling it, she was peeling her fingers off the arm rest so I figured I should keep it there.

"Well, last year, one of the rookies offered to remain a virgin for the rest of the season if he scored a hat trick in his first game."

She went silent for at least a full half minute. "Did it work?"

I snorted. "Course not. So he lost his V-card the next night and scored a Gordie Howe hat trick at the next game."

I stole another glance and found her looking bemused and amused.

"A what?"

"It's when you get a goal, an assist and a fighting penalty in the same game."

"And that's a good thing?"

"Yep. Especially in our league."

Another silence. "Is there something different about your league? I don't know that much about hockey, sorry."

"No need to be sorry. I can teach you everything you need to know."

I flashed a smile, but she didn't appear to be falling for my charm. I could respect that. Didn't like it, but I could respect it. Just meant I had to work harder. And I was nothing if not a hard worker.

"Our league is different than other leagues you might know. Like the NHL. Sure, they make a hell of a lot of money, and they get a lot of press. But we have a hell of a lot more fun."

"And how do you do that?"

"We don't take the game as seriously, so it moves faster. We give a better show."

"So it's more of a hobby league."

My back cranked into a straighten line, and I had to remind myself she wasn't dissing me or my game. She honestly just didn't know.

"No. We just think the game should be more fun." Damn, I sounded like I had a stick stuck up my ass, so I made a conscious effort to relax. "We make it more fun for everyone. Our league doesn't have some of the rules the NHL does. I mean, we have rules. We're just a little more, uh, lenient when it comes to some things."

"Like what?"

"Like penalties. There's not a lot of penalties in our league. And we do a lot of fun stuff for the fans during the game."

"Like what?"

She sounded genuinely interested, and I flashed her another grin, which still didn't land with the impact it usually did.

Losing your touch in your old age, man. And not just with women.

"Well, all the players have a certain thing they do when they score a goal. Like Rebel. He does this stupid dance that everyone loves, and the Angels toss Devils' underwear into the crowd. KooKoo grabs a Thor hammer from the bench and circles the ice with it while the girls throw lightning bolts."

"Girls?"

Shit. I glanced over, not surprised to find her staring at me with raised eyebrows. "Uh, the Angels. So, I've known some of the, uh, women since birth, so, yeah. Sorry."

"You've always lived here?"

"Except when I went to college. Penn State." I shrugged. "Never wanted to live anywhere else."

Which probably sounded pretty pathetic to this woman. Then again, I really didn't know anything about her, so…

"What did you go to college for?" she said.

There was that interest again, that tone in her husky voice that felt like her fingers running down my back. And not in a weird way. No, I really wanted her to run her fingers down my naked back while I—

"Political science with a minor in psychology."

I knew exactly what she was thinking. Which kinda pissed me off. Yeah, I was a professional athlete, and my parents owned the team. And, yeah, I'd inherited enough money from my grandparents to live comfortably for the rest of my life if I never held another job again.

But I wasn't some lazy-ass hick with no brains and—

"I always wanted to study poly-sci," she said, "but I knew I'd never be able to use the degree, so I went for boring. Business management."

Okay, not what I'd expected. I stole another glance and found her staring out the window with an expression I could only describe as wistful. Again. Not a Neanderthal. Sometimes an asshole and sometimes the life of the party but never a complete dick. My mom had taught me better.

"So what do you do for a living?"

She didn't answer right away, a long enough pause that I thought she wasn't going to. Then she took a deep breath, like she was bracing for impact. Or giving her answer some serious thought.

"I manage a talent agency."

Now, I might not be the brightest bulb in the shed, but that sounded like a dodge. I was willing to give her some leeway because obviously, she'd had a rough time of it last night.

"Were you at some fancy party last night with your clients?"

Yes, I was digging for info but, honestly, could she blame me? She stumbled into the bar last night and fell into my arms. It was a scene straight out of the movies Rain liked to watch, the sappy ones with happy endings where no one ever took their clothes off.

Another short, sharp breath. "Yes. But I... I had a fight with... someone, and I decided I needed some time away."

I felt the sudden need to growl. "Did someone hurt you?"

She glanced at me, her gaze narrow, probably because I sounded like I wanted to punch whoever had dared to upset her.

"No. It wasn't like that."

Her answer didn't sound that convincing and my hands tightened around the steering wheel.

"Who—"

"No one hurt me physically."

This time her answer was much more assured. My hands relaxed, slightly, on the wheel.

"Some asshole break your heart?"

Yep, still fishing, but I couldn't help myself. It was like pulling fucking teeth. I knew I should let her keep her secrets, knew it wasn't any of my damn business.

And still…

"No. Nothing like that."

That still didn't tell me whether she had a guy in her life or not. Maybe I should just come out and ask. Usually, I couldn't shut up. And caution wasn't in my vocabulary. This woman, with her quiet reserve and a princess dress that probably cost more than I earned playing hockey for a season, had the power to make me think about every word that came out of my mouth. When my mom figured that out, she'd want Tressy to stay forever.

I waited for her to go on, biting my tongue and focusing on driving. When the silence dragged on for more than thirty seconds, I heard her release a heavy breath.

"My mom and I have a pretty…contentious relationship. She did something that—" She shook her head. "I just needed some space. So I grabbed Krista and we left. Probably not the smartest thing to do when you're pissed off and upset. Definitely not the most adult."

That last was said mostly under her breath. My hands relaxed a little more, and I breathed easier. Family shit. I understood that.

Hell, I'd had enough fights with my dad growing up that it was a mystery how I'd made it to the age of thirty.

"Family can be a blessing and a curse."

"Your family seems wonderful."

I heard something in her voice that almost sounded like longing, which would make sense if what she'd said about her mom was true. And I had no cause to doubt anything she said. Just because she didn't want to talk to me didn't mean she was lying. It just seemed like she had secrets. Then again, maybe that was just my over-active imagination.

"They are. They're also annoying, frustrating, nosy, loyal and the only people who love me unconditionally."

"You make it sound like you're unlovable. That's not the vibe I got last night."

I flashed her a quick grin and saw her gaze drop to my mouth for a hot second. Maybe I hadn't lost my touch, after all.

"I guess they think I'm a decent guy."

"I got the sense that the women I met last night think you're more than just decent."

Was that a little hint of jealousy I heard?

No, you're just an idiot.

"I guess if you stick around for a few days, you can decide for yourself."

———

As I suspected, Donny wouldn't be able to get the rim until Monday, which meant Tressy and Krista would be staying a few days longer.

Tressy had nodded and thanked Donny as she handed her keys over like she was giving up a beloved pet. Then she climbed into my truck and slumped into the passenger seat.

"Sorry about the tire." Though I wasn't really. Actually, I was pretty damn elated.

She sighed, shaking her head. "Not your fault I didn't know you shouldn't drive on a flat for as long as I did. I just didn't want us to be stranded on the side of the road. I had to get Krista somewhere safe."

"And you did. Take a few days off and enjoy yourself."

She fell quiet again, and I had to bite my tongue to stop while I was ahead.

I had three days to get her to trust me. To show her how to have a good time. To show her how much fun we could have. Fun that involved kissing. And yeah, more than kissing. We would have amazing sex. I could just tell. We'd click together like Lego bricks. Close and tight and… Yeah. Better stop that train of thought now or I'd head into the arena with a hard on.

Which was a definite possibility because I'd just pulled into the driveway to the parking lot. The players' area was filled with trucks and SUVs. It looked like almost everyone had beaten me here. Shit, I hoped like hell I wasn't the very last or I'd have to do the toilet run, and there was no way in hell I wanted to do that with Tressy here.

I'd just put the truck in park when I saw Bonesaw come flying up the street.

With a grin, I looked at Tressy. "Gotta move it. Can't be the last one."

I hopped out of the car and hustled around to open the door for her. Bonesaw laid on the gas and tore into the parking lot when he saw me get out of my truck. Apparently, Bonesaw didn't want to do the toilet run either.

Reaching in, I grabbed Tressy around the waist and lifted her out of the car. Couldn't wait for her now. I didn't even have time to enjoy the feel of her in my hands because we had no time left. Grabbing her hand, I tugged her toward the players' entrance, and she followed me with a startled laugh.

"What's going on?"

"If you're the last guy to get here on the first day of the season, you have to do the toilet run. I've never had to, and I ain't starting today."

She had to run to keep up with me as I hustled toward the door.

"Am I going to regret asking what the toilet run is?" She didn't sound out of breath.

"Absolutely."

Behind me, Bones cursed as he got out of his truck, just as I opened the door and waved her through ahead of me.

Bobby "The Bonesaw" Brassard was six-feet-one of solid bulky muscle from head to toe. The guy was a tank in human form. But surprisingly fast on his feet. I just managed to shut the door before Bones made it to the entrance.

And when he realized I'd locked the door on him, meaning he had to go around to the front, Bones lifted his hands and gave me both middle fingers.

At the same time, Bones yelled, "Sorry, ma'am," through the glass, giving Tressy a smile that made him look like a kid due to the missing front tooth. Then he glared at me and made a gesture with his arm that was universally understood to not be a compliment.

Tressy made a strangled sound, and I glanced over my shoulder at her. She had one hand over her mouth, covering a laugh. And damn if she didn't look even prettier. I would've continued to stare if I hadn't seen Bones snap his head around to look over his shoulder. Following his gaze, I saw Dryden Hollowell, one of the rookies, cruise into the parking lot.

I immediately unlocked the door, let Bones saunter through, then locked it again when Denny ran up to the door.

"Hey, man, how's it going?" Bones said as he shook my hand, his smile trained on Tressy. "Hello, ma'am. Sorry for the language just now. Heat of the moment and all."

Tressy's smile had widened until her eyes were almost closed. "Not a problem."

"I'm Bobby. Nice to meet to you."

"Tressy."

After she'd shaken Bones's hand, she turned to me and that smile grabbed hold of my gut and twisted. "Are you all so…?"

Vaguely, I heard Bones laugh, in a way that should warrant some type of retribution. Like an elbow in the gut. But honestly, I couldn't take my eyes off her. When she smiled like she was now, I felt bathed in warm light.

Of course, that was probably the lust pumping through my veins, but it all kinda went hand in hand. And honestly, lust had never felt like this before. This…soft.

"So what?"

"Crazy."

She said that word like it could infect her, like she wanted nothing to do with it.

"Hell, this isn't even bad." Bones offered helpfully. "Just wait until the season actually starts. Then it gets insane."

I wanted Bones to disappear into the floor, the wall, the next dimension. Anywhere away from here. Because Tressy looked like she suddenly wanted to be anywhere but where she was.

"Um, hey, guys? The door's locked."

The rookie knocked politely, looking confused as all hell. Bones started to laugh, which made me laugh, which made Tressy shake her head, probably because she thought we were all insane.

Then she turned to me and Bones and said, "I'll give you to ten, then I'm opening this door."

I snorted out a laugh while Bones whooped and gave her a gentle pat on the shoulder.

"Thank you very much. You're a true lady," Bones said before sprinting down the hall.

Leaving me smiling down at her, her grin doing weird and wild things to my insides. Without thinking about it too much, I leaned down and pressed my lips to her cheek. I carefully didn't get too close to her mouth, even though I desperately wanted to kiss her, hard and deep and heavy. And I didn't linger.

But, damn, her skin was soft, and she smelled amazing.

The fucking rookie knocked on the door again, and I pulled away, my gaze locked with hers. She didn't look angry.

"Uh, Rowdy…?" the kid said from the other side of the door.

Tressy's lips twitched at the corners.

"Ten," she whispered.

"Come down to the ice after you let Denny in."

"Nine."

I gave her one last grin and took off, before I said, "fuck it," and kissed the hell out of her.

CHAPTER SIX

Tressy

WHAT THE HELL had I gotten myself into?

I watched Rowdy stroll away, toward the buzz of loud voices coming from somewhere down the hall. I couldn't hear exactly what they were saying. Or maybe I couldn't understand because I was more interested in the way Rowdy's jean's clung to his muscular ass and thighs.

The man had muscles on muscles in all the right places, though he didn't come off like a muscle-bound jock. It'd be better for me if he did. I could ignore him more easily.

"Ma'am, can I come in now?"

I gasped, "Oh, geez," as I turned back to the door to see the younger man staring at me with a confused smile. "I'm so sorry."

"No problem." He nodded his head at me. "I just don't want to be late for my first game day."

"Then don't let me hold you up any longer."

He gave me a big smile as I walked through the door then

waved as he headed down the hall. Unknowingly headed toward his doom of the Toilet Run.

Shaking my head, I took a deep breath, the unfamiliar scents of the arena making my nose twitch. The smell wasn't unpleasant, it was just…different. Like day-old popcorn and an industrial ice maker.

A loud cheer sounded from the end of the hall. The locker room, I guessed. Whatever the Toilet Run was, I had a feeling it wouldn't be fun for Denny.

I grinned, a little surprised at myself. After last night, I hadn't been sure I'd find anything funny for a long time. As a kid, I'd laughed all the time. It'd been my trademark, giggly and joyous. It's also made me one of the most bankable child stars on TV.

Until that giggly child became a sly, snarky teenager. And my career had taken a hit. I'd played a few goth best friends, overdosed a few times as drug addicts on Grey's Anatomy and Law & Order, and had one memorable three-episode arc as a dying cancer patient on an HBO miniseries that won a couple of awards.

By the time I'd turned seventeen, the roles had dried up. And my sister had never been able to duplicate my success, much to our mom's chagrin and my sister's bitterness.

Last night's event was supposed to have been the start of my sister's big comeback. But my mom and sister hadn't counted on me saying no and fucking up their big plans.

Roiling anger and that awful sense of betrayal hit me again, deep in my gut where it burned and made me feel like I wanted to throw up.

With an effort, I took a couple of deep breaths and shoved all of that out of my head. If I let them, those thoughts would consume me, take me back to that dark place I'd been in during my teens.

Not today.

There was a handsome man down that hall who looked at me

like he wanted to kiss me. Surprisingly, I wanted to kiss him back. I might be crazy. I might just be horny. Right now, I didn't care. I wanted to be a woman who could answer the question in his eyes. Yes, I liked him. Yes, I wanted—

Another whoop went up from the locker room then the door at the end of the hall flew open so hard, it smashed against the brick wall, and Denny sprinted though it. In nothing but his underwear. His expression was part resignation, part determination.

He was running flat-out by the time he reached the end of the hall and took the corner. I sucked in a gasp when he nearly wiped out, but he righted himself and took off down the concourse.

And holy crap, the guy was ripped. My mouth fell open as I caught sight of his muscular ass and thighs as he disappeared around the corner of the elliptical arena.

"I think I'm offended."

Blinking, I turned to find Rowdy coming up behind me. "What?"

"You don't look at me the way you just looked at him."

I heard the flirtation in his tone but also a bit of jealousy.

"You didn't just run by me in your underwear."

His brows arched and his eyes widened just a little. "Are you saying you want to see me in my underwear?"

He was flirting. And a little ball of heat exploded in my gut when I realized I wanted to flirt back.

But should I? *Could* I? I couldn't remember the last time I'd flirted with a guy. The last time I'd *wanted* to flirt with a guy. Taking care of Krista and building my career had consumed my life for the past six years. The moment the nurse had put her in my arms, I'd known my life was going to change. And it had. There were so many good things about my life now. But a man was not one of those.

It's not like you're going to marry the guy. Just loosen up and have a little fun.

Taking a breath, I deliberately looked him up and down. "Will you look that good?"

His smile slowly widened into an all-out grin that made my stomach flip and my core clench.

"If you think the rookie looks good, you've never seen a real man."

I was beginning to think he was right. Not that I'd tell him that, but damn, I'd love to see Rowdy in his underwear. Oh, hell, I'd totally prefer him without the underwear.

"Sorry to ruin your little fantasy world, but I have seen naked men before."

"Rowdy! You're supposed to be making sure the rookie hits all the bathrooms. Not talking to the beautiful lady."

I turned to find the entire team watching us. And grinning. A few of them were outright laughing. And wow. I didn't think I'd ever seen a group of men this…big. Like lumberjack big. Tall. Broad. Muscular. Handsome. So many good-looking guys. Maybe they only hired the handsome ones.

Then again, I'd never been around a lot of athletes before. I spent most of my days with child actors and their parents. None of them looked like these guys. Not a single damn one.

"The rookie ain't back yet." Rowdy yelled over his shoulder, never taking his eyes off of me. He crossed his arms over that broad chest. "So you wanna see me naked?"

When he arched his brows even higher, I began to laugh, which turned into a snort when I tried not to snort. Covering my mouth with my hand, I just shook my head while Rowdy chuckled, looking pleased with himself. Out of the corner of my eye, I caught a glimpse of movement and turned to see Denny sprinting up the hall behind me, carrying…something.

"Y'all are sadistic motherfuckers." Denny panted as he stopped next to Rowdy. His well-muscled chest heaved, six-pack abs clenched. "Sorry for the language, ma'am."

Rowdy burst out laughing, as did the rest of the team.

"You get them all, rookie?" Rowdy had to raise his voice to be heard over the whoops from the rest of the team.

Breathing heavily, Denny raised his right arm, gripping something in his hand.

"I wanna know who put that last one in the damn trashcan." Denny scowled. "You're a sick bastard."

I couldn't tell what he held right away, then had to take a second look to make sure I was seeing what I thought I was seeing.

I leaned a little closer to Rowdy, so he could hear me. "Are those…"

"Yes, they are," Rowdy said, his amusement clear.

My nose wrinkled. "Ew."

"Hey, at least they're clean. The sadist who came up with the Toilet Run made sure they came straight from the dirty laundry."

Denny clenched six jock straps in his hand, still breathing like a freight train.

"What the hell am I supposed to do with them now?"

"Well," Rowdy said, "now you have to keep the one that fits and wear it tonight for good luck."

Denny's whole face scrunched, making me cover my laughter with a cough.

"All right, Devils." Rowdy clapped his hands. "Let's go. We still gotta do the offering."

Breaking off into smaller groups, the guys turned and headed back toward the locker room, herding poor Denny with them. A few of the guys turned to give Rowdy the eye but kept moving, leaving us alone.

I looked up at him, smiling. "Is it like this all the time?"

"Like what? This much fun?"

His expression made it clear he was being serious. Then again…

"This chaotic," I said.

Now his grin burst wide, and my heart beat a little fast. "Nah.

Sometimes we actually play hockey."

CHAPTER SEVEN

ressy

I MADE my way down to the ice from the concourse. I didn't see anyone else in the seats, although I could hear the guys in the locker room, their voices loud and laced with enough profanity to make my ears burn. It actually made me a little nostalgic for my performing days, when I'd huddle in a dark corner of the set watching the crew set up. They'd become used to me hiding there from my mom and the PR people who had "just one more interview."

The arena was colder than any set I'd been on, and I stuffed my hands in the pocket of the sweatshirt. It wasn't a very big arena, probably only held four thousand people. The auditorium my mom had rented for my sister's concert last night held six thousand. At the time, I'd been amazed that it'd been sold out, because my sister didn't have that big of a following.

I hadn't questioned why my mom had wanted to hold my sister's concert in New York. Tiff wasn't as well known in New

York, didn't have some of the baggage she would've carried in L.A. And when my mom had guilted me into showing up, I had grudgingly admitted that I really should make an appearance.

But then my mom had sprung her trap. Even though she knew how much I hated performing now. How it made me physically ill to even think about getting on stage. It'd felt like a knife in my back when my mom had told me how she'd managed to sell out that auditorium. By promising the return of Teresa Sinclair to the spotlight. Along with a special guest.

"We need you to do this for your sister. All you need to do is this one concert. That's all she needs to get back on her feet."

The sound of men's laughter drew my attention to the tunnel that led out from beneath the seats, pushing away the memories of last night.

My heart began to beat faster, and my lungs squeezed tighter. But this was totally different from the feeling I got just thinking about performing. I wasn't going to think about why that might be. Instead, I forced myself to look around the arena, instead of staring at the entrance, waiting for a glimpse of Rowdy.

Nope, I was not obsessing over the guy. Not at all.

My gaze slipped to the short walls around the ice, covered with advertisements for local businesses. Tommy's Auto Service. Martin's Farm Stand, complete with a map that looked like it'd been drawn by a child. The Daily Register, where you could read all about your favorite teams. The local John Deere dealer and the local hardware store and the local restaurant.

Maybe I really had landed in an alternate reality, where people lived in small towns and actually enjoyed it. I couldn't imagine living anywhere without round-the-clock delivery and decent Thai food. And the anonymity that came with living in a city of millions.

You're a snob.

Probably. But I wasn't enough of a snob not to drool over brawny hockey players with messy hair and scruffy chins, because, *oh my god*. My breath caught in my throat and my heart did a wild jig when the first guys stepped out onto the ice.

But none of them were Rowdy.

The men began to skate around the ice, but my eyes stayed glued to the entrance. And then there he was. The hair flowing around his shoulders and that smile that could totally sell millions for a toothpaste company. The slightly crooked nose and those dark eyes that made me want to stare into them like a lovesick idiot.

The crowd let out a cheer, but he looked up and looked straight at me, his grin widened, as if he knew exactly what I was thinking. I deliberately looked away, watched the guys circle the ice a few times before breaking off into pairs and trios, laughing and talking with one another.

Rowdy and Rebel peeled off with a couple of guys at the other end of the ice from where I was, so I couldn't hear them. Rowdy leaned on his stick, shaking his head, his mouth curved. Whatever Rebel was saying, Rowdy thought it was pretty damn amusing. And when he was amused, he smiled. This smile was open and free and totally easy.

Why now?

With everything going on in my life, why did I have to catch feelings for a man now? One I didn't even know. Who was so totally outside the small bubble of my life. Was it a response to the stress from yesterday? Maybe my mind was trying to distract me with lust. If that was the case, it was working like a charm.

A loud bang, almost like a gong, made me start, my gaze snapping back to the entrance the guys had used to get on the ice. A member of the team was rolling out a metal barrel from beneath the stands. He smacked the side with a log again, making that gong sound.

Flames emerged from the top. It looked like the kind of thing you'd see at a campfire. Were they going to roast marshmallows?

Make smores? Burn all those jock straps the rookie had collected?

I smiled, shaking my head as I remembered Rowdy's laughter. And feeling that heat in my gut move lower.

"Mommy, did we miss the rishual?"

I turned with a smile to see Krista running down the stairs toward me. She looked happy, her normal reserve wiped away by joy.

"What have you been up to this morning, baby?"

Scooping Krista into my arms, I hugged her close, loving the way my daughter's arms wrapped around my neck and squeezed.

"Miss Raffi and I went shopping, and we got stuff for the rishual."

"And what stuff did you get for the ritual?"

"Stuff to eat! She said we had to have sussefance."

I smiled at Krista's adorable mispronunciations. "And what kind of sustenance did you get?"

"Well, Miss Raffi said we had to have some good stuff, but we got popcorn and gummy bears too, because Miss Raffi said we gotta be a little bad."

"What I said was, you have to be a little bad *sometimes*. Oh good, we didn't miss anything. They're just getting started."

Raffi smiled at me in a way that couldn't help but make me feel wrapped in a warm, fuzzy hug. I don't know how she managed that. The woman just seemed like every cliché ever written of the perfect wife and mother. Of course, she couldn't be. No one was that perfect.

"Why don't we sit down and get ready for the festivities to start."

I moved over so Krista and Raffi could sit next to me. By the time they were settled, the guys had moved the flaming tub to the center of the rink, where the team formed a circle around it. All of the guys held something, mostly pieces of paper. Some of the guys had what looked like stuffed animals, and there were a few things I couldn't make out. And yes, the rookie was holding the jockstraps.

I still wasn't exactly sure what was going to happen, but strangely, I couldn't wait to see. I wouldn't admit it to anyone, and I barely wanted to admit it to myself, but I was fascinated by Rowdy. Big, boisterous, loud. Someone I never would've found attractive before but now couldn't seem to look away from. What did he always find so amusing? I'd never met anyone who smiled as much as he did. He couldn't be that happy all the time. It just wasn't possible.

"Do they do this every year?"

I spoke in a near-whisper as I saw other people sliding into seats throughout the arena. No one sat too close to the ice, as if they were giving the team privacy.

I felt like a voyeur, watching something forbidden. Or sacred. Which was totally ridiculous. They were playing a game, not fighting fires or curing cancer. But as more and more people filtered into the stands, the quieter it seemed to get. It almost felt like church, or at least what I remembered of church from the few times I'd been in one.

"Yes. It's been a tradition since the second season." Raffi kept her voice low, as well. "The boys don't like to admit they're superstitious, but they don't mess with traditions."

"Rookies, listen up!"

Rowdy's voice rang through the arena, make a little shiver run up my spine and…lower.

"Hockey is a game, but it's also a way of life."

I snuffled a laugh, my eyes wide as I turned to Raffi to share the joke. But Raffi wasn't laughing. And neither was anyone else in the arena. Luckily, Raffi's attention was firmly fixed on the ice, so she hadn't seen my reaction. Quickly, I refocused my gaze. Back to Rowdy.

"We are family. We take care of each other. We watch each other's back. We kick the shit out of anyone who messes with our family. We help each other reach our goals. We score goals!"

The guys cheered, though it sounded more like a roar, raising their sticks in the air.

"And today, we offer the hockey gods our sacrifices for a great season."

Another roar, this one louder.

"Rookies, did you bring your offering?"

A few of the younger guys looked at each other, shaking their heads, their expressions ranging from disdain to confusion. But none of them said a word, just held up whatever they had in their hands. Rowdy pulled something out of the front of his pants. And damn, if that didn't make me think about putting my hands there, as well.

I shoved that thought out of my head as fast as it'd popped in. I didn't need that floating around, giving me ideas I couldn't do a damn thing about. Because we weren't staying long. Just a few days. I couldn't sleep with Rowdy. Okay, sleep was not what I wanted to do with Rowdy, but I couldn't have sex with him either.

Why not?

Because I couldn't. Just nope-nope-nope.

"My offering to the hockey gods," he continued. "The x-ray of my torn ACL two years ago. I've been holding onto this since then, knowing I would need it. I burn this as insurance against injury this season."

Rowdy threw the x-ray into the flaming barrel and a few of the guys began to chant, "Burn, burn, burn" as it caught fire. After Rowdy, it was Rebel's turn. Then Bobby. One after another, until every member of the team had thrown something into the flames.

It was both absurd and weirdly compelling. I'd never seen anything like it, and I worked with actors, who were some of the most ridiculously superstitious people on the planet. If they picked up their coffee mug the wrong way or their hairbrush was on the wrong side of the makeup table, it'd send them into a panic spiral.

I really hadn't known what to expect, but it hadn't been this serious, almost religious experience. By the time Denny tossed a handful of jockstraps into the fire—except for the one he was supposed to wear tonight, I assumed—the entire team looked stoked. Completely committed. And they all looked at Rowdy to lead them.

Rowdy no longer had a smile, his expression completely serious. And compelling. And way too damn handsome.

Swallowing hard, I tried not to fidget in my seat. Raffi was too perceptive. Or maybe she really could read minds. I definitely didn't want Rowdy's mother to read mine right now because it was filled with x-rated visions of her son.

"All right, boys, let's skate a few laps, loosen up and go over the game plan for tonight."

Another whoop went up and the circle broke apart as the guys skated around the perimeter of the ice. Someone I assumed was from the ice crew took the burning tub away. The spectators began to talk amongst themselves.

And Rowdy skated over to the entrance onto the ice, where there was no glass, looked directly at me and crooked his finger.

If it'd been any other man, I would've given him a different finger and ignored him. I couldn't ignore Rowdy. Didn't want to ignore him.

"I think I'm being summoned." I turned to give Raffi a look that I hoped conveyed my amusement and not the heat coursing through me.

"Can I come, too?"

Krista's question kicked me back to reality. Nothing was going to happen here. Nothing could happen. We were only going to be here a few days. I had too many responsibilities at home, first and foremost…Krista.

"Of cou—"

"Krista, honey," Raffi said, "why don't you come with me to help decorate the family suite?"

"What's a family sweet? Is there candy?"

Krista's attention immediately turned to her new best friend. I couldn't blame her. Raffi was the cool mom my mom would never be. My mom was too driven, too hardened by a rough early life and too bitter about what she didn't have that she thought she deserved.

Raffi laughed and took Krista's hand. "There *is* candy. Why don't you come with me, and I'll show you. I really could use your help."

Raffi looked at me and winked as Krista glanced at Rowdy before deciding candy trumped hockey player and taking Raffi's outstretched hand.

"Tell Rowdy I'll see him later," Krista said with a look that made me bite back a smile. Krista's natural sass was finally rising back to the top. Where it should be.

For years, I'd been the good girl. The one who followed the rules and gave a hundred-and-ten percent of myself to everything. Who let my mother dictate my life because it was best for the family. Not always best for me.

I vowed not to let that happen to my daughter.

"I'll be sure to do that," I said. "Be good for Raffi."

"No need to worry about that." Raffi laughed. "I raised four ruffians. Krista is definitely not a ruffian."

"But I wanna be a Ruffy Ann, too."

I snorted and Krista looked at me with wide eyes.

"You can be whatever you want to be, honey. I just want you to be a good girl for Miss Raffi, okay?"

"I can do that."

I laughed even harder when I realized Krista had mimicked me perfectly. I said that exact phrase at least five-hundred times a day when I was working and, since I worked at home with Krista most of the day, she'd obviously picked it up from me.

"All right, sweetheart." I directed my next words to Raffi. "Thank you. I can't—"

"Stop right there." Raffi held up the hand that wasn't holding Krista's. "No need to say anything else. Honestly, Krista's been the bright spot in my day. There aren't enough little ones in my life right now, so thank you for letting me borrow her."

Raffi sounded so honestly grateful, I didn't know what to say. Krista's own grandmother loved her but never treated her like a precious gift.

I nodded, biting my tongue against the threat of tears as Raffi and Krista turned and headed out of the row and up the stairs. I had no idea where they were going, but I knew Krista would be fine.

I couldn't say the same for myself. That man's smile made me feel like my bones were jelly. Taking my time down the stairs so I didn't trip, I reached Rowdy, who was leaning against the boards, dark eyes shining with amusement.

"Have a good time?"

"It was…interesting." I smiled, hoping he wouldn't think I was trying to make fun of him but not wanting to fawn all over him. "It looked like you all were having a good time."

"It's a good team-building exercise. And it gives the veterans a chance to get to know the rookies better."

I stopped on the last step, wondering if this guy was for real. He seemed…decent. Nice. Down to earth. All wrapped in a bad-boy exterior that was catnip to my inner Bad Girl. I knew he wasn't perfect. No one was, myself included. As a kid, I'd been too trusting, too ridiculously naïve. Now I trusted no one, because everyone wanted something from you. Nothing came without strings.

What did Rowdy want from a woman he didn't even know?

Same thing you want from a man you don't know.

It couldn't be that easy, could it? A random flirtation, maybe a little covert making out? And if I was lucky, a couple of orgasms that led to nothing more than a quick smile and "thanks so much, have a good life," the next morning. I couldn't even remember the last time that had happened to me, but I couldn't stop thinking about it now.

"How long have you played for the team?"

Small talk. Sure, that's really gonna take my mind off the strong neck I want to lick.

"Come to the game tonight and you'll find out all you need to know. Then let me take you out for a drink after."

Oh, yes, please.

"Won't you be too tired to go out?"

His smile widened. "I'm not ancient, and I'm never too tired to buy a drink for a beautiful woman."

My brows rose at his blatant flirting, making him huff out a laugh.

"You're gonna be hell on my ego, Tressy, but I still want to get that drink after the game. Say yes. Please."

I wanted to. He was the first man in years I'd wanted to spend time with. The first man to stoke my dormant sexuality.

Say yes, already.

But I was staying with his parents, and it almost seemed disrespectful to want to have hot sex with the son of the woman letting me and my daughter stay in her home.

"You know your little girl has my mom wrapped around her finger. Mom's probably already making plans for her and Krista tonight."

I shook my head. "You're pretty damn sure of yourself."

Rowdy huffed out a laugh, his grin slipping for a quick second. "Only on the ice. Solid ground gives me more of a problem."

"I don't believe that one bit." I crossed my arms over my chest. "You're one of the most confident men I've ever met."

And I didn't mean that in a bad way. Rowdy's confidence was sexy, not pretentious or a pitiful cry for attention.

"Stay for a while."

This time, his words were quiet, sincere.

I paused, though I knew what my answer would be. "I think… I'd like to."

Now his smile returned. "Good. I'll see you at the game. The team always starts off the season with a private dinner before the game. Mom and Rainbow usually do dinner together, so I'm sure you and Krista will be invited along with them."

"You all spend a lot of time together. You work together, eat together, live near each other." I couldn't imagine having to live with my mom now. Or even live in the same state. "Doesn't that get…stifling?"

He shrugged like it was nothing. "Nah. They're family."

I didn't know what to say to that. My family was nothing like his. And I was almost ashamed to say anything else. It felt disloyal. And pathetic. For so long, I'd lived like my family was a necessary evil. Maybe it would be good for Krista to see how a real family functioned.

"I would love to go for a drink."

His smile warmed every part of my body from head to toe.

*owdy*

"HEY, SON. GOT A MINUTE?"

"Yeah, Pop. What's up?"

"Everything go okay this morning?"

The Colonel sounded distracted, which wasn't unusual. The opening game of the season was always hectic. All the opening-night festivities plus a meeting with the visiting team's owner, in addition to the team dinner and the after-party. It was a lot, but my dad thrived on being over-worked.

"Of course. The rookies got into it after a while. Nessy and Reb helped me keep them in line."

"And Tressy and her little girl? How are they settling in?"

My brows rose as I slid into the chair on the other side of my dad's desk. Pop wasn't oblivious, but my mom's strays didn't normally warrant notice until they'd been around for a few weeks.

"I think they might be staying a little longer."

Pop nodded, as if he'd expected that. "Your mom'll be happy to hear that. She's taken a real liking to those girls."

"Something bothering you, Pop?"

His brow drew down. "No, no. Nothing's bothering me. It's just…"

I waited a second for my dad to continue. But he just kept staring out the window of his office on the second floor of the arena, like he saw something I didn't.

"Just what?"

My dad shook his head, mouth pursed. He looked like he had something weighing on his mind, but I couldn't believe it was connected to Tressy and Krista. It had to be something else. Something he didn't want to discuss. Which was strange because my dad always talked to me.

When he finally turned to me, his pursed lips turned into a half grin, but it still didn't look completely genuine. "She just reminds me of someone, I guess. I just can't figure out who."

"Tressy? You think you know her?"

Pop shook his head "No. That's the weird thing. I know we've never met. Just a weird case of déjà vu, I guess. So, you ready for tonight?"

I shrugged. "Of course."

My dad leaned back in his chair. "You don't sound all that excited."

Now I had his full attention, like a ray gun of intense heat focused directly at me.

"Why are you looking at me like that?"

My dad's focus intensified. "You haven't seemed yourself lately. Something you want to talk about?"

"Nothing's going on, Pop. Why do you ask?"

"You just don't seem…here all the time."

I returned my dad's stare for a few long seconds. "What does that mean?"

"It means your attention isn't here, on the team."

Well, shit. I'd thought I was keeping my secret pretty well. But that phone call I'd gotten three weeks ago had been weighing on my mind. Not that I was seriously considering the offer. It'd been a pity toss from an old friend. I was doing what I loved right here. And when I didn't love it anymore…

I'd figure that out later. When my dad retired. Which was something I could never imagine happening.

"What's going on here, Pop?"

My dad shook his head. "We're just having a conversation."

"Yeah, but why are we having *this* conversation?"

"You ever think about doing something else?"

My eyes rounded, and my brain blipped. My dad usually left the deep conversations to his wife, because the Colonel was a bull in a china shop.

"Like…something other than hockey?"

My dad rolled his eyes, which just left me more confused.

"Well, yeah. What the hell else would I be talking about?"

I threw my hands in the air. "Jesus, Pop, I don't have a clue. Why would I want to do anything other than play hockey?"

"Maybe because you want more than to live here all your life."

"Why would I want to live anywhere else?"

My dad shook his head, his exasperation growing. "Rowdy. I love you, son, but you're the most damn stubborn kid."

"Well, at least you know I'm definitely yours."

My dad's laughter filled the room, making me breathe a little easier. Now my dad sounded more like himself and less like he wanted to dig into things I didn't want to discuss.

"You're a chip off the damn block, kid. Which is how I know you got something on your mind."

"Anyone ever tell you you're a pain in the ass, old man?"

My dad's grin grew. "All the damn time. But that doesn't mean I'm wrong."

"Well, if there's something on my mind, it's gonna stay there." I gave my dad my best determined glare, which just made my dad's grin widen. "Honestly, there's nothing wrong, Now, do *you* wanna talk about whatever's got you in this mood?"

"Well, I guess you do have some of your mom in you. She'd good at turning the tables on me." My dad huffed. "I'll tell you what's on my mind. You are. You seem lost lately, and I'm worried."

Well, damn. This wasn't good. My mom was usually the one who worried after me and my brothers and sister. She called for no reason other than to reassure herself we were still alive and had clean underwear, although I was pretty sure she didn't ask my sister that. Growing up in a house full of boys, Rain had learned to carve out her own space and make her own way. Independent was an understatement with that one.

But I must have done something pretty damn blatant for my dad to realize I had something on my mind. Didn't mean I had to spill my guts, though. Especially not on the first day of the season.

"Always a few nerves before the start of the season. Maybe I'm getting smarter with age."

"You've always been smarter than you give yourself credit for."

"Okay, Pop, now I know there's something wrong. Did you hit your head recently?"

I hid a grin when my dad scowled. "Goddammit, Rowdy, I'm trying to be serious here."

"You've got nothing to be worried about, Pop. I'm fine. Everything's fine. We're all fine."

Except I wasn't. Not completely. But it'd pass. It always did. Just part of living in a small town.

The Colonel gave me another long look before he nodded, not so much accepting but agreeing to let it go. For now. I figured my mom would be checking in sooner rather than later. If I was lucky, I'd take a hard hit in the game tonight, and Mom would take pity on me. Maybe I'd get some sympathy from another pretty woman, as well.

At least I'd gotten her to agree to go with me to the afterparty, even if that meant having it with the entire team and family, friends and fans.

"This season's gonna be one for the books, Pop."

"THIS JOCK'S TOO DAMN SMALL."

Raucous laughter bounced off the cement walls of the locker room followed by increasingly ridiculous and profane suggestions of what Denny should do with the allegedly too-small protective gear.

"You sure you don't mean too big?"

"Are you sure you're putting it in the right place?"

"Maybe you need help finding your dick. Let me get you a magnifying glass."

"Dude," I said, "your brain's not that big. It'll fit."

Denny held up his hand with the offending equipment. "I don't wear it on my head, asshole."

That prompted another round of laughter, mostly from the guys who got the joke. Denny just looked at me like I was an idiot. Which made me laugh all that much harder.

As the guys continued to razz the rookie, I just shook my head and continued to get ready.

The first game of the year was always a fun night for the guys. It was a clean slate and a leap into the unknown. Anything could happen. Hell, we could start with a win and maybe have a winning season.

Not that it'd happened for a while, but there were more important things than winning,

Like women. And tonight, that meant only one woman.

"Rowdy! You planning to go out there in your jock? I mean,

the crowd would love if you did it again, but maybe wait for the middle of the season when we've lost a couple games."

I didn't give my brother the dignity of a verbal response, I just flipped him the finger and went back to dressing.

"Hey, man, never known you to have opening night jitters."

I shook my head at Bobby's quiet comment. My longtime teammate, who'd earned the nickname Bonesaw for using his stick like a precision instrument to slash and sometimes score goals, sank onto the bench next to me.

Bonesaw was the only one of the guys who'd actually played in the NHL. Before his demons got the worst of him. The Colonel had signed him the month he'd gotten out of rehab.

"No jitters. Just ready to get started."

Bobby kept staring at me. "Or ready for the game to be over. Hear you have a date afterward."

Oh, for fuck's sake. "Dude, who are you? My mother? And where did you hear that?"

Bobby smiled, white teeth gleaming against his dark skin. "So, you do have a date?"

"No. It's not a date. I just invited a little girl and her mom to the afterparty."

"Little girl, huh. Must really like the mom if you're willing to spend the night with someone else's kid."

I figured I should take offense to that. "What the hell, man? I like kids."

"You don't usually like women who have kids."

Okay, valid point. Still...

"You really wanna talk about this now?"

Bobby shrugged, grabbing his helmet off the bench next to him and tapping his stick blade against my pads. "Just thought I'd find out what's up. You ready for the game?"

"I was before you started asking me questions like we're in junior high."

Bobby huffed. "Neither of us have been in high school in a long time."

"Jesus, now you're calling me old. Next you'll be telling me I need to retire."

"Don't get ahead of me. Just saying we're not getting any younger."

"Now you really sound like my mom."

Bobby's smile was designed to get a rise out of me. "I like your mom."

I threw an elbow hard enough to make Bobby grunt. "Don't even go there."

Bobby shrugged. "I like your sister, too."

"Oh, for fuck's sake." I stood, my skates an extension of my body, my uniform a second skin. "Devils! Are we ready?"

"Yes, Captain!"

The cheer rose up from the team, who stood and slapped their sticks on the floor.

I looked around the room, at the excitement on the rookies' faces and the smiles on the veterans' faces. And if the sight didn't make me as excited as in years past, well, I'd just keep that to myself.

ressy

"Mommy, can I have popcorn? Or ice cream? Or cotton candy?"

"How can you still be hungry? You just had dinner. And we're going to a party afterward. You don't want to have an upset tummy for that, do you?"

Krista pouted, her face screwed up with little lines. "No, but—"

"Krista, honey, if it's okay with your mom, we could go check out the kids' area. There are all kinds of games and lots of other kids to play with."

Krista and Raffi looked at me with almost identical expressions of expectation. I would've laughed, but I didn't want to offend Raffi in any way. The woman had seemingly fallen in love with my daughter overnight, and my daughter had decided Raffi was her best friend. The bond between them was practically visible. I would've felt slighted except for the fact that Raffi treated me like another one of her children.

Dinner tonight had just been Raffi, Rain, Krista and me. With the Colonel, Rowdy and Rebel eating with the team, I had insisted on taking Raffi and Rain out to dinner as a thank-you. The four of us had gone to a small Italian restaurant where everyone knew Raffi by name and the chef came out to say hello then invited Krista back to the kitchen to watch her make the sauce.

Raffi had kept the conversation on neutral ground, not digging for information. I had found myself wanting to spill my guts, to confide in this woman who seemed to want nothing more than to help.

But I couldn't find the right words. At least, I couldn't find the words that wouldn't make me sound like an ungrateful daughter and sister.

"Sure, honey. Be good for Miss Raffi."

"You could come with us, Mommy."

I would've thought Krista actually wanted me to join them, if not for the fact that I knew my daughter and knew that look on her face. Krista wanted her new friend to herself. Krista loved her Gigi—because, of course, Bebe Meyers wouldn't want to be called Grandma—and her Aunt Tiffy, but they didn't see her often because they lived in Los Angeles.

Krista made the same face when our neighbor, Rosa Santiago, who was nearing sixty, took Krista for their weekly brunch date on Saturday. Which reminded me that I needed to contact Rosa and let her know we were okay. And to somehow not tell her where we were so Rosa didn't feel obligated to lie to anyone who might ask.

"That's okay, sweetheart. You and Miss Raffi have a good time. I'll be fine."

Krista's smile could brighten the darkest day.

"Okay. See you later, Mommy. Come on, Miss Raffi." Krista tugged on Raffi's hand. "Let's go play."

Raffi smiled as she let Krista drag her back to the entrance to the suite, leaving me to settle into a seat. The suites were located just above the general seating. People were already starting to filter into the arena, most of them wearing Devils jerseys, sweat-shirts, t-shirts, baseball caps, scarves, gloves. Some wore camou-flage-print pants in the Devils colors of black and red. Every single person wore something with the Devils logo on it.

The merchandising alone had to rake in hundreds of thou-sands of dollars. Which is probably where the team, or the Lawrences, made most of their money, because it definitely wasn't on tickets. I'd noticed the prices listed above the ticket windows and, even though Raffi had mentioned that the game was sold out, I knew enough about the economics of ticket prices to know that, even if they sold out every game this season, they couldn't make enough to cover arena upkeep, player salaries, not to mention staff salaries and all the other costs that went into maintaining a venue like this.

So either the Lawrences were pouring money into this team and facility, or they made a shit-ton of money on merch. I guessed the answer was somewhere in the middle.

Once again, I wondered if I'd fallen down a rabbit hole and ended up in some backcountry Wonderland.

And I really had to stop thinking about St. David as back-country. Was anywhere on the East Coast truly backcountry? The town had cell service and running water. It wasn't like they were living in the Middle Ages. Although I had seen a horse and buggy on the road today. I'd stared at it for way too long then laughed when the little boy sitting next to the driver made a face at me.

A feminine growl of frustration from the hall announced Rainbow's entrance. The curvy brunette whirlwind stomped into the suite, threw herself onto the chair next to me and looked for all the world like someone had told her she couldn't play with her favorite toys anymore.

"Don't ever work with athletes, your brothers or your father. They will find ways to piss you off that you would never think of in a million years. They will treat you like a twelve-year-old and tell you not to worry your pretty little head about things and then expect you to design and order an entirely new line of merchandise for next year."

Rain let out a low scream of fury that should've made any grown man cower in fear. I had only met Rain this afternoon at her parents' house, when she'd stopped by to drop something off and had made me feel like a forever friend within five seconds. She'd complimented my hair, my skin and, weirdly enough, my battered and well-loved Chuck Taylors sneakers.

Then she'd asked if I wanted to join her and a few friends for Sunday brunch. No men allowed, Rain had said. Just gossip, mimosas and enough food to soak up the alcohol.

My head still spinning from the torrent of words Rain had unleashed, I had paused only a moment to say, sure, I'd love to. Which was totally not like me. I didn't like to be thrown into intimate situations with strangers. I ended up quiet and awkward. But I couldn't deny I wanted to go to brunch with this woman. She seemed a lot like her mom, who gathered people into her orbit with her heart and smile.

Now, Rain took a deep breath while I tried to figure out how I should respond to her barely leashed fury.

"Do you have any brothers?" Rain said before my brain had stopped working.

"No, just a sister."

Rolling gorgeous brown eyes that appeared to be a Lawrence family trait, Rain shook her head. "You're so damn lucky. Don't get me wrong, I love my goddamn *annoying* brothers with all my heart, but if I ever get the chance to lace their beer with castor oil, I will laugh as I watch them run to the bathroom every two minutes."

By this time, I was laughing so hard, I actually snorted. Covering my mouth with one hand, I had a flashback to my childhood and my other life, the one I'd lived in front of a camera and an audience.

Rain lifted her brows as she watched me try to contain herself.

"Well, I'm glad someone thinks I'm funny instead of cute when I'm pissed off. When you're cute, everybody thinks you're harmless."

Rain wasn't wrong about the cute part. She looked like she could walk on set and immediately everyone would know she was the girl next door. The one who pined after the hot neighbor boy, the captain of the hockey or football team.

"I don't think you're harmless at all. And besides, if they think you're harmless, they'll never see you coming."

Rain's smile took over her whole face now, wiping away the last of the faint bitterness. "I knew I liked you. I definitely think you should stay a while. I mean, like, after Monday."

Raffi had been careful all day not to bring up the subject of when Krista and I were going to leave. And frankly, I hadn't wanted to think about it. The mess I'd left back in New York wasn't going anywhere and, since I hadn't even peeked at my social media since before I'd left, I didn't know how bad it was.

I liked being disconnected. Out of reach. And the more I thought about it, the more I was leaning toward maybe taking a few more days next week to stay.

"I mean, I'm not trying to pressure you or anything," Rain said, "I just figured maybe you might want to take a real break."

I arched my brows and looked at Rain, who was practically biting her lip, trying not to ask invasive questions, even though I knew she could barely contain herself. Raffi seemed more than willing to let me keep my secrets, at least for now. Rain... not so much.

And I found I wanted to talk to someone. Not that I wanted to spill the whole truth, which was kinda shitty. But I'd grown so used to protecting herself and Krista from a world that would want every little piece of us they could get, that it was second nature now.

"I'm actually considering maybe staying a few days next week. It's…quiet here."

Just at that moment, "A Night on Bald Mountain" began to blast through the speakers as the lights brightened throughout the arena and the fans began to cheer. I knew the game wasn't supposed to start until seven p.m. so this must be warmups.

Lasers shot around the roof of the arena and light projections of flames surrounded the Devils logo at center ice.

Rain leaned forward so I could hear her over the music.

"It's certainly not quiet all the time. But don't let this scare you away. This is how we blow off steam all winter. Not much else to do around here."

I watched as the other team skated onto the ice to boos from most of the crowd. Their jerseys were a bright blue with white trim and, if I was right, their logo was a set of antlers of jagged ice.

"We've been playing our home opening against the Deer Run Stags since the league started." Rain had to raise her voice a little more. "It's tradition. And we take our traditions pretty fucking seriously around here."

"Everyone, please be aware that pucks and other objects may fly into the crowd and could cause injury." The announcer sounded older. And female. Someone's grandmother. Who smoked about ten packs of cigarettes a day. "So make sure you're ready to catch them! Throw small children out of the way. Don't be afraid to throw a few elbows. Our boys sure aren't!"

And that was my first clue that this wasn't going to be a normal hockey game.

The music segued into "In-A-Gadda-Da-Vida." The flames around the center of the ice began to move toward the home bench then burst across the Devils end of the ice until they began to whirl in a circle and then disappeared in a flash. Every light in the arena went out for a split second and the Imperial March from "Star Wars" began to play.

Then the Devils skated out onto the ice.

The goalie entered first, followed by Rowdy, and the crowd, which now filled almost the entire arena, cheered. They rang cowbells and stomped on the concrete stands until I was sure the place shook. As the rest of the team followed, I noticed the music blended into "Carmina Burana."

The guys began to skate around the perimeter of their end of the ice, their jerseys a bright purple with black trim and their logo of a grinning devil head over crossed hockey sticks on the front.

I laughed when I saw the back of the jersey, a devil's tail snaking up the spine, the spike pointing to their name across the top. Some were obviously nicknames. Rowdy's was Sheriff. I'd have to ask him about that later. There was also Bonesaw, Cudgel, The Fed, KooKoo, Admiral, and Jedi. The rest of the team had regular last names, like Wellar, Kruse and Solow.

The guys took a couple of laps, took some shots on net, then lined up on the center line. The other team hadn't shown up yet, and I was just about to ask Rain what was going on when the music changed to something instrumental. Something I recognized but couldn't place.

Then the lights dimmed, and a spotlight hit the visiting team's bench, just as their players started to take the ice. But they didn't skate around like the Devils had. They lined up on the other side of the center line across from the Devils' players. Goalies on either end, everyone paired up.

I glanced at Rain, who was grinning like she'd won the lottery. Without taking her eyes off the ice, she leaned forward so I could hear her over the music.

"Do you remember the scene in Dodgeball where the two teams line up at the start of the championship game?"

And that's where I recognized the music from. Dodgeball was one of the movies I put on when I needed to laugh.

"That's where I got the idea." Rain had to raise her voice as the music swelled.

The music cut off and the arena announcer said, "Welcome, Deer Run Stags. We're happy to see you this year."

The crowd booed again, which made Rowdy's grin even bigger. That grin made heat settle low in my body and between my legs. My brain started to imagine how he would look taking all that gear off. How his muscular arms would flex as he pulled the jersey over his head. How those big hands would easily strip away the protective gear underneath. And how he would look at my—

"Will the captains please choose their sacrificial—Well, excuse me. I'm so sorry for that slip of the tongue. I mean, will the captains please send their teammates to participate in the rookie shootout."

I tore my attention away from Rowdy to glance at Rain, who looked at me with raised brows, asking a question I didn't want to answer.

"Is this something you came up with, too?"

Rain's mouth twisted into a grin, before answering my question.

"Yeah, it was one of the first things I suggested when I started working with the team. I was sixteen or seventeen, something like that, and I wanted the team to do a fundraiser."

When the rest of their teammates started to bang their sticks on the ice, I turned my attention back to them. Okay, back to Rowdy, but no one would be able to tell that's who I was ogling. Except I still felt Rain's attention like a laser beam on the side of my face, trying to burrow into my secrets.

Not today, sorry

When the rookies stood on the center line between the two teams, Rowdy and the other team captain skated together, meeting in the center circle. They shook hands, though they didn't smile at each other, which was curious because Rowdy smiled at everyone.

"Don't they like each other?"

Apparently, I didn't have to explain my question, because Rain answered immediately.

"Not anymore, no."

There was something in Rain's voice that made me want more of an explanation, but Rain wasn't looking at me now. Guess my questions could wait for another time.

When I turned back to the ice, I realized someone had put a board over the goal with a tiny opening at the bottom.

And the announcer, with her whiskey-and-gravel voice, said, "All right, you know what's coming next. And if you don't, where've you been? This league's been around for nearly fifteen years. For all you newcomers, each of our rookies is going to show off their best moves on the ice, and for every goal, the teams donate a hundred dollars to charity. For off-ice moves, well, you're gonna have to figure that one out on your own."

The announcer's voice took on a sly tone that made my smile widen.

"All right, boys. Show us what you got. And make it good."

I had a feeling Rowdy would be happy to show me exactly what his moves were. And not on the ice.

CHAPTER TEN

ressy

"Mommy, I'm not sleepy. I wanna go to the pawty."

"You can barely keep your eyes open."

The game had ended almost fifteen minutes ago, and Krista stood in a corner outside the locker room, little arms crossed over her chest and the most adorably stubborn expression that nearly made my heart melt.

But my little girl was dead tired after a long day, and I was trying to be a good mom. Krista needed to go to bed. No matter how much I wanted to go to the after party.

My inner bad girl, who was slowly awakening from a self-induced coma, really wanted me to go to the party. That girl hadn't been out and about for years. She didn't want me messing things up.

Would it hurt to have a little fun? Just for one night? In a town where no one knew who I was?

Apparently, it would.

"I can so…" loud yawn, "keep my eyes open."

Except, no matter how hard she tried, Krista's eyelids kept falling lower and lower.

Looks like that bad girl would need to go back to her coma for now.

"Come on, baby. Let's get you—" I almost said home then remembered we were nowhere near home, "to bed."

I picked up Krista, who immediately did her wanna-get-down wiggle. My daughter was normally a good-natured kid, but she could throw a tantrum like a champ, especially when she was tired. I could sense it coming, could feel Krista gathering her remaining strength to begin crying when Raffi walked up to us, seemingly from out of nowhere.

"Hey now, what's the matter, sweet girl?" Raffi leaned in to speak to Krista, still trying to wriggle out of my arms. "What do you need?"

For a second, I held my breath, wondering if Krista would start to scream bloody murder, and everyone would think my baby was a monster, and they would judge me as a bad mother, and no one would want to be around us.

And then I realized that was my mom's voice in my subconscious. I thought I'd evicted her from living rent-free in my head years ago.

"I wanna go to the party."

Krista's voice was ratcheting up, and I winced, trying to reposition Krista so I didn't drop her on the floor in front of a gathering crowd that I was sure was staring at us.

"Well, I'm not going to that party, so maybe you and I could have our own."

"Oh, no, Raffi, you don't have to—"

Krista stopped wriggling. "We could?"

I shook my head, looking at Raffi with complete and utter mortification.

"Well, of course, we could, sweetheart. How does you, me, a

couch and 'The Little Mermaid' sound? That's always been my favorite."

"Raffi, I can take her ho—back to the house myself. You don't have to—"

Raffi's smile was directed at both Krista and me. "I can think of nothing I would like more than spending time with Krista."

She sounded so sincere that I almost caved immediately. But what kind of mom would that make me if I did?

The kind of mom your *mom is?*

"I really don't think you want to deal—uh, spend time with her when she's like this."

Krista looked at me with slitted eyes and pursed little lips and still looked adorable even if she was about to have a full-blown tantrum.

"Like what?" she asked, though it took a second for me to understand what she was saying. My girl was too smart by half and maybe not as far gone as I'd thought.

I chose my next words carefully. "When you're tired, sweetheart."

"But Miss Raffi wants to watch movies and that's what we do when we're tired."

Now Krista sounded like cotton candy wouldn't melt in her mouth. My lips started to twitch, trying to curve into a smile.

"Hey, Mom, you heading home? Sure you don't want to come out with us tonight?"

My stomach caved in on itself, and heat made the top of my head tingle. As well as some other places on my body. I turned and looked over my shoulder.

Rowdy stood in the door to the hallway, arms crossed over his broad chest, messy hair still wet and curly (curly!), and wearing a white t-shirt that stretched over that broad chest like a lover after she'd been satisfied twice and was asking for more.

And that smile on his face for his mom made my heart melt. Like seriously, it was just a squishy little ball of goo in my chest.

"You know I haven't gone to the first-night party for years. Too much noise for me."

So Raffi really had been going home? Does that mean I'm off the hook?

"I wanna go with Miss Raffi."

Still, I hesitated. Krista was my daughter. I should be taking care of her. What if—

Oh, hell, it's just one night. Let's go have some fun.

I didn't honestly know what do here. But obviously, my mouth was working faster than my brain. "Are you sure you don't mind?"

"Not one bit." Raffi sounded like it was the absolute truth. "Come on, Krista. Let's go watch some movies."

Raffi stretched out her arms, and Krista jumped ship faster than sailors on a sinking boat.

Then my little girl gave me the biggest smile, as if she hadn't just been about to melt down spectacularly.

"Night, Mommy. Love you."

Raffi gave me the look every mom knew and understood. It was the "I've got this. No worries," look. And I felt tears begin to well. It'd been so long since it'd been anyone but me and Krista. Sure, I'd hired babysitters when I needed them, and our neighbor at home, Mrs. Santiago, was always there to lend a hand. But most of my friends in New York were single and childless. And kinda miserable most of the time if you asked me. They worked all the time. And if they weren't working, they were attending parties or gallery openings where they hoped to make business connections. Or they went to off-Broadway shows to support friends who'd managed to get cast.

And with my mom and sister living a continent away, I didn't have a lot of women I could talk to about being a parent. I'd become one at such a young age, with no one to help. Not even my mom, who'd been too busy managing Tiff's career. The same way she'd managed mine once upon a time.

I nodded at Raffi, swallowing down the lump in my throat before I could speak.

"Thank you. I…" I didn't know what else to say.

"No worries, hon. Have fun tonight." Raffi spoke like it was no big deal, like she was used to caring for stranger's kids. Then she turned her gaze on her son. "But not too much, Rowdy. I don't want to have to drag this baby out of bed in the middle of the night to pick you up at the police station."

Rowdy winced. "Damn, Mom. You make it sound like I was arrested. Hell, I was just there because Dougie thought it'd be hilarious to make you pick us up there."

"At least you were smart enough not to drive when you'd been drinking. Make sure you make good choices tonight."

Raffi gave him a look that made Rowdy's grin widen even more. "I plan to make great choices tonight. Love ya, Mama."

Shaking her head, Raffi turned back to me. "Have a good time, hon. Enjoy yourself. Krista and I will be just fine. We'll see you tomorrow morning."

I nodded, feeling free in a way I hadn't in a long time. Not free from a burden, but free to have fun. Bad-girl fun.

"Be good, Krista. Love you."

"Bye, Mommy. Miss Raffi, can we have more popcorn with the movie?"

"Didn't you already have some tonight?"

I didn't hear the rest of Krista's conversation with Raffi because they moved out of earshot, but my daughter was all smiles now.

"You ready to have some fun?"

Rowdy's voice was raw meat to that bad girl I'd had to suppress for years. It called to me, seduced me. Made me want to be that girl again. Even if, when I'd been that girl, my life had been heading toward disaster. A disaster I'd narrowly averted.

But I was older and wiser now. And I knew how to control myself.

"Yes, I think I am."

Rowdy's smile returned. It'd been missing while he waited for me to respond. But now it spread like wildfire over his face, which had a distinct bruise forming below his left eye.

"Does that hurt?"

His smile turned into a smirk. "Oh, it hurts. But the face, not so much."

I wanted to roll my eyes, but I refused to give him everything he wanted. Because I knew he would want everything. And there were things I couldn't give him.

"Then I guess maybe you should go home and take care of it."

I realized I'd crossed my arms over my chest in an exact mimic of him.

"I plan to. Later. First, I'm gonna celebrate our first loss of the season with my teammates."

Walking up to my side, he held out his hand, which also looked swollen. I hesitated a second before taking it, gently.

"Do you always celebrate the losses?"

He didn't answer right away, leading me down the hall toward the exit to the parking lot. A few of the other guys began to file out of the locker room now, saying "See you there," as they passed.

I did a double take when I realized a few of those guys were from the other team.

"Sometimes that's all you've got. In this league, we've learned to celebrate everything. Hell, sometimes we celebrate the fact that we made it on the ice without a major incident."

"What kind of incident?"

"Hey, Rowdy. You buying the first round?"

Rowdy stopped and turned, his smile morphing into the one I recognized as for friends. "Of course. Tressy, this is Brian Fiskers, otherwise known as Mr. Whiskers."

The player I recognized as the assistant captain of the other team held out a huge, battered hand. The guy was taller than

Rowdy, with auburn hair that hung below his shoulders, hazel eyes that nearly disappeared when he smiled and a face that showed a matching bruise to Rowdy's from the fight they'd gotten into in the second period.

The crowd had loved it, banging on the glass, stomping their feet and egging them on. Both men had looked seriously intent on killing one another as they fought. But then, after the referee broke them up, they each skated around their end of the ice, on their way to the penalty box. The theme to "Titanic" played as the crowd cheered Rowdy and booed Fiskers. And, when Rowdy got to the box, he picked up the championship belt waiting there and made a production of putting it on, to the delight of the crowd. I could honestly say I'd never seen that at a hockey game before.

While Rowdy had been beaming at the crowd, Fiskers had continued to call him out, which the crowd loved even more. And when they left the box after serving their penalties, they knocked gloves on the way to their benches, and the game continued as if nothing had happened.

I shook Fiskers' hand. "Hi. It's nice to meet you."

He nodded, his gaze meeting mine for a brief second before sliding back to Rowdy. "Same. See you at the bar, later?"

Okay, not a talker.

"Yeah. We'll see you at the game, right, Tressy?"

My tummy tightened then did a happy little jig. "That sure of yourself, huh?"

His grin slowly disappeared, until just the intensity of his eyes was all I could see.

"Not at all. Just hoping like hell that if I say it enough, it'll come true." He paused long enough for me to take a deep breath. "Wanna have some fun?"

Absolutely. Yes. Just...yes.

"What are you offering?"

Beside us, Fiskers huffed out a laugh. "I'm just gonna... Yeah, I'll see you later."

Rowdy's intense gaze never left mine, making me feel like there was no one else in the room, even though I knew we were gathering a small crowd. Hockey players and a few of the Devils' Angels had stopped to watch us, not even bothering to pretend they weren't.

Leaning closer so the crowd couldn't hear him, making them groan in disappointment, he spoke directly into my ear. "As much fun as you're willing to let me give you."

His words weren't dirty, but my brain immediately translated all those innocent-sounding syllables into "I will make you hot and sweaty and come so many times, you will want me to stop, but I won't until you pass out from the pleasure."

When I pulled away, my expression must have given me away because his gaze dropped to my lips, a slow slide that felt like a promise of things to come.

"Is that a guarantee?" I spoke barely above a whisper.

"Absolutely."

"Then I guess we should get started."

He waited a beat, staring into my eyes like he could read my mind. Then he winked and took a step back. Any other guy and that move would've been cheesy. I would've rolled my eyes and written him off. But Rowdy…

"Brace yourself. We don't party like fancy people in big cities."

He had no idea how hard I used to party. And how hard it had been to drag myself out of that pit. But when you become a mom at twenty-one, your life isn't just your own anymore.

"And how do people in big cities party?"

I realized I'd put my hands on my hips and raised my eyebrows. Challenging him. Letting him know I wasn't going to be a pushover.

Unless he pushes me over a chair and fucks me until I can't see straight.

I really wanted him to do that.

"Like they're more worried about how they look than how they feel."

That was so *not* what I'd been expecting him to say. But I couldn't really say he was wrong.

"When we party," he continued, "we make sure everyone's having a damn good time."

Why did everything he said sound like word porn? Like we were alone in a dark room and were about to—

"Hey! If you two are finished flirting, the rest of us are ready to blow off some steam."

I don't know who spoke, but the masculine voice bounced off the concrete walls around us. The next voice belonged to a female.

"Jesus H. Christ, Rebel, shut your damn mouth, or we'll never get out of here."

Rowdy held my gaze for another long second, his eyes sparkling with laughter. How did he make them do that? I'd only known the man for a day, but it felt like decades.

I liked him.

I didn't know if it was the circumstances, or the fact that he wasn't a city guy, that he had a few rough edges, and I was sick of smooth. Or maybe it was because, for the first time in years, I felt free enough to let go, if only for a little while.

No one knew me here. I could be whoever I wanted to be. Tonight, I wanted to be just a little bit bad.

"Are we done flirting?"

Now his grin was wider than the one he'd had when he'd skated off the ice after the fight.

"Oh, hell, no. We're just getting started."

"Then finish it at the damn bar."

Rebel again, but the crowd gathering behind us added their two cents. Most of which was grumbling about wanting to get a drink.

"I guess we better get out of here before the heathens get even more restless."

Rowdy nodded, grabbed my hand, then turned to the crowd, which consisted of both hockey teams and both team's dancers.

"Let's go have some damn fun."

CHAPTER ELEVEN

THE DRIVE to The Church wasn't long enough.

I had Tressy all to myself, and I didn't want to give that up.

Locked together in the cab of my truck, I considered reversing course and heading to my house. But I knew I had to show up at the bar for the team. My team. Still, I was already counting the minutes until I could get her alone again.

Tressy, on the other hand, couldn't stop talking about how much she was looking forward to spending time out with other people. I couldn't tell if she was having second thoughts about the heavy flirting in the hall, or if she was nervous about being alone with me.

Then again, she'd been flirting right back at me—

Jesus, what the hell's wrong with you? You sound like a fucking teenager at a high school dance.

"This is a bar?"

Tressy stared out the windshield at the only place in St. David that could accommodate two hockey teams, the Angels and the Does, the Stage Run dance team, and the fans. The Tea Room, where we'd met last night, didn't have enough space.

"Yep."

"Wow."

"Yep."

Without waiting for her to say anything else, I got out of the truck and walked around to open her door. She gave me a look I couldn't interpret before she took my hand and let me help her out. We stood there, inches separating us, her lips slightly parted, eyes staring right into mine.

Then she said something under her breath that sounded an awful lot like, "Fuck it," and leaned forward to kiss me.

Since I was already on my way to meet her, we collided with a shock wave of heat that exploded through my body.

With my hands on her shoulders, I pulled her closer, right up against me, until the warmth of her body seeped through my clothes. Her lips were a little cool, but they moved against mine like fire. She kissed like she knew exactly what she was doing, and I was fast becoming aware that she could tie me into a neat little bow and wrap me around whatever finger she'd like.

She knew exactly how to make me beg, with her lips pressed hard against mine, like she was learning everything about me. Then her lips parted, and she flicked her tongue against my lips, looking for entry.

Who was I to deny her? Especially when I wanted exactly what she was asking for. I opened to her in, let her tongue slide into my mouth and curl around my tongue. Then I put my hand on the back of her head, held her steady and took over. I chased her tongue back into her mouth and tasted her the way I wanted. Hungrily. Completely. My other arm wrapped around her waist, locking her body against mine, and my lips moved over hers. Hungry. Too damn hungry for only knowing her for a day.

Then again, I knew what I liked, and I liked her.

The way she tasted. Hot and sweet. And hungry for me. Everything she did made it clear we were on the same page. And that page apparently included standing in the damn parking lot making out like horny teenagers. Because that's exactly what I felt like right now.

Tilting my head, I opened my mouth even wider, wanting to consume her. But she wrapped her arms around my shoulders and short-circuited my brain. My cock immediately wanted to join the party. I'd been semi-erect since we'd gotten in my truck at the arena. Now it was a full-blown hard-on. And not even the cold was helping to calm me down.

Not that I wanted to calm down. My hand at her back was sliding around to her hip to urge her even closer. She was several inches shorter than me, so my cock nestled up against her belly. And was enjoying the hell out of being there. Same with my lips on hers. My fingers curled into her hair streaming down her back. I held her tight, even though I didn't think she wanted to go anywhere. Not if the way she kissed me was any indication.

No, she seemed to be just as into this kiss as I was. Her breath hot against mine, her hands curved around my hips, fingers biting into my flesh. Yeah, I liked that a lot.

I also liked the way she arched into me, her head falling back just a little more so I could taste her even deeper. If I wasn't care-ful, I'd be trying to fuck her up against the truck and that was not cool.

So not cool.

But damn, it'd be hot as hell.

"Hey, you two. You gonna join the party or you wanna freeze your asses off out here?"

The laughter that followed wasn't enough to break us apart. At least, not at first. I kept my lips glued to hers, turning my head and deepening the kiss.

Christ, I could do this all night. Her lips were soft and so were her curves. I wanted to run my hands all over her, but I didn't want to put on a show for my so-called friends.

"Dude, let the lady breathe, for chrissake."

Her lips curved in a smile beneath mine, and I pulled back so I could see her. Her eyes remained closed for a split second before she opened them and stared straight into mine as her smile widened.

"For the record," she spoke softly, I had to lean closer to be able to hear her. And since I was this close, I wanted to kiss her again. "I could breathe."

I let my gaze drop to her lips, slightly swollen from the kiss. Fuck, that was hot.

"Then I guess I'll have to work on my technique."

"Your technique is fine." Her voice rasped against my libido, made my cock throb in my jeans. "I think we just need to find somewhere a little more private."

I felt like I'd just scored the winning goal of a championship game. Something I didn't think I'd ever do. And I wouldn't care if she kissed me again…then used her mouth on other parts of my body.

But I was probably getting ahead of myself. Unless I was reading the look in her eyes right. Then all bets were off.

"I can make that happen."

Her eyes crinkled at the corners as those lips curved in the sexiest smile I'd ever seen.

"But I gotta buy a round first."

Her gaze flipped over my shoulder for a second, at the gathering crowd. I wondered if she'd be embarrassed by their PDA. Hell, we hadn't known each other more than a day, and we were already trying to suck each other's face off. But I wasn't complaining. And I hoped like hell she wasn't going to, either.

When she looked back at me with a grin, I knew she wouldn't.

"Then let's have a drink."

CHAPTER TWELVE

*Tressy*

"SO YOU'RE STAYING WITH ROWDY?"

Nursing my second beer, I shook my head at Olivia, one of the Angels. I hadn't had more than a glass of wine with dinner in months, and I didn't want to embarrass myself by being a lightweight.

I wanted to be alert and ready for whatever might come my way later tonight. And I really hoped there'd be something good coming my way.

"No. I'm staying with Raffi and The Colonel. They were kind enough to give Krista and me a room with them while..."

While what? What should I say? Especially to someone I'd only met a day ago? At home, I would never consider spilling my guts to a practical stranger. Hell, I didn't talk about some things with my closest friends. Only Denee would've been able to get me to talk, but Denee was gone and had been for years.

Olivia reached across the table and put her hand on top of

mine, resting on the table. "I'm not digging for info, hon. Honest. I get that you don't want to talk about whatever you're going through. I just want you to know you're not alone. A lot of us have stories about how we found our way to St. David."

"I didn't exactly find my way here. My car blew a tire and left me stranded."

The younger woman's smile widened, golden-brown eyes striking against her darker-toned skin, as she waved a hand. "Same diff. My parents moved here from Miami because my dad thought the name was a sign." She rolled those eyes as she shook her head. "My dad is…unique. Don't get me wrong. I love him. But he wasn't born in the right decade. You remember the dad from 'Valley Girl?' I mean, who doesn't, right? That's my dad. He's one-of-a-kind. He makes furniture. It's a good thing my mom runs their business, or they wouldn't eat. Anyway, after one too many hurricanes, he and my mom decided they wanted to move somewhere where it snowed instead. They literally threw darts at a map. One of them landed on St. David. My dad's name is David. He called it fate."

Surprisingly, I'd kept up with all of that, including the "Valley Girl" reference, because I'd once been up for role in a remake that had never gotten made. But before I could say anything, Olivia continued.

"Now, I don't know about fate, but when we moved here, I wasn't happy. Like, at all. And I made sure everyone knew it. So here I was, a teenager from a big city where I had everything to do, living in a town where the only thing to do in the winter is hockey. And the only thing to do in the summer is fish. Yeah, no. That ain't happening. But then Caity decided she was going to be my friend and told me to join the cheer squad. And what do you know? I was damn good at it. And if we hadn't moved here, maybe I never would've known how much I loved it. What about you, Tressy? Do you love what you do?"

It took a second for my brain to catch up with the conversation. Between Olivia's rapid-fire delivery and the relentless stream of pop music from the eighties, it'd been hard to keep up. But that last question had rung out during the slow section of "Come On, Eileen."

"I do."

"Well, that's good. And it's clear you love that little girl. She's adorbs, by the way. Not prying, but she's got a little Latina in those genes. Those eyes... So gorgeous. I'm guessing you're not still with her daddy, and I still ain't prying," She splayed her hands in front of her, "but if you're gonna tangle with Rowdy, I figure you should know he has kind of a reputation. The guy's a cinnamon roll. All that sweet icing on the top and soft and squishy on the inside but boy, does that man have layers."

I had to bite my tongue against a torrent of questions because I knew if I kept quiet, Olivia would just keep talking. The woman seemed to have no filter or off button.

"He doesn't want anyone to know, of course, but you can tell. You'd think someone like him, who had everything handed to him, would be a real asshole. But The Colonel and Miss Raffi, they raised those kids right. Hell, the man makes sure old Mrs. Garfield gets to her weekly hair appointment, even if that old buzzard was the meanest teacher in high school."

By this time, I thought I might be halfway in love with Olivia and wondered if the woman had any aspirations to act, because with her looks and her attitude, I could definitely find her work, even if she was at least fifteen years older than most of my clients.

"So what do you think?"

I didn't have a clue what Olivia was asking. "About what?"

"Do you think you're going to stay in St. David awhile? I mean, it looks like you're doing okay for yourself wherever you came from, but you could've ended up somewhere way worse."

I bit my lip for a second before answering. "I am thinking about staying a little longer."

"I'm glad to hear that."

Rowdy's voice startled me, and I turned to see him standing behind me, hands in his pockets and dark green henley stretched across his broad chest. Did any piece of clothing this man owned not fit him well? Seriously not fair.

"Livi, you spilling all my secrets?" He slid a glance at the other woman.

Olivia scoffed. "You know nobody has secrets in this town. But I haven't told her anything that's not common knowledge. You're just an open book, aren't you?"

If I hadn't been watching him so closely, I might've missed his slight wince. What was it about Olivia's words that made him look like that?

"Of course. No secrets here."

Oh, now that was definite bullshit. Everyone had secrets. And if they said they didn't, they were lying. So Rowdy was lying. I wanted to dig into those secrets, wanted him to tell me all about them. Even while keeping my own. No, it wasn't fair but life wasn't fair.

"You want another beer?"

I raised my half-full bottle and shook my head. "I think I'm done after this one."

"And I've already hit my limit," he said.

That definitely felt like a hint. With Olivia hanging on his every word, he leaned a little closer. "I'm ready to head out whenever you are."

I'd been waiting for him to say exactly that for three hours. Not that I hadn't been having a good time. I'd enjoyed talking to everyone and the last half hour or so with Olivia had been enlightening. I understood that Rowdy had obligations to his team and the fans. To be with them to celebrate opening night. And he was good at it.

From the moment we'd entered the former church, now bar, I'd watched him work the room. I hadn't expected him to stay by my side the entire time we were there, but he hadn't made me feel like the outsider I was. Even after I'd said I was going to sit at a table for a while, he hadn't forgotten me. He'd circle back every so often to check on me.

And it wasn't like I lacked company. The Angels must have set up a visiting schedule so I was never alone. Which I totally appreciated. It just meant I couldn't blatantly watch Rowdy all night. Even though I had as much as I could.

I'd watched him interact with the fans, watched him talk to each person as if he knew them, which he probably did. Watched him talk with his teammates and the other team's members, laughing and smiling like they hadn't battled it out on the ice just a few hours earlier.

He smiled, shook hands and slapped backs and laughed.

But the more I watched, the more I thought his smile slipped every now and then. That his laughter wasn't completely genuine. I had to be wrong, though, because these people knew him better. They'd grown up with him. Then again, maybe it took an outsider to see what those around him couldn't.

Turning my head so I could look into his eyes, I said, "I'm ready."

The slight tension I'd seen in his smile melted away, but it made the tension that'd been lurking inside me build. I wanted to cross my thighs to ease the ache throbbing between them.

But I also wanted to jump out of my chair, grab his hand and run for the door. And wouldn't that fuel the gossip around town. Which wouldn't matter to me because I'd be gone.

Hell, everyone was looking at us now. They could see what was going on between us and, if they couldn't, well, they weren't looking. Or they were blind.

"Then let's get the hell out of here."

I stood, grabbed the sweatshirt I'd taken off earlier, and took the hand he held out to me. His warm fingers wrapped around mine, completely engulfing them. His hands were so big. Like the rest of him. My hand curled at my side because I wanted to touch him. It'd been so hard to rein in the urge to compulsion whenever I was in range. But now that I'd taken his hand, I didn't want to let go.

And I didn't want to look back. Everyone in the bar would be watching us. I wasn't worried about what they thought. I just didn't want to second guess my own decisions.

No one stopped us on the way to the door. No one cat-called us or leered or anything like that. But they all knew Rowdy and I were going to exchange more than phone numbers.

Back in his truck, the heater going full blast because it had to be almost freezing outside again, I sank into the heated seat and watched Rowdy as he got us on the road.

"Did you have a good time?" His lips curved into a smile as I nodded. "Good. Because all everyone wanted to talk about tonight was you."

I winced. "I guess my entrance last night was kind of spectacular."

"Yeah, but that's not what they were talking about. The girls all like you. Said you're chill."

"Oh?"

"Yeah, and not stuck up like girls from the city usual are."

I huffed out a laugh. "I guess that's fair. They're pretty great for being cheerleaders."

"Don't let them hear you call them cheerleaders, though. They're dancers."

"Yes, that's right. Olivia told me their squad wins competitions all the time."

"Yep. Wherever they compete, they win. Can't say the same for the Devils."

"Maybe you just need time for the team to come together."

"Nah." He shrugged. "We're pretty much always in last place."

"Does that bother you?"

"Used to. Now it's just…what we do."

"It doesn't sound like you enjoy losing."

"Who does? But life's not all about winning."

"Sounds like you've been thinking about this a lot."

Rowdy didn't answer right away, as we drove through town. Main Street was deserted, the sole traffic light blinking yellow.

"I've had a lot of time to think about it."

"What are you going to do when you can't play anymore?"

Shrugging, he flipped the blinker and made a left, heading down the road I recognized as leading to his parents' place.

"Coach, I guess."

"Don't you want to use your degree?"

"Maybe. I guess I'll see what happens when it happens."

I shook my head, wondering what it would be like to have that kind of freedom. To make decisions as they came rather than worrying about the future and trying to plan out everything six months, a year, two years in advance.

Did that make me anal? Or was he a stunted man-child who knew his parents would be there to back him in whatever play he made?

And wow, was I being bitchy or what? Where had that come from?

You're such a wimp. You want him. Don't freak out now.

Bad Girl was right. I'd let myself forget how fearless I used to be. How fearless I'd had to be to navigate the Hollywood system as a child actor. How I'd become a mother at twenty-one. How I'd gone to college and started my own business with a toddler in tow.

I'd been so damn good for seven years.

As we passed his parents' home, I let my gaze linger for a second on the warm light coming through the front window. I couldn't help the slight twinge of guilt I felt at leaving my daughter in the care of someone else.

Rowdy took an immediate left onto a road I hadn't noticed before. It went past his parents' house and into a wooded area. The trees closed around us, cutting us off from the rest of the world. It got so dark, I couldn't even see the moonlight through the trees.

"Where are we?"

"Still on my parents' property, so we're technically still in town, but my property straddles the township and the borough line."

None of that made much sense to me because the most beautiful home I'd ever seen came into view. It had two stories, was made of stone with four double windows and a covered porch that ran the entire length of the house.

"Did you build this?"

I huffed out a laugh. "No. This was built more than a hundred years ago. It was a mess when my parents bought the property. They considered tearing it down but never got around to it. Rain and my brothers and I used to play here when we were kids, even though we weren't supposed to. It was the one secret we were all able to keep. I'm sure my parents knew but they never said anything. I think they were just happy we had somewhere to play that wasn't under their feet all the time."

"Can't say I can't blame them with four kids."

I turned away from that gorgeous house to catch him staring at me with the most serious look I'd seen on his face yet. But it vanished in a second, replaced with his normal grin. I was beginning to think that grin covered a multitude of sins.

"We were angels."

I laughed so hard, I snorted, covering my mouth with my hand as his grin widened.

When I could talk, I said, "I call bullshit."

His exaggerated gasp made me laugh even harder. "I think I'm offended."

"No, you are definitely not."

"No, I'm not."

That smile took my breath away and, even though I tried not to let it show, I knew he could tell. I wanted to kiss him, but I was enjoying the anticipation almost too much to break it.

"I also can't take credit for all of the work that went into getting this place to where it is now."

Was he teasing me? Drawing out the anticipation? I could barely breathe now, and I had to put conscious effort into my response. Which basically consisted of, "Oh?"

He nodded. "It took me five off-seasons to get it to the point where I could actually live in it."

"Did you do the renovations yourself?"

"Yeah, but I had a lot of help. My dad and brothers helped when they could, but Rain is better than all of us with a hammer and saw. She can build in bookcases in a couple of days and make them look like they're original."

"Are you going to show me around?"

"Are you asking to see my etchings?"

My lips curved again, falling a little harder for this guy with every word he said. Why? What was it about him?

No, no, no. We're not going to overanalyze this now.

Bad Girl was right. No over-thinking. Just go with it. Whatever "it" is.

"Do you have etchings?"

"I guess you'll have to come in to find out."

"I'd love to see your home."

"Then come with me."

He opened his door and climbed out. The overhead light made me blink, but it was only for a second, and then he opened my door. He reached in for my hand, and I took it without thought. It was only after the warmth of his skin seeped into mine that I realized I was expecting it. Looking forward to it.

Sliding out of the truck, I looked up to find him watching me with that intensity I'd noticed earlier. Again, it quickly disappeared, replaced by that grin. As much as I found that grin enticing, the intensity made my blood heat and my stomach clench.

This time, he didn't release my hand immediately, and I didn't pull away. I liked the feel of him, liked the way my fingers slid between his and his curled around mine. His hands were large and rough. They'd feel amazing against my naked skin.

Swallowing hard, I held his gaze but didn't return his smile. I wanted him to know I was serious when I said, "Yes."

He must have known what question I was answering, the unspoken one that lingered between us. His smile shifted, became a little sharper, a little harder. A whole lot sexier. He didn't speak, just tugged me with him toward the front door.

The crunch of the gravel driveway beneath our feet was the only sound now. There was no traffic noise, no wind, no leaves rustling. Just stillness. We reached the porch, and he released my hand to open the front door with the keypad. I turned to look back down the road, marveling at the brightness of the moon that painted the woods silver.

I heard the door open and turned to see him leaning against the frame, soft light from the house spilling out around him. My breath caught as I thought about the fact that I was going to be naked and have his man wrapped around me sometime in the near future.

Unless I was seriously off-base, and he really did just want to show me his house.

But, of course, I wasn't wrong.

"It's so quiet."

He nodded slowly, never taking his gaze off of me.

"This is my refuge. When everything else gets too noisy, I know it'll be quiet here."

"I don't think I've ever been anywhere more quiet. New York is always loud. And I've never been bothered by it. There are always sirens and car traffic and horns and people. Even in the Village, it's never silent."

I realized I'd just told him where I lived, not that he looked surprised. The man wasn't stupid. My car had a New York license plate, and I'd looked like a freaking princess doll when I'd fallen into his arms last night.

And now, I was ready to go to bed with the guy.

Who was I?

Someone who knows what they want and goes for it.

And someone who only had a limited amount of time to get what I wanted.

"Have you always lived in New York?"

I shook my head slowly as I closed the distance between us. "No. I used to live in L.A."

His gaze narrowed. "Are you an actress? Should I know you? I'm sorry, I don't go to a lot of movies, and I don't watch a lot of TV."

He sounded so guilty, I felt sorry for him.

"No, you wouldn't know me." Which wasn't a complete lie. Unless he'd watched one of the silliest sitcoms ever to air on network TV. But not *everyone* in the world had watched it. And even people who had watched the show didn't recognize me now. I wasn't that kid anymore. I didn't live in that world. I'd never belong in that world again. I didn't really know where I belonged anymore. But at this moment, I knew I belonged right here.

He didn't respond right away, just let the silence build. Then he tilted his head to the side, inviting me in. I dipped my head and broke the connection, walking by him into the house. Trying not to reach out and let my fingers trail across that broad chest, I focused my attention on his home instead.

A stone, wood-burning fireplace dominated the center of the room, comfy leather chairs and couch in prime position in front of it. Built-in bookshelves flanked the fireplace, filled with books and only books. No pictures or tchotchkes. I wanted to explore those shelves, but there was so much more to look at. The walls on either side of the room were almost covered with pictures.

Many of them with his family, but many others were hockey related, of course. Team photos, solo photos, photos of Rowdy with his arm around another player's shoulders. So many other players.

I turned to the left, drawn to the photos of his hockey career. He was smiling in every photo, except a couple, and those were the ones I went to first. They'd been taken during games and that intensity was front and center. Tonight during the game, I'd noticed how, even though he was having fun, he played with so much heart.

And more skill than most of the other guys on the ice. I couldn't believe he'd never been asked to play for a higher-level team. Then again, maybe he hadn't wanted to leave. His dad owned the team. Rowdy was the captain. He had it good here.

Still…

I felt him stand behind me, not crowding me, but close enough that I could feel the heat radiating from him. My fingers curled, nails digging into my palms.

"Do you want something to drink?"

I shook my head, feeling my hair swing against my back.

"Do you want to continue to make small talk?" Humor laced through his voice. "I mean, I can, if you want."

Biting my lip against the urge to turn and devour him, I took a step forward then turned to meet his gaze. He stayed in place, sliding his hands into his pockets. He was waiting for me to make a move. Wanting me to be sure.

My lungs tightened and my core clenched. I was sure. I was really damn sure of exactly what I wanted.

"I don't want to make small talk. I want to kiss you."

His lips barely curved, but I knew he was smiling, and it felt like another of his teases. Then he withdrew his hand from his pocket and crooked a finger at me. If another man did that, I'd turn and walk out the door. It should've seemed sleazy. Why, when Rowdy did it, did my breath catch in my throat?

"If you want to kiss me, princess, you're going to have to come closer."

It was my turn to smile.

"Maybe I want you to come to me."

"All you have to do is ask."

I took a page out of his book and crooked my finger at him.

His smile sharpened, and I suddenly needed air desperately. I almost wanted to turn, knowing he would chase. Wanted to be caught.

Who are *you?*

Good question. One I'd ask myself tomorrow.

I took a step back and then another, until I sensed the wall at my back. Flattening my hands against the surface, I tipped my head back and watched him close the few feet between us, until there were only inches. And then centimeters.

He leaned down until our foreheads were almost touching and said, "Your move."

He just couldn't help himself. He had to push.

Don't lie to yourself. You like it.

Okay, but I didn't have to tell him I did.

"Kiss me."

The words came out as more of a plea but seeing the look on Rowdy's face was worth any hint of weakness. I watched his control falter and disappear as hunger took over. His mouth was on mine a split-second later. His hot kiss demanded, and, for a split second, I wasn't sure I should give him what he wanted. What I wanted. I wasn't sure about him or me or about any of this. Then the Bad Girl muttered, *Fuck, yes,* in my brain, and my lust became a red-hot flame that licked into every part of my body.

His closed mouth pressed against my lips for several long seconds, until I was holding my breath, waiting for him to push me farther, harder. To open his lips and slide his tongue into my mouth and really taste me.

My hands found his shoulders, clenching into the muscles, feeling them bunch under my fingers. I wanted to melt at his strength, to press myself against him and let him hold me up. But he wasn't moving fast enough. I needed more. And he wanted me to work for it.

Fine.

Pulling back, I looked him in the eyes and said, "Chair."

A corner of his mouth kicked up. "Yes, ma'am." Then he turned and sprawled into the nearest chair. I followed, taking a deep breath as I let my gaze crawl over him. Like I wanted to.

How did just a look from those dark eyes make my heart beat faster? And my thighs clench?

Only one way to find out. No more hesitation.

Settling my knees on either side of his, I sank down onto his thighs, my hands landing on his shoulders. I took a deep breath, inhaling the scent of soap and clean male and just a hint of something darker. I wanted to lean forward and kiss my way from that hollow in his throat to just behind his ear and along that scruffy jaw.

Instead, I rubbed the tip of my nose against his jaw, the rasp of his whiskers making me shiver. I sucked in a breath and held it as I tilted my head to let my lips brush against his cheek. The sensitive skin of my lips tingled, and I bit them between my teeth as I pulled back.

His gaze darkened even more, and there wasn't a hint of playfulness now. Just sharp, total focus.

Mesmerized, lungs grasping for air, I leaned forward and pressed my lips against his, kissing him hard before drawing his bottom lip between my teeth and giving it a tug. His breath released on a harsh sigh and his hands grabbed my hips, fingers sinking in and anchoring me. I liked the feeling of being held tight, like he wouldn't let me slip and fall.

With my gaze caught with his, I slid my hands up his strong neck to his hair, sinking my fingers into those messy curls.

"Do you ever comb this?"

"You mean with an actual comb?"

My lips curved, and I looked into his eyes again. "Guess that's a no."

He shrugged as I wound those silky curls around my fingers. It wasn't fair that a guy had such great hair.

"Why bother when it's just gonna do its own thing anyway?"

Kind of how he lived his life.

Nope, not over-analyzing anything right now. Leaning forward, I kissed him again. He was ready for me this time, giving me just enough to make me want more, need more. Making me come closer, until my breasts were pressed against that hard chest and my lips moved over his. I wanted him to kiss me harder, but he refused to cooperate. He seemed content to let me lead. Frustration built, making me kiss him a little harder, crush my lips against his until his mouth opened enough for my tongue to slip inside.

He made a sound almost like a growl when my tongue touched his, wanting more. He tasted like whiskey, heat and desire. *Not enough.* Scooting forward, I settled my sex over the ridge in his jeans, inviting him to rub against me.

Now he groaned, a rumble in his chest as his hands slid around my waist, flattening against my back and pressing me closer.

Yes. This is what I want.

Need built, licking through my blood like a slow-moving flame. My thighs clenched, but with my knees on either side of his legs, I got no relief from the ache in my core. And I couldn't stand that he didn't seem in any hurry to get naked and get busy.

He kissed me slow and steady, even though I was trying my damnedest to rile him into moving faster. Tugging at his hair, I tipped my head to the side and kissed him with more urgency, my tongue curling along his, wanting to push him into losing a little bit of his control. Instead, the damn man seemed to slow even more. Like he was learning every little bit of me and wasn't going to move on until he had.

With a little growl of frustration, I pulled back, though his hands held tight, not allowing me to move too far away.

"What's wrong, princess?"

His voice held an almost soothing tone, that only served to rile me even more.

"You need to get with the program."

"Oh, I'm definitely on board with the program."

"Then you need to kiss me."

His smile was slight but taunting. "I am kissing you. Am I not doing it right? Maybe they do it differently in the big city? You know I'm just a country boy."

Damn his teasing. It'd been a damn long time since someone had played with me. Did I remember how to play this game? The male-female, flirty-sexy game. I'd been out of practice for so long, which was ridiculous considering I was twenty-seven. But I'd never really had the opportunity to learn the rules of this game when I'd been a teenager. I hadn't had regular dates. Most of my "dating" had been with other actors, specifically chosen for that particular moment in time.

Sure, I'd had crushes and had thought myself in love once or twice, until I'd realized they were all playing a part, even me, though I hadn't known it at the time.

That had been another life, and the life I'd been living lately hadn't included a man.

"And I'm just a woman who hasn't done this in a long time."

The words came out raw and a little too truthful. I immediately wanted to take them back. Mortification began to set in, but Rowdy's grin made it disappear into steam.

"I'm glad to help you back on that horse."

I immediately burst into laughter, raising my hand to cover my mouth when I started to snort. His grin just kept growing.

"Oh my god. I'm sorry, I'm not laughing at you—"

"Hey, nothing to be sorry for. I just love to hear you laugh."

No man had ever said that to me before, and I blinked in sheer and utter confusion.

"Seriously?"

"Yeah, and I'm gonna make sure you do a lot of that tonight."

"You want me to laugh at you in bed?"

"Well, I certainly hope you don't laugh when you see me naked, but otherwise, I'm good with it."

I couldn't stop smiling. "I like you, Rowdy."

"I like you, too, Princess."

I scoffed. "I'm pretty damn far from being a princess."

"When you walk into a bar in the middle of nowhere, dressed in a ballgown and high heels, with your hair studded with diamonds, I get to call you Princess."

I'd had other people call me princess before. It came with the job. Creepy directors who wanted little girls to like them. Clueless publicists who considered children a necessary evil of the job and didn't bother to learn their names. Crew members who were too busy to learn their names.

I'd come to hate the nickname. Except when Rowdy said it… I wanted to go down on my knees right here and unzip his jeans. And I wasn't that kind of person. I'd never been that kind of person. But right now, I wanted to do all the naughty, bad-girl things I'd only read about in books. And Rowdy was the person to let me be that girl.

"Fine. I'll allow it. For now." My smile continued to grow, along with the heat in my blood. "Kiss me, Rowdy."

"Whatever you want, Princess."

He cupped my head in his hands and sealed my mouth against his. This time, his kiss stole every drop of breath in my body. Open-mouthed and wet and hot. His tongue licked between my lips, teasing and playing. But this felt different. He kissed with purpose now.

And the purpose was to make me melt for him.

Yes. This is what I want.

I wanted to drown in heat, so I let it take me over.

My head tilted to the side so he could kiss me deeper, let my body sink into his, until his erection pressed against my core, exactly where I wanted him to be. Wrapping my arms around his shoulders, I crushed my breasts against his chest and heard him make that low rumble again. It sank straight to my clit, which was already highly sensitive and throbbing.

Inching even closer, I rocked against that ridge in his jeans, trying to ease some of that ever-increasing ache. Until his hands gripped my hips and lifted me just high enough that we were no longer touching.

"None of that yet," he said as he tore his lips away from mine and kissed his way down my throat. "You're gonna have to beg for it, now."

Holy shit. Why did that make my nipples tighten so badly they hurt?

But that was a dare, and I had to respond.

"Not if I make you beg first."

He nipped at the sensitive skin where my neck met my shoulders, causing me to shudder. Shoving my hands back into his hair, I tugged hard on the strands, until he pulled away and met my gaze. The heat in his eyes stole my breath.

"So make me beg."

The edge in his voice gave me the push I needed. Holding his gaze, I slid my hands to his shoulders then continued to his chest. The warmth of his body made the tips of my fingers curl into the hard muscle there before I reached for the first button on his shirt. The green and black cotton flannel was silky soft, the buttons giving way to expose a t-shirt beneath. Biting my lip with frustration, I undid the rest of the buttons quickly, shoving it off his shoulders.

"Take this off."

"Ask nicely."

I leaned forward and bit his left earlobe, hard enough to make him wince.

"Keep pushing me," he growled, "and we're gonna end up on the floor."

"I'm good with the floor. Just move faster."

A split-second later, he shoved his hands under my ass and set me on my knees on the floor. I was reaching for him as he joined me, my hands helping him shed his shirt. I threw it to the side when he grabbed his t-shirt and yanked it up, exposing rock-hard abs and chest. Jesus, I wanted to pet him. Instead, I leaned forward and pressed my lips right in the center of his chest. The silky soft hair there felt rough, but his skin was soft and hot.

"Hang on. Let me—"

He ended on a groan as I caught the hard tip of his nipple between my teeth.

"Fuck, Tressy."

Yes. Please, yes.

Need made me frantic as I grabbed the button on his jeans and worked it open, but I was thwarted a millimeter from my prize when he grabbed my hands.

"Oh, no, you don't." Rowdy's voice was a low rumble. "You touch me now, and I'm done."

"I think I might like to see that."

"*Shit.*"

I let out a little yelp when he grabbed me around the waist and my thighs and laid me flat on the floor then started to laugh as my back hit the floor. My laughter cut off as he kissed me again, coming down on top of me as he grabbed both of my hands and held them above my head.

Groaning at the unfamiliar and totally hot sensation of being unable to move, I let my body relax, let my eyes close as he slowed his exploration of my mouth. I loved how he kissed me, like he was enjoying the hell out of it and didn't want to rush.

With his shirt gone, I ran my hands down his back, his

skin silky and sleek. His muscles bunched and flexed as he moved both of my hands to one of his then used his free hand to glide down my body. He skirted my breast, which just made me want his touch that much more. My back arched, but I couldn't move because he had me pinned to the floor.

This shouldn't feel this good. Why does this feel so good?

His hand moved to the waist of the jersey I wore. The one with his name and number on the back. Then his hand slid beneath, and I stopped breathing as he finally touched me skin to skin. As his fingers danced along my side, making my skin erupt in goosebumps, his mouth moved down my neck again.

When he drew away, my eyes flew open, and I blinked at the shadowed ceiling beams for a second. When he released my hands, I almost protested before I realized he was sitting up, his hands working the jersey up and over my head.

His grin when he saw what I was wearing underneath made me smile.

"You look good with my face on your chest."

The line was so cheesy I had to laugh, which cut off with a gasp when he gripped the hem and tugged it up my body.

"But I'm sure you look much better without it."

Now I arched my back to help him get the t-shirt over my head, and his gaze burned as he took in the see-through lace bra. It was the only bra I'd packed, and I wasn't sure it was going to survive the night the way he was looking at it.

"I think you need to take that off so I don't rip it, okay, Princess?"

"Since it's the only one I brought with me, I think you're right."

Crossing my arms, I pulled the straps off my shoulders then arched off the floor so I could unsnap it. Tossing it aside, I lay back down, lifting my arms above my head again and stretching. I loved how his gaze followed my every move. It felt almost reverent, like he was worshiping me with his eyes. But I wanted more.

"Touch me."

"Say please."

My lungs seized, and I parted my lips to draw in more air.

"I guess I could just do it myself."

I heard him suck in a breath then his hands clenched into fists at his sides before he stretched his fingers out.

"Go ahead. I'll watch. And learn."

Bad Girl practically purred at the rough edge to his voice. I loved the way he swung from playful to growly in the space of seconds. Loved the way he looked at me like I was special. And when he smiled at me, I felt the weight of the world lift off my shoulders.

I felt sexy. Desired.

Lifting my hands to my breasts, I squeezed the mounds then pulled at my nipples, rolling them until I felt the ache in my pussy sharpen. My eyes closed as I played with my breasts, my lungs straining harder with each tug, the thought that he was watching, urging me on—

"Not so fast, Princess. Won't it be more fun if I make you come?'

He grabbed my right hand, shackling my wrist with his fingers and holding it firm on the ground several inches from my hip. My eyes opened to find him popping the button his jeans. The ridge behind his zipper had grown even more, and I reached for him with my free hand.

"I wanted to do that."

My voice sounded husky, seductive, and his jaw tightened as my finger gripped the zipper tab and began to tug it down. His erection made it difficult, and I didn't want to hurt him, because I definitely had plans for that part of his anatomy. Sitting up on my knees made it easier for me to reach my goal and, when I finally reached the bottom, I bit my lip at the sight.

He wore black briefs, and the tip of his cock had worked its way out of the elastic band. When I touched a fingertip to it, his abs contracted into the most fascinating display of muscles.

"Push them down."

My voice held power now, even though it was barely audible. He heard me, though, because he released me and put both hands on his waist. But he only shoved them down a little, grinning when I huffed at him and flashed him a look.

"Nah, I think I'm going to strip you naked first."

I went wet at the matter-of-fact way he said it, my pussy clenching and my nipples tightening to almost painful points. Managing to bite back an embarrassing moan, I pushed myself up onto my elbows and stared at him with narrowed eyes.

"Only if I get to return the favor."

"I don't have a problem with that. But be a good girl now and lay back."

My mouth dropped open at the way those words hit me. Why did I want to mindlessly obey?

Shock. I had to be in shock.

But a second later, I found myself flat on my back again as his hands reached for the waistband of my pants. I wasn't wearing jeans. I didn't usually wear them. But I had packed a couple pairs of yoga pants and my favorite cargos. Luckily for both of us, the cargo pants had an elastic waist and slid right off without any effort at all, taking my underwear with them. Almost as if I'd planned it.

How could you have planned for this?

I was naked and horny and about to get fucked by a guy I'd only met yesterday. And I couldn't fucking wait.

"Rowdy. Your turn. Now."

I could barely get enough air into my lungs to speak, and I didn't wait for him to respond. Reaching for his jeans, I grabbed the waistband, made sure his briefs came with them, and shoved them down his thighs. Holy shit, the man's thighs were massive, roped with muscle and the perfect frame for his thick cock.

I let myself stare for a few long seconds, hoping I didn't literally drool. He was hard and ready. And my brain took that moment to remind me how long it had been since I'd had sex. Like, a year, at least.

"I love the way you're staring at me," his voice was barely a rasp, "but I want you to touch me. Now."

I had to swallow before I could answer. "You're getting awfully bossy."

"I have a feeling you like it, Princess. And you know you want to."

Fuck it. I did. I really did.

"Lay down."

His mouth quirked at the command, but he did what I wanted, shoving his pants and socks off along the way. Now he lay naked with his arms crossed beneath his head, his erection hard and angled away from his stomach, and that grin that made me want to straddle his thighs and take him in immediately.

Instead, I took a page out of his book and forced myself to slow down. Getting up on my knees, I let my gaze stroll down the length of him. He had a few tattoos, one on his left upper arm, another on his right pec and one down his right thigh. I'd explore those later, because right now, I had other ideas. Like easing the ache between my legs.

"Are you going to—"

I put my hand over his mouth. "I'm going to do whatever I want."

He sucked in a sharp breath, then released it on an amused huff. "Guess I deserve that."

"Oh, you definitely do. Don't worry. You'll get what you need."

"I appreciate that, Princess. But I'd really like if you could hurry it up a little. My dick's getting cold."

Another laugh caught me by surprise, and I shook my head. "Are you ever serious?"

"What's there to be serious about? This is the most fun I've had in a damn long time. You're just about the most fun I've ever had."

That last part hit me dead center in my heart. No one had ever said that to me. Not one single person had made me feel like his best time.

Before I got too sappy and declared my undying devotion, which I'd never do anyway, I swung my right leg over his hips so I could straddle those thick thighs. Damn the man was *built*. And I didn't mean like obscenely so. Just muscled enough to make me want to kiss my way from that stubbled jaw all the way to his kneecaps, because, okay, shins didn't really do much for me.

Settling my hands on his stomach, I felt his muscles tighten as I curled my hands then dragged my fingernails up to his pecs.

Groaning, he said, "Fuck, I like that. Do it again."

I considered letting him wait, but I liked playing with him too much. Raking my hands down to his waist this time, I didn't stop until I reached his thighs, then dug my nails in as he blew out a breath.

"Goddamn, I like that, too."

I repeated the motion several times, watching as he tipped his head back and closed his eyes, jaw tight. Leaning forward, I put my hands on the floor of either side of his chest.

"Don't move."

I intended to get up to grab the sling bag I'd taken to the game, where I'd stashed the condom I'd had in my makeup bag, but his eyes opened, and he grabbed my hips.

"Back pocket."

Turning my head, I saw his pants only a few feet away. I reached for them—at the same time I dragged my sex over his cock.

My eyes closed and I shuddered at the sensation of his heated shaft sliding through my sensitive folds.

"Get the condom, Princess."

I felt another rush of wetness at the rough growl in his voice.

"And hurry, because I'm fucking dying to get inside you."

Oh, god, yes, I wanted that, too.

I snagged his pants, dragging them closer as he continued to tease me. Anticipation electrified every nerve in my body, my heart beating so fast, I felt it in my throat. Finally finding the right pocket, I extracted my prize and tore open the packet.

"Rowdy." Holy shit, he hit the exact right spot on my clit to make me moan. "Put this on."

He met my gaze for a brief, hot second before taking the condom from me. I moved just far enough away to allow him to roll it down his shaft. I barely gave him time to move his hands before I shimmied into position, lined up his cock and sank down.

My eyes closed as his heated groan made flames lick through my blood. He was almost too much to take. It'd been a long time for me and the toys I'd been playing with didn't match his width. Like, at all.

With my hands on his abs, I held myself in place, letting my channel clench around him and my clit tighten with anticipation. His heavy breathing and mine filled the air, and I opened my eyes to find his closed, his expression tight and filled with lust.

My body wanted to move, to ride him hard and fast, but I didn't want it to be over too soon. I wanted to have sex with him all night, even though I knew I'd walk funny tomorrow. Even though I knew his mom would know I'd spent the night having sex with her son. Right now, nothing else mattered but what was happening here between us.

"Princess." His eyes opened and his gaze snagged mine. "You gotta move soon, 'cause if you don't, I'm gonna take the reins."

"I might like that. Later. Right now, you're mine."

I started to move, slowly at first, taking an infinite amount of time to draw myself up his cock until only the tip remained inside. Then I slid back down, just as slowly, every ridge of his shaft rubbing against my inner flesh.

Damn, this was so much better than any toy.

Beneath my hands, Rowdy's abs moved in time with his harsh breaths, then flexing as I moved his hands to my hips. He didn't try to control my movements, but just the feel of that warm flesh on my skin was enough to make me clench around him.

"Fuck, Tressy. Do that again."

My breath hitched at the growl in his voice, my body unconsciously giving him what he wanted. What I wanted. My pace picked up because I couldn't help myself. I chased my pleasure, knowing he was right there with me. But I needed more.

Leaning forward, I draped myself over his naked chest, my clit finding the angle I needed for a short, sharp orgasm. It sparked like electricity, my moan ruffling the soft hair on his chest.

His arms rose and wrapped around my back, holding me in place.

"Goddamn, do that again."

Yes, I really wanted to, but I wanted even more.

"Move with me, Rowdy."

As if he'd been waiting for my permission, he thrust, hard, burying himself inside me until my clit could barely take the pressure. Then he started to move in earnest.

"Kiss me, Princess. And hold on."

I didn't move right away, enjoying the sensation of his cock moving inside me too much to think straight. Then I did put my hands on either side of his shoulders and lifted up just enough for my lips to be within reach of his. He tilted his head down to reach my mouth, nipping at my bottom lip before kissing me hard, his tongue sliding against mine and demanding control.

One hand slid down my back to cup my ass, and he squeezed me before he gripped my hips, held me steady and began to thrust hard, sinking as deep as he could before drawing out and seeking to bury himself even deeper the next time.

My body went slack with surrender. I let him have whatever he wanted. And he wanted everything. His kiss demanded my full attention, but the way he moved between my legs held me captive. So many sensations, so much pleasure.

He held me so tightly, I felt each individual finger sinking into my flesh. He controlled my movement, and I let him, loving the sense that I could give myself to him and he wouldn't let me falter.

When he ripped his mouth away from mine, I whimpered. Actually fucking whimpered, but I couldn't care less. And when he rolled us over so that I was on my back and he was stretched out over me, I sank my hands into his hair and held on.

Now I felt the full strength of his body as he thrust into me, starting slow but building in power and strength. But it still wasn't enough. And he must have sensed it. Before I knew what he was doing, he pulled out and leaned back, making me protest with a frustrated moan.

"Rowdy—"

"Hang on, Princess. Just one sec."

He didn't move far, just enough to grab a pillow off the nearest chair, which he shoved under my ass to tilt my pelvis.

"So fucking pretty."

His gaze traced fire between my spread legs, which turned into a blaze of lust as he put his hands on the inside of my thighs and pressed them even farther apart.

"I can't wait to watch you come like this."

My pussy clenched, aching to be filled again. So I reached for his cock, wrapping my right hand around it and tugging on him.

"Fuck, Princess, you do that too much, and I'm going to come on your stomach."

"Then you better move, because I'm not stopping until you—"

He tugged me closer, making me yelp in surprise, then

replaced my hand on his cock with his and lined the tip with my entrance. His eyes never left mine as he thrust inside. This position made him feel twice as wide, and I sucked in a breath, even as my legs wrapped around his thighs and tried to pull him even closer.

"Play with your nipples while I fuck you, Princess. Give me a show."

I didn't think twice. Lifting my hands, I cupped my breasts and plumped them together, making circles around my nipples with my index fingers until they hardened to diamond-sharp tips, so sensitive I felt every touch go straight to my clit.

With a groan, he began to thrust harder, keeping one hand on my hip to hold me steady and moving the other to my stomach, using his thumb and forefinger to play with my clit. My breath caught as my entire focus became the coiling anticipation in my sex. Every flick of his index finger and press of his thumb pushed me closer to an orgasm.

My eyes closed as I chased it, every sensation becoming more intense. My stomach contracted as my sex clenched and rippled around his cock, wanting more. He swore under his breath as I moaned, my hands releasing my breasts and reaching for his wrists to hold myself steady.

"Come on, Princess. Come for me."

Whether it was the words or just his voice or the combination of both, I finally went over the edge. My back arched as I came, raw undiluted ecstasy pouring through my veins as I spun out.

With another rough curse, Rowdy stretched out on top of me and fucked me through my orgasm until I felt him shudder and shove himself as far into me as he could get, then he held still. He nuzzled his head into my neck, his breath hot on my skin and his body heavy. A good heavy, like an anchor I needed to keep myself grounded.

We lay there, breathing like we'd just run a marathon. Our skin, silky with sweat, melded together. I didn't want to move, didn't want Rowdy to move, but I released my hold on him when he rolled to my side. After he took off the condom, he scooped an arm around me and draped me over his chest.

Ridiculously relieved that he didn't get up and move away, I settled my head on his still-rapidly rising chest and put my hand over his heart, feeling it pump hard and fast.

Damn, this was way too comfortable.

I might just have made the most incredibly stupid mistake of my life. And one of the best.

CHAPTER THIRTEEN

owdy

THE LONGER I HELD HER, the more I was convinced this was the best damn night of my entire life.

It'd definitely been the best sex I'd ever had. And I couldn't wait to see if we could top it.

But I knew I couldn't ask her to stay tonight. I wanted to, but she'd want to go back to my parents' house so she could be there when Krista woke up in the morning. And yeah, I knew that could be awkward as hell for her with my mom. I knew my dad was probably oblivious to the situation unless my mom said something. And I didn't think she would. Because my mom liked Tressy. And she really liked Krista.

If my mom could adopt them, she would, because… well, that was my mom's M.O.

With every passing second, Tressy relaxed against me even more, until she released a long breath that made goosebumps rise all over my body. And my cock stir.

Down, boy.

"I really should think about getting back to your parents'." A few seconds passed. "And wow, that sounded really weird. Not as weird as it's going to be facing your mom tomorrow morning, but still…"

I tightened my arms around her. "Mom won't say a word. She's not going to be waiting up for you in a chair by the door. She's not going to make you feel like you did anything wrong. Or that she's entitled to know what you're doing. And, contrary to popular opinion, she can't read minds. You're allowed to be an adult, Princess. I mean, she manages to stay out of her kids' sex lives, so she's definitely not going to stick her nose in yours."

She stilled, like she was thinking really hard about something. I didn't push, knew it wouldn't work with her. Tressy didn't give up anything easily or willingly. I'd learned in the two days I'd known her that, if she didn't want to tell you something, she wouldn't. She had walls.

And that was okay. I was pretty decent at tearing down walls. You didn't always have to use brute force. Sometimes, they just needed a little encouragement to fall on their own.

So I waited. Tightened my arm around her and made sure she knew I wasn't one of those guys who shoved a girl out of bed after sex. Hell, I actually liked to snuggle.

"My mom's not like that."

Is that who she was running from? Not everyone was lucky enough to have the family I did. What had her mom done?

"So, what's she like?"

A deep breath then a long exhale, cool against my chest. She was debating what to tell me, how much to tell me. Damn it, I wanted to know everything about her, but I'd rein myself in because I sensed she needed to get this off her chest. Or at least, get some of it out.

"Demanding. Driven. Tough. Always working an angle."

"Your dad in the picture?"

Another pause, thinking through her response. "No. My mom left him when she was pregnant with my younger sister. He was…abusive. Mainly to my mom, but when he gave me a black eye when I was five, she packed up and left. She had three hundred dollars in cash and pawned her wedding and engagement rings for another couple hundred. We drove from Tampa to L.A. and crashed on an old friend's couch. The old friend turned out to be a sound technician for a television production company, and he got my mom a job in craft services. Gerry was a good guy. Had a good heart. My mom broke it, of course, but that's my mom. I cried for days when we got our own apartment."

"Your mom didn't stay in craft services for long, did she?"

She shook her head. "She wanted more. And she wanted to do it on her own. Luckily, she had two really photogenic daughters. My sister started doing print ads almost from birth. I booked a few, but mostly I did tv spots."

"And what'd your mom do?"

I had a clue where this was going, but I wanted her to keep talking. Wanted her to know I was listening.

"She managed. Our careers, our lives. Everything."

"Did you like it?"

"At first. Yeah. Then it became a job."

"How old were you then?"

She shrugged, and I felt every inch of her skin pressed against me like a hot iron.

"Eleven. I started to realize how much I was missing. I wanted to go to school with other kids my age. I wanted to do normal things like skateboard, but I couldn't because, what if I fell? What if I broke an arm or skinned my knees and I had to shoot that week?"

"So what'd you do?"

"Nothing. I did nothing. Because my mom and sister relied on my income."

"You were a kid. That shouldn't have been on you."

She rose up on an elbow and looked down at me, her smile twisted. "I know that now. But I felt guilty that my mom had to leave my dad because he hit me."

My mouth dropped open. "What the fuck—"

She shook her head. "I was a kid, Rowdy. Sometimes, that's how kid's brains work. At least, that's what one of my many therapists told me. My mom never made it my fault. She isn't a monster. She's just…driven. She wants us to succeed, probably because she thinks she never did. She's never had a successful relationship with a man because she could never trust them enough. Especially around her kids. And honestly, she has the worst taste in men. We used to be able to laugh about it. Then she just stopped looking, and it became all about us. Me and Tiff."

"That's your sister?"

She nodded, biting her lip as if trying to keep herself from saying more.

"Yeah. She's a singer."

She said that like maybe I was supposed to know her, but the only Tiffany singer I knew was older than forty, and her sister couldn't be.

"A good one?"

Her nose crinkled in a way that made me want to kiss her and roll her back to the floor and start loving her again. Fucking adorable.

"Not good enough. I mean, yes, she can sing, but she'll never be great."

"Do you sing?"

Another face. "Yes. But again, not good enough to be more than…okay. If you know what I mean."

I nodded. "Story of my life, Princess."

Her brow creased. "What do you mean?"

Shit, I didn't want to make this about me, but she'd asked. "Don't get me wrong, I love hockey, but if my dad didn't own the team, I wouldn't be playing."

Her mouth twisted. "No way. I saw you tonight. You were one of the best players out there."

Yeah, the compliment sounded great coming from her, but I was a realist. "There's a reason I haven't moved up another level."

"Have you tried?"

Tricky question with a tricky answer, but I didn't want to shut her down.

"Once. Went to an open tryout for an ECHL team." My turn to shrug. "Didn't make it. And the Devils actually had a winning season that year."

"And you never tried again?"

"No. Why would I? I've got my team here."

"And you're happy."

It wasn't a question, but I nodded anyway.

"Yeah. I'm happy." And if I wasn't ecstatic every day… Hell, no one was. Didn't mean I was going to abandon my team and run off to chase a pipe dream. "Aren't you?"

"Most days. I mean, no one's happy all the time, right?"

When she said it like that… I wanted to tell her she deserved to be happy all the time. That, if she let me, I'd try to make her happy every damn day.

But I couldn't just blurt that out. She'd run so far and so fast, I'd never see her again. Hell, we'd only met yesterday. I'm not stupid, but I can be too much sometimes. I know that. I also know she'll think it's too soon. Which is why I keep my damn mouth shut.

For, like, a second.

"You can try, though."

She looked like she wanted to say something, something I probably wouldn't like, then she must have thought better of it.

"Sure, you can try."

Sighing, she looked away, toward our clothing lying in a haphazard pile on the floor.

"I think it's time for me to go."

She said it so matter-of-fact that, for a second, I thought she'd shut down on me completely. Which would suck.

Then she turned back, released a sharp exhale and bent down to kiss me again. And, oh hell, this was not a goodbye kiss. This was definitely an "I will see you later and we will be naked" kiss.

"Thank you," she said before she pulled away completely, "for making tonight so much…fun."

"Glad I could help." Damn it, I really wanted her to stay, but I knew she couldn't. "Bathroom's that door over there."

Her smile widened, and she pressed another sweet kiss to my lips before she got to her feet, grabbed her clothing and headed for the bathroom.

While I lay there and watched her perfect naked ass as she walked away, I had to stop myself from waiting outside the bathroom door and taking her to my bed. But, when I looked at the clock on the side table, I knew she'd want to be back to the house before one a.m., because she could reason that she hadn't stayed out all night. And that maybe my mom would be asleep and wouldn't notice when she came in. Which she wouldn't because Tressy would enter through the door directly into her bedroom.

Hell, she could slip in before dawn and my parents wouldn't know a damn thing, but, yeah, I got it. Appearances mattered to her. And she was a good mom who wouldn't want her kid to know she'd been out all night.

But I'd be damned if this was the only time I got to spend with Tressy naked and horizontal.

This called for a plan.

CHAPTER FOURTEEN

ressy

I THOUGHT the drive back to Rowdy's parents' house would be awkward, full of weird silence and a need to fill the silence that just made everything worse.

It wasn't. Rowdy put his hand on my thigh as he drove, a warm weight that just made all the loud voices in my head shut down and purr. I felt like a damn cat who wanted to rub up against him and have him pet me.

Maybe I'd think about the implications of that later. Or maybe not. What I knew was that I didn't want to leave here anytime soon. And I didn't know how I was going to make that happen. I had a life, a career, people who needed me.

I also had two partners who could handle things for me for a week or so while I figured out my shit. Or got him out of my system. Because Rowdy had seriously gotten under my skin.

And there was also the problem of my mom and sister.

"You're gonna come to the game tomorrow, right?"

It was the first he'd spoken since we left his house, and I could see the lights from his parents' house through the trees just ahead.

I didn't even stop to think about my answer. "Of course."

I turned in time to see his smile. That smile that did amazing things to my breathing and heart rate and made practically every part of my body tingle, including the parts that still ached and begged for more.

"Good. Maybe we'll even win one for you."

He smiled, but I heard something in his voice that didn't vibe with the smile. But it was late, and I wanted nothing more than to crawl back into his arms and go to sleep. But I couldn't because I had to be there when Krista woke up.

"I'd like to see that."

"Yeah, so would we."

And there was that tone in his voice again, the one that held a secret I couldn't crack.

"Rowdy…"

He pulled to a stop at the side of his parents' house, at the path that led to the side door that opened directly into the rooms Krista and I were sharing. No one would know what time I came home, because that door had a keypad for entry. No sneaking through the house like a guilty teenager after curfew. Something I'd never done, by the way.

"Yeah?"

I looked at him and couldn't help but smile. He hadn't bothered to comb his hair, just raked his hands through it, and it looked messy, all those soft waves. I loved it. And even though his eyes were shadowed in the dark, I knew I'd remember the exact shade of them forever.

"I had fun tonight."

His smile turned into a wide grin. "Me, too, Princess."

That nickname was growing on me. If anyone else had tried

to call me that, I would've ripped them a new one. But Rowdy… The rules were different for Rowdy.

"I'll see you tomorrow."

Then I leaned across the console, and he met me halfway, our lips coming together harder than either of us intended. But the second we touched, that fire in my blood burned hotter than ever. My hands rose to cup his face so he couldn't pull away, not that I thought he would. No, he kissed me deeper, his mouth more demanding, until I couldn't breathe, and my heart pounded against my ribs. Until I was ready to crawl over the divider and onto his lap.

Just when I thought I might actually do it, he pulled away, that grin gone but the heated intensity in his eyes letting me know he wanted more.

"Not that I don't want to continue this, but before I strip you naked, and we end up pretzel fucking in my truck, you should go inside."

I laughed at the wry humor in his voice, but I could also hear the promise, too. And no, I really didn't want either of his parents to accidently look out a window and catch sight of me and their son fucking in his truck. I would never be able to look either of them in the eyes again.

Hell, I wasn't sure how I was going to face Raffi in the morning as it was.

With that thought in mind, I watched him get out of the truck and walk around to my door. He gave me his hand to help me out, and I had a momentary panic when I realized I didn't want to let him go.

When I tried to release him, he curved his fingers around mine and walked me to the door, hand in hand.

"You and Krista want to go to brunch with the team and the Angels tomorrow? It's another tradition, but mostly it's just to gossip about what happened the night before."

He must have seen the look of panic on my face because he

immediately added, "Trust me, no one'll give you a hassle. You're new. You get a pass. At least for a few weeks, anyway. The girls will make sure of it."

I wanted to go. I wanted to spend more time with him. Wanted to be part of this world, if only for a few short days.

"Sure. What time?"

"Be back around eleven." Then he leaned over and pressed his lips against mine for all of two seconds before he pulled away. "See you tomorrow, Princess. Sleep well."

He walked back to the truck but didn't get in until I'd opened the door and shut it behind me.

———

"Mommy? Are you okay? I'm hungry. And it's, like, almost lunch."

Krista's voice made my eyes fly open as I shot from sleep to instantly awake.

"Are you okay? What's wrong?"

Krista laughed as she bounced on my bed before snuggling in beside me. "I'm hungry. You've been sleeping for so long. I thought you'd never wake up. I wanna eat."

Turning to look at the clock on the bedside table, I groaned when I saw the time. "Baby, it's only seven-thirty. And it's Saturday. We can sleep later on Saturdays and Sundays, remember?"

"But I'm awake, and I'm bored. Can I watch TV until you get up?"

A yawn caught me off-guard, making Krista giggle again. "Mama, you must have gone to bed late."

Heat flooded my cheeks as I remembered exactly what I'd been doing last night that had kept me awake late.

"You know what, hon? You can watch TV. If you do it in the other room."

Krista smacked a kiss on my burning cheek then scrambled off the bed to run to the sitting room where the TV was located. I figured she'd call for me in a few seconds because she wouldn't be able to find the remote or wouldn't be able to work the TV. But I was proven wrong when I heard the distinctive sound of cartoon voices filter into my bedroom.

With a tired sigh, I flopped back down on the bed and closed my eyes again, though I knew I couldn't fall back to sleep. Yes, I was tired, but Krista needed me. A little alone time with my thoughts was not too much to ask, though, right?

Was I having regrets about last night? *Should* I have regrets about last night?

No. Because I wasn't a child, and sex wasn't dirty. And, oh my god, it had been the best sex I'd ever had. Ever. I wanted to have sex with Rowdy again tonight and the next night and—

Krista and I couldn't stay forever. Not even for a month. I had made a commitment to my business partners. Our agency was only four years old. I had clients who depended on me, who trusted me with *their* children. And even though my business partners would cover for me for as long as I needed, I had to go back to the city because that's where my clients needed me to be.

But did they really?

Most of my work was done over the phone or by video call now. Sure, I took in-person meetings when I had to, but I spent at least two days a week working from home because I didn't want to make the trek across town to our office. My partners and I had even considered shutting down our office or getting one in a shared workspace. Jen and Leon had pushed for it, while I'd been the hold out. We'd agreed to talk about it again at the end of this year after we had some hard data to justify getting rid of the space.

So, why couldn't we stay a little longer?

So now you're letting one night of sex get the better of you?

Rational Girl was back. Bad Girl must still be sleeping.

Shit. I needed a shower.

"Krista, honey, I'm getting in the shower."

I made sure I heard her say, "Okay, Mommy," before I forced myself out of bed and into the bathroom. Krista and I had a date with Rowdy this morning and I wanted to be presentable. But when I saw the tub, I knew I couldn't pass it up. It was huge, could probably fit at least two people, and had one of those over-the-tub trays where I could put my phone so I could read through my email and socials while I soaked.

I'd skimmed my emails a few times last night at the game, just to be sure I didn't miss anything important, but my inbox was about to become unmanageable. I filled the tub and dumped in bubble bath I found on the counter. I climbed in before it was full and let out a sigh as the hot water immediately started working on my tight muscles.

I lay there for several long minutes, eyes closed, body starting to loosen, before I even touched my phone. Then I took a deep breath and opened my messages. And nearly shut the app, because, holy shit, I didn't want to deal with this now.

But I was an adult, damn it, and I had to act like one.

I started with the messages from my partners.

JEN:

OMG what happened Thursday night

You disappeared

U ok

What'd your mom do this time

LEON:

Are you ok? Heard you never made it to your sister's show.

Hey, you ok? Call please. We need proof of life.

I HAD several messages from client's parents, questions I definitely needed to answer before end of day. Two messages from casting directors looking for talent. Those could wait until Monday. A message from a director asking specifically to see one of my client's reels. I needed to get that out this afternoon. Luckily, that text had come in late last night.

Mrs. Santiago, our neighbor, was the only person I'd contacted last night because I knew she'd be looking for Krista for their weekly Saturday brunch

That just left my sister and mom.

Just rip off the bandage.

I clicked on my sister's messages first and was surprised when I didn't have to scroll back that far to get to Thursday night's messages. They started out how I'd expected, with a lot of all caps and some serious "woe is me, you ruined my big night" energy. But the last couple were unexpected.

TIFF:

Hey, are you okay

I'm sorry. I didn't mean to go off on you. you know how mom gets when things don't go to plan.

Please get in touch. mom's freaking out and I'm worried about you.

WELL, that was different. My sister had never been worried about me. She was younger by five years and had always been self-involved. Mom had kept her busy with auditions and classes and every part she could book. She'd been a teenager when Krista had been born, and I'd been so wrapped up with having a baby at twenty-one that my relationship with my sister had become secondary. So maybe I was mostly to blame there.

I wish we'd all been closer, but life hadn't turned out that way. It was nice that she actually sounded worried about me now. But before I answered her back, I had to read through my mom's texts.

They started out pretty much as I expected. Wanting to know where I was going. How could you do this to your sister? Why are you acting like a child? Then came the guilt. How I'd ruined Tiff's big night. How I couldn't let Tiff shine on her own.

Which was bullshit. I didn't want the spotlight now. There were secrets I needed to protect, and they weren't mine.

Finally, she hit me with the concern and the apology. Was I okay? She was sorry. She'd been under a lot of stress. Where was I? When was I coming home? Was Krista okay? Did I need help?

It was the last question that made me close my eyes and sink a little farther beneath the water until my chin was covered and my lips could blow tiny waves across the water. I wasn't being overly sensitive, and I wasn't overreacting when I say that last question negated every other concern she might legitimately have.

My mom had never been able to accept that I'd willingly leave acting to do anything else. She'd never understood that that world had become toxic to me. That I'd left to save my sanity and, when Krista had come along, to save her from that world. I didn't want her growing up like I had. I wanted her to have a normal childhood, whatever that meant these days. At our home in New York, it meant pre-school and a highly organized structure of playdates at carefully chosen events and hours-worth of classes from dance to sports to arts.

I tried to make my schedule predictable, but it didn't cooperate all the time. And maybe I overcompensated because I wanted Krista to have all the things, and there were things I could never give her. Like a father. And at least one grandparent who wasn't more concerned with her children's success than she was with being a loving parent.

With a groan, I let myself sink completely under the water, holding my breath for several long seconds before I came back up for air.

Only to let out a startled yelp, when someone knocked at the door.

"Tressy, are you okay?"

Raffi. "Yes. Sorry. I didn't hear you. Did you need something? Is Krista being too loud?"

Raffi's laughter carried through the door. "Oh, hon, that single child could never be as loud as three boys and a girl fighting over what cartoons to watch on a Saturday morning. I just stopped by to see if you and Krista wanted to have breakfast with Reston and me?"

"Mommy, I'm hungry."

I huffed. Of course she was. She was always hungry.

"Or I could just feed Krista a little something? Rowdy texted that he was taking you both to the team brunch, but I figured Krista would be hungry until then and you can have some extra time to get ready."

Was this woman a literal saint? Seriously, there had to be something wrong with her.

"Mommy? Are you okay? Do you need help?"

I'd taught Krista not to open the bathroom door when it was shut, and to always ask if she could come in first. For some reason, Krista thought that meant I was in trouble.

"No, sweetie, I'm fine."

"Then can I go with Miss Raffi? She said she's gonna make muffins. I like muffins."

"Sure, you can go. Make sure you thank Miss Raffi."

From the other side of the door, I heard, "Thank you, Miss Raffi. Can we go now?"

"We'll be in the kitchen, Tressy. Take your time."

Faintly, I heard the entry door open and close and then all was silent. And, oh my god, I don't think I ever enjoyed a soak in a tub more. Krista was safe and taken care of. Not even our neighbor at home made me as comfortable as Raffi did. And that felt disloyal.

But walking out on your sister's big night didn't?

Not fair, I told Rational Girl. Totally, not fair.

Shoving all of that shit out of my head with an effort, I allowed myself the sheer pleasure of a half hour thinking of nothing. Just absolutely nothing. Not last night. Not Rowdy. Not Krista or my mom or my sister. Just blissful peace.

Until the tapping started. A quiet rap on wood. But not coming from the inside door. Definitely coming from outside.

My heart started to pound harder, but not from fright. Excitement made my breathing shallow out, and I got out of the tub and was reaching for a towel when my phone dinged.

ROWDY:

Hey, beautiful. You awake?

THOSE FEW WORDS made me feel giggly and bubbly, like a teenager talking to her first crush. It was stupid and juvenile. And amazing.

Instead of answering, I ran out of the bathroom in just a towel and went straight to the outside door. My wet hair probably made me look like a drowned poodle, but I couldn't help myself. I didn't want him to get away.

He was turning away as I opened the door, but his head whipped around when he heard the knob turn. His smile was all I needed to see to know last night had not been a mistake. And maybe it was my over-acting libido or maybe it was sheer stupidity, but I had the crazy thought that maybe Krista and I should stay just a little while longer.

Like maybe forever.

CHAPTER FIFTEEN

owdy

I'D NEVER BEEN SO happy to see a woman smile at me than I was right at this second.

Women smiled at me all the time. Older women. Younger women. Girls. Babies. Women who wanted to sleep with me. Even women who wanted to smack me usually smiled after they thought better about it.

But this woman… Fuck, this woman made me want to fall to my knees and pledge my undying devotion. And that was before I noticed she was soaking wet and wearing nothing but a towel. And that smile.

"Hey." Her voice held a little bit of a rasp that made all the small hairs on my body stand straight up in excitement. "Sorry, I was in the tub. I'm not late, am I?"

Late? For what? Oh…

"No. I just wanted to say good morning."

Jesus, I'm an idiot. If that wasn't the absolute worst—

"Good morning."

Her smile widened and, okay, maybe I wasn't that much of an idiot. Except I didn't know what else to say that wasn't, *"Damn, you're gorgeous. Can you drop that towel and I'll worship your body?"*

"You sleep okay?"

She nodded, her smile softening. "Yes, although Krista woke me up a little earlier than I expected. Your mom took her so I could get ready."

"I think my mom likes that little girl more than she does her own children."

Her laughter made my cock stir. "I think your mom would love to have grandchildren."

"Believe me, I know. She hasn't exactly been subtle the past couple of years." And I hadn't been anywhere close to granting her wish. But then this woman had stumbled into my arms two nights ago. And I thought, now, I might be ready.

Rebel would tell me I was an idiot for even thinking about this. Rain would tell me I was an idiot if I didn't. And Rocky… well, Rocky would ask what I wanted.

I wanted her.

"It's nice, and Krista loves the attention." She shrugged. "We don't see my mom a lot and," she readjusted her grip on the towel, and, sue me, I wanted her to just let it drop, "your mom's kind of a rock star."

I couldn't argue with that, so I just nodded. "So can I come in?"

She paused, and I wondered if she was going to say no. Then she gave me a look that sealed my fate and waved me in with the hand currently not holding her towel together.

"Sure. Just let me get some clothes."

I caught her free hand, wrapped my fingers around her wrist and brought it to my mouth. Pressing my lips to the pulse beating under her soft, warm skin, I watched her eyes narrow and her lips part.

I wanted to linger, her skin soft and warm beneath mine, and, damn, she smelled good. But I wanted to taste her lips. Her breath hitched and the hand on her towel tightened its grip.

Then she leaned in and pressed her lips against mine and stole my breath. And my sanity. Because right now, I didn't care if my parents were in the same house, I wanted to rip that towel away, pick her up and lay her out on the bed. Then I'd kiss my way down that luscious body and make her come with my mouth before I ripped off my jeans and fucked her until neither of us could walk.

When she pulled away after only a few seconds, I clenched my hands at my sides so I wouldn't just grab her. That'd be a dick move, and I didn't want to be a dick.

"I need to get dressed."

I bit my tongue so I couldn't say she didn't need them. Instead, I nodded.

She turned and headed back to the main bedroom, but not before she sent me a look over her shoulder that made my blood snap, crackle and pop. Fuck, I really hated being the better man and not following her into the bedroom.

"I thought you said brunch wasn't until eleven?"

Her voice drifted out of the bedroom, and I closed the door behind me before I walked into the sitting room, heading for the couch.

"It isn't. I'm early." I thought a few seconds before adding, "I wanted to see you."

Silence. Okay, maybe I'd shot myself in the foot by being too honest.

"Rowdy?"

"Yeah?"

"Come here."

I turned to find her standing in the doorway to the bedroom in just a bra and panties. They weren't lace or silk, just pink cotton that probably covered more than a bikini would. But my heart raced and every nerve ending in my body burned. And the look on her face…

Holy shit. She wasn't exactly smiling, but she definitely had something good on her mind. And when she crooked a finger at me, I couldn't get across the room fast enough. I didn't exactly run, but…

When I reached her, she grabbed the front of my shirt, tightening her fingers in the cotton and dragging me even closer. I had plans to resist. She wanted to control the situation, and I didn't have an issue with that. In fact, I kinda liked it.

"I'm glad you came by."

Her lips whispered against mine, and I rethought the whole control issue. Maybe I could just—

Her lips pressed against mine, her body melding into mine as she kissed me. And yeah, I put my hands on her ass and dragged her even closer, right against the erection that throbbed behind the zipper in my jeans.

If she pulled away, I'd let her go, but damn, she felt so right here. Plastered almost naked against me, every soft curve begging to be touched. Kissing me like she wanted to inhale me.

But just as I was about to lift her up and press her back against the wall, she pulled away. My eyes flew open, and I stared into hers, the blue almost a stormy gray right now.

"Sorry, that was—"

"Amazing. Don't apologize." Though it almost pained me to do it, I released her and stepped back. My momma raised me right. "Let's just call it a preview for later."

Her laughter seemed to surprise her. "I thought we had the full show last night?"

"Oh, no, Princess. That was just a taste. Like the spoonful of ice cream you get at the shop. Just makes you want more."

"So what flavor are you?"

"I guess you have to decide that for yourself. But you're definitely Birthday Cake."

Her expression turned confused. "Why Birthday Cake?"

"Because you're sweet…" I pressed a kiss to her cheek, just to the left of her lips, "and made for a party."

She got that look again, the one where her lips parted and her eyes widened, and I could tell she was thinking something, but I couldn't tell what. Then she laughed again, that full-belly sound that eventually led to that delicate snort I found so fucking adorable, but that she obviously felt embarrassed by. Her hand came up to cover her mouth, and she turned away for a second, shaking her head.

"I don't know what to make of you."

She sounded genuinely perplexed, but I just shrugged because I'd heard it before.

"I'm just a guy, standing in front of a girl—"

"Wait, wait, wait. You are *not* going to quote 'Notting Hill' at me?" Now she looked astounded and amazed, and I bit back a smile.

"What's that?"

She stared for another few seconds, her mouth hanging open in shock, before she smacked me in the chest with one of those delicate hands of hers.

"I honestly don't know what to do with you."

"I have a few suggestions."

And all of them had to do with her naked and me worshipping every inch of skin on her body before I fucked us both into oblivion.

Her eyes got brighter, and her expression transformed with sheer joy. *Absolutely beautiful.*

"And I really hope we get to do a few of them tonight."

"I'm looking forward to it."

Another pause, another smile, but this time, there was something else there, something a little sad.

"I guess I should get dressed."

"You don't have to on my account."

"I think I might be a little cold if I go out in this. And I think I might shock your parents."

"Princess, my parents have owned a minor league hockey team full of misfits for the past two decades. They wouldn't be surprised if you walked out of here naked."

Her brows arched. "Are you trying to tell me something?"

"My life's an open book. Ask me anything."

I thought she'd make a joke. Instead, her eyes narrowed, and I could tell she was working something over in her head, and that I should probably be worried. I'd just given her a free pass to my life. And I'd meant it. I just hadn't expected her to take me seriously.

"Do you ever think about moving away from here?"

Damn, it's like she know exactly what I'm hiding. "Sometimes, yeah."

"Have you never thought about playing for another league?"

"Once or twice, yeah." Or, like, five hundred times in the past few weeks.

Her head cocked to the side, and she looked at me like she could read my mind.

"Why do I think that's not entirely true?"

Because I was a pretty shitty liar, and everyone around here knew that. But I was damn good at telling people what they wanted to hear without answering a straight question.

I shrugged, letting my lips curve in a grin that usually allowed me get away with almost anything. "So maybe I've thought about it more than a few times. But, I love it here. I wouldn't want to live anywhere else."

But would I like to play somewhere else? Play for a team that actually gave a shit about winning? And leave behind a group of guys who counted on me to be here, to be the one stable thing in their lives?

"But would you *play* somewhere else?"

Maybe she could read minds.

"My team depends on me. My dad depends on me." Hell, the town depended on me, to some degree, because I was the face of the team and the town depended on the team. And that wasn't ego. That was just the way it was.

She continued to stare into my eyes, and I could practically see those wheels turning. "But what do you want?"

"You." Hell, I didn't even have to think about that answer. Right this second, she was the only thing I wanted. Not hockey. Not to play for another team. Not anything. "I want you."

For a second, I didn't think she was going to let me get away with the dodge. Because even though what I'd said was true, I hadn't really answered her question.

Putting my hands on either side of the wall so I wouldn't grab her again, I leaned forward and nuzzled my nose against her neck, breathing her in. She sucked in a quick breath before leaning forward and tilting her head farther to the side, inviting me to do more than run my nose along her warm skin.

I pulled back before I decided to take her up on the offer.

"You better get dressed or risk Krista finding you in a compromising position."

She huffed out a laugh and put her hand on my chest, though she didn't push me away. She petted me as she smiled up at me, those blue eyes sparking with amusement.

"Then you need to leave."

Nodding, I took a few steps back. "See you in a few, Princess."

I forced myself to walk out and around the house to the front door, smiling all the way.

Tressy

As I excused myself to use the restroom at the restaurant where we were having brunch, I couldn't help thinking that Rowdy was hiding something.

After our talk this morning, all I could think about was the fact that Rowdy had a secret he didn't want to tell me. And I wanted to know. I wanted him to trust me enough to tell me. Which was ridiculous, because we barely knew each other. And I had a pretty big secret myself.

Which was getting harder and harder to justify keeping.

When we'd arrived at the restaurant, almost everyone had greeted me like a long-lost friend.

The Angels cooed over my "absolutely adorable" daughter and introduced her to their children, a few of whom were the same age. She was now happily playing in a special corner of the restaurant rigged out just for kids, with coloring books and crayons and toys, watched over by a revolving stream of parents.

Rowdy's teammates had welcomed me with smiles and not one had said anything even slightly snarky about my relationship with their captain. Rebel might've started to say something, but Rowdy had stuck an elbow in his side before any words had escaped.

Only Rain had been preoccupied and not very talkative, her attention clearly somewhere else.

And Rowdy had been…Rowdy.

"Hi. I know you."

The voice brought me out of my thoughts, and I looked down at the boy standing in front of me in the hallway where the restrooms were located. I smiled down at him, the only thought on my mind was getting back to Rowdy and Krista. He wasn't much older than Krista, maybe eight or so, his little freckled face intent as he stared up at me.

My smile widened. "Hi there. Are you looking for the men's room?" I pointed down the hall. "I think it's the next door."

"I know you."

He looked at me with wide, hazel eyes and the most self-assured look I'd ever seen on a child's face. Panic twisted my gut into a knot, and my lungs froze for a split second. Then I immediately tried to dismiss it. This little boy had no idea who I was. I needed to calm down.

"I don't think so, sweetie. I'm not from around here. My name's Tressy."

"No, I know that. But I know you. You're on my favorite TV show."

You've been caught.

Okay, don't panic. Deep breath. He probably thought I was someone else.

"What's your favorite TV show?"

"You're Mabel Ann. On 'Broad Street.' I recognize your voice."

Shit. Shit. And double shit.

I kept a smile on my face, but it was tough. Damn it, I didn't want to lie to this baby. I didn't want to tell him he was wrong. Make him doubt himself. Because he was right.

But damn, I really didn't have to like it.

"Broad Street" had made me one of the most recognizable child actors in America for a brief period of time. Until the show runners' egos had gotten too big and killed the show with their outrageous demands.

That'd been more than fifteen years ago and, until recently, it'd held cult classic status because there'd been copyright issues with some of the music, which had kept it from being syndicated or licensed.

Until recently, when the producers had gotten those problems worked out, and "Broad Street" had become something of a sensation again. Mainly because of Denee.

The excitement on this little boy's face made my chest tight and my pulse beat faster. It'd been years since I'd been recognized as Mabel Ann. My hair had been red back then, and I'd been this little pudgeball of energy, the perfect sidekick to the perfect girl-next-door Denee Henning, who'd become so famous and then died so tragically.

It still hurt my heart to think about everything she'd lost. Everything she'd never get to do.

Noting the small bench along the wall, I lowered myself onto it and gestured for him to sit next to me. He scrambled up onto the cushion, still staring at me with that adoring smile.

My lips curved, though my heart beat like a trapped bird. "What's your name?"

"Brandon, but everyone calls me Bud."

"Bud, if I tell you a secret, do you think you can keep it?"

He nodded so hard, I thought he might hurt himself. "I won't tell anyone. Not even my mom and dad."

Damn it, that hurt. I didn't want this baby keeping secrets

from his parents. I wouldn't want someone telling Krista to keep secrets from me. *Shit.*

But self-preservation had become second nature.

"That was me, but it was a really long time ago. I was about your age when I started on 'Broad Street.'"

"I knew it! I knew it was you."

He didn't exactly shout the words, but I winced because it sounded really loud in the hallway.

For the next few minutes, Bud talked my ear off. In a good way. About everything he loved about the show and how he had watched the whole thing in, like, two weeks, and it's the only show he wanted to watch now and, then he went into detail about episodes I'd long forgotten filming.

But I smiled and nodded and let him talk. And let his enthusiasm infect me. That show held so many good and bad memories for me. It was impossible to separate them now, they were all so tangled together in a mess that sometimes it still hurt to think about it.

Finally, he had to take a breath, and I could get a word in.

"I'm so glad you enjoy the show, Bud. That makes me really happy. But I do need to ask you a favor."

He nodded again. "Sure!"

You're a horrible person.

"I would really appreciate it if you could please not tell anyone who I am."

I held my breath as I waited for him to react. I was expecting more questions, maybe a few tears. Instead, Bud grinned from ear to ear.

"It's a secret."

I winced inwardly. "Yes, it's a secret."

Damn it, I felt like a pervert, though I wasn't asking him to do anything weird or illegal. I was simply asking him not to reveal my past.

Bud bounced off the bench, promising again not to tell

anyone and how great it had been to meet me. Then he headed back down the hall, leaving me sitting there, feeling like an awful person.

This sucked. I wanted to go after Bud and tell him to go ahead and tell his parents, tell whoever he wanted. I didn't have anything to hide. Who would even recognize me anymore? More importantly, who would care?

So, I used to be a child actress. A fairly successful one, yes, but never a household name. Not like Denee. And then it all went away. I hit puberty, and I hadn't been cute anymore. I hadn't been small and adorable and chubby. I'd been skinny and had acne and boobs. I didn't fit the Hollywood teen stereotype.

My mom had tried… God, how she'd tried to make me the next big thing. Dyed my hair. Hired a dietician. A personal trainer. Weekly dermatologist appointments. Daily acting classes.

She'd tried to make me into someone I wasn't. And I'd gone along with it. Because I loved my mom and sister, and I wanted to provide for them like I always had. Until it wasn't enough. I wasn't getting the roles my mom thought I should be. I just had to try a little harder, do this differently, do that differently. Until it'd all become just so much noise. Too much noise for a teenager with an attitude and a chip on her shoulder. A teenager who wanted to go to college.

"Tressy? You okay?"

My head popped up to see Rain walking down the hall with Caity, the Angels' captain, their expression almost identical. Frowns and concern. Jesus, how bad did I look?

"Yeah," I smiled. "I'm fine. Is Krista okay? I'm sorry. I didn't mean to leave her for so long—"

"She's fine. No worries." Caity waved a hand next to her head like she was stopping traffic. "I think the team wants to hire her as their mascot. She's certainly cuter than anyone else in the organization."

"Tressy, did something happen?"

Rain continued to study me like I was bug under a microscope. It made me want to squirm. I wasn't used to people questioning me. Being concerned about me. It was as uncomfortable as it was unusual.

"No, nothing happened. I just sat down for a second and I guess I lost track of time."

Caity shrugged it off. "Everybody needs a few minutes to themselves sometimes. Anyway, I'm just gonna…"

She pointed to the bathroom door and disappeared. Leaving me with Rain. And the questions she wasn't asking.

Rain just stood there for a few seconds, before she sat next to me on the bench.

"You know I don't care if you sleep with Rowdy. I mean, he's my brother, and I think he's an idiot, but he is a good guy."

I didn't know what to say to that, so I just nodded, my cheeks flaming red, and all the other shit that I'd been thinking about still rolling around my head.

"But he can really be blind to some shit. And he totally thinks he's needs to fix everything for everyone. Sometimes, he forgets not everyone needs something from him. So, do you?"

I had no idea where she was going with this. "Do I what?"

"Do you *need* something from him?"

Do I?

"No, I don't."

"Are you in trouble? I know you said you're not but—"

"No, I'm not. Honestly. It's just… my mom and I are having issues. Our relationship is a little more complicated than most." I didn't even think about what came out of my mouth next. The conversation with Bud must have loosened my tongue. Or maybe I was just tired of holding it all in. And I didn't want to tell Rowdy and have him look at me differently. "Many years ago, I was an actress. A pretty successful one, actually. I supported my mom and sister. We lived really well. For a while. And then I grew up."

I waited for Rain to ask the question, the one I didn't want to answer. I could see it forming there behind her sharp, dark eyes.

"You know you're allowed to have a life of your own life, right? At some point, you have to live for yourself."

I blinked, because that was *so* not what I'd expected to hear.

"I mean, yes, I know that. But when you grow up with your entire family depending on you, you develop some weird phobias of your own."

Rain shrugged, like we weren't having a pretty heavy conversation outside the bathroom. "Hell, you can develop those anywhere. I feel like my family would fall apart if I weren't here to keep them all in line. Parents included. And maybe they would. But that's not on me. You know? And it's kinda shitty for your mom to put you in that position."

I knew that, but it still brought up the old defensiveness. My back went stiff, and it took me a few seconds to shove those feelings back down. Because she wasn't wrong.

"I know that. But… she's my mom."

"And family comes first." Rain's smile sharpened. "Trust me, I get it. The Lawrences are nothing if not family first. But sometimes you gotta do what you need to do for yourself."

"And if that means hurting those you love?"

Rain shrugged. "It sucks, but sometimes you can't help it. If they love you, they'll forgive you."

I thought back to those texts from my sister and the ones from my mom. "Or they'll guilt you into thinking it's all your fault."

Rain's nose crinkled and her expression turned sympathetic. "Ugh. That sounds…not fun. Is that why you don't want to go back? I mean, St. David is a good place to hide out. But most everything catches up with you."

"Sounds like you have some experience with that."

Rain's lips twisted, and I knew my observation was right.

"Maybe a little."

"So why do you stay?"

"Maybe I have nowhere else to go." She shrugged. "Maybe I just like it here."

"Where *would* you go?"

"I don't know." Rain just smiled. "I haven't given it much thought."

"Bullshit."

They both turned to see Caity leaning against the open door to the bathroom, arms crossed over her chest. The dance team captain looked young enough to have just graduated from high school, but she had to be at least twenty-one because she'd been drinking last night. Toned, tight and perfectly put together, Caity made me feel like a grandma in my black cargo pants and slouchy green shirt.

Red hair in ringlet curls and green eyes flashing, she stared at Rain with serious attitude.

Rain arched her brows and stared back. "I don't know what you're talking about."

Caity rolled her eyes. "And again, I say bullshit."

She sang that last word, and when I turned back to Rain, I saw her eyes narrow down to slits. Then she gave Caity the finger and turned back to me. "You ready to get back to the party? I'm sure Rowdy's missing you by now."

Nodding, I walked back to the dining room with Rain, who looked tense, and Caity, who looked way too satisfied with herself.

And as soon as I stepped out of the hallway, I caught sight of Rowdy, holding Krista's hand like it was the most natural thing in the world. My daughter looked up at him like he was this amazing shining toy she'd just discovered. I couldn't remember my daughter ever looking at anyone like that. Not my mom, not my sister. Not anyone in our small group of friends at home.

"He gets that look a lot." Rain had stopped next to me, and I glanced at her, just to make sure we were on the same page. Rain wore an exasperated grin now as she shook her head. But the love she had for her brother emanated from her like a physical force.

Everyone loved Rowdy. So, of course, it wasn't a shock that I'd fall for the guy.

The hard part would be leaving him.

CHAPTER SEVENTEEN

Krista held my hand like she'd been doing it since birth, and she hadn't left my side since Tressy had taken off for the bathroom. It seemed like she'd been gone for a while, but she'd probably got stuck talking to someone. I wasn't worried. She'd be back.

"I don't know about you, man, but I might be getting too old for this shit."

Brian Fiskers was the only Stag team member here today, but only because he'd once been a Devil. And once a Devil, always a Devil.

I continued to scan the crowd, watching for any situation I might have to step in to diffuse. Most of the guys knew the drill for these outings. Have fun but don't start any shit. We were in public, for fuck's sake. Save the drama for the ice.

But there were always unknowns with the new guys. Nineteen-year-old Wellar had earned a reputation as a hothead in one of the toughest junior leagues in Canada. Brock Mingo had been a second-round draft pick by the Philadelphia Colonials eight years ago but had never managed to make it to the NHL because of a plague of injuries. The guy was a walking accident waiting to happen, but he could stick handle like a seasoned pro.

And Denny Hollowell had been a high-ranking junior player in the American system, a shoe-in for a top draft spot, until he'd been one of the victims of the worst hazing incident in modern hockey. Not many people knew the whole story, and Denny wasn't talking. At least, not to me or my dad or any of the other guys. And I had to respect that. But damn, it's been hard not to want to find out who had hurt this absolute puppy dog of a kid and beat them to a pulp.

Yeah, I was aware of the contradictions in that scenario, but it didn't make me any less willing to do violence to anyone who'd put that haunted look in that kid's eyes.

Anyone who knew me knew that if you needed a wingman, I'd be there. If you needed a helping hand, I'd give you one. And if you deliberately hurt someone I considered mine, well, prepare to face my wrath.

"Man, we were too old for this about five years ago," I finally responded to Brian's comment after making sure there was nothing going on.

"I really think this is the last year for me."

Shaking his head, his too-long hair brushing his shoulders, Brian looked out over the crowd like he was looking for someone. I had a feeling I knew who, which was proven true when his gaze stopped moving. Following his stare, I saw Rain and Tressy emerge from the hallway to the restrooms.

"You know you could just ask her out." I leaned a little closer to Brian, so no little ears would hear. "I promise I won't cut your balls off for touching her."

Brian went rigid beside me. "I don't know what you're talking about." He paused. "And if I wanted to ask her out, I would."

Which was bullshit, because Brian—

Tressy's eyes met mine again, and she stared at me like she was seeing me for the first time, taking my measure. When her lips curved in a smile, my heart started to pound, and I grinned like a lunatic.

Beside me, Brian shook his head. "You're toast, man."

Yep, I knew that.

"Can I have some more pancakes?"

Krista's voice drew my attention away from her mom. "Okay, if you're sure it won't make you sick. You must've had twenty already."

Krista giggled, the sound hitting me right in the feels. "I haven't had twenty. I only had ten. And they're so little. May I please? And can I have whipped cream?"

I had no defense against Krista's pleading. She was just too adorable. Those big dark eyes and dusky skin and the pug nose with those freckles. And it wasn't because I saw Tressy in Krista's features. As a matter of fact, I saw nothing of Tressy in Krista's features. She must really take after her dad.

Was he was still in the picture? Neither Krista nor Tressy had mentioned him, and I knew Tressy wouldn't be the kind of woman to screw around on a boyfriend or husband. I just knew.

"Exactly how much sugar have you fed my child already?"

The smile in Tressy's voice made all the hair on my body stand on end. I turned to find her grinning at me. With her hair loose and shiny, and those blue eyes gleaming, I wanted to kiss her from head to toe and everywhere in between, and it was probably a good thing she couldn't read my mind. Although the heat in her eyes made me feel like I'd been scorched.

"Obviously not enough to turn her into a sugar monster because she hasn't started to scream yet."

"Krista, can you come over to my house this afternoon to play? My mom said it's okay."

The little girl who'd run up to Krista's side and grabbed her hand was one of the Angels' daughters. Mandy was a carbon copy of her mom, from her head to her toes, but I still saw a little of her dad there, too, in the shape of her mouth and the way she smiled. Her dad, Derek, worked as a local firefighter and ran his own handyman business. He was on the payroll at the arena.

"Mommy, can I?"

Tressy looked at me, as if I had a say in the decision. Then I realized she was asking my opinion.

"Hey, Mandy, why don't you ask your mom to come over and talk to Krista's mom?"

"Okay."

And off she ran back to her mom, Daisy, who'd been talking to Rebel and a few of the other players. Daisy smiled, waved and said something to Rebel, then took Mandy's hand and walked back to us.

"Hey, I don't know if you remember me from Thursday night, but I'm Daisy. You met Mandy already. She said she'd like to have Krista spend the day with us, and I'm totally fine with that if you are. My husband's a firefighter, so he knows CPR, and Mandy's gluten-free so we're used to food intolerance. Mandy's been begging to have friends over for weeks but with school and sports stuff with our older kids, we just haven't had time. But today would be perfect. If it's okay with you. Rowdy'll vouch for us, won'tcha, Sheriff?"

Daisy and Derek were two of my best friends from high school. "How come you never invite me over for playdates anymore?"

Daisy slapped a hand on my chest, hard enough to sting. "Because you're worse than a teenager. You eat all our food and drink all our beer and make my husband get banished to the couch because he ate too many damn hot wings and gets indigestion that annoys the crap out of both of us."

I laughed. "That was a good night."

Daisy gave me a look. "Not for him, it wasn't."

I just shook my head because, yeah, Daisy had condemned

Derek and me to sleeping together in the guest room. I'd had too many beers to drive home, and the guest bedroom would've been mine alone if Derek hadn't gotten the worst case of indigestion. We'd laughed practically all night, like teenagers and woke up with matching hangovers.

"Not for me, either, hon."

"You deserved whatever you got that night, Rowdy."

Tressy watched the interplay, the discomfort I'd seen a little earlier disappearing as her smile made its return.

"Are you sure?" Tressy asked. "I know you have a game tonight, and I don't want to interfere with—

"Oh, gosh, no." Daisy waved that thought away with her hand. "Actually, it'll be good for Mandy. She sometimes gets the short end of the deal. She's six years younger than her older sister, and they fight like cats and dogs sometimes. You'd be doing me a favor."

Tressy bit into her bottom lip, sliding me a quick glance before smiling back at Daisy. "If you really don't mind…"

The two little girls began to giggle and jump up and down, holding hands.

"Krista, honey, you need to be good."

"I will, Mommy. Bye!"

Krista didn't look back as she and Mandy linked hands and took off across the room to Derek, while Daisy gave Tressy a smile that was clearly grateful.

"Thank you. Mandy doesn't make friends easily and she's really taken with Krista. Your daughter is a sweetheart."

"Thanks. She doesn't get to do a lot of playdates at home. I work and there aren't a lot of kids her age in our building—"

"They'll have a great time." Daisy reached out and squeezed Tressy's hand. "We have a big backyard and a playset that doesn't get used nearly enough. We'll bring her to the game with us, if that's okay with you?"

My brain was already calculating how many hours I'd have alone with Tressy. And I was liking that math.

After a second, Tressy nodded. "Sure, that would be great. Thanks again, Daisy."

"Oh, no problem at all."

Tressy waved again to Krista, who barely glanced back as she and Mandy headed for the door hand-in-hand with Daisy and Derek, then stared at the door for several long seconds before turning back to me.

"Derek's one of my oldest friends from school," I assured her. "He and Daisy were childhood sweethearts who had their first kid when they were twenty. There are a lot of good people in this town, but those two are great."

I wanted to reassure her that St. David was safe. That the people here were some of the best in the world. She could find a haven here, if she wanted one. Because she'd been running from something. And she still hadn't told me what. But now we had the entire day to ourselves. And while I wanted to spend some of it alone and naked, I didn't want her to think that's all I wanted.

"So since we have some time on our hands, you wanna see something cool?"

Her expression lightened in a way that made me grin, because I knew exactly what she was thinking.

Her brows rose, challenging. "I think I saw a lot of those cool things last night. What else is there?"

"I think you'll be surprised how much more there is to see. Are you ready to get out of here?"

She paused. "You're sure Krista will be okay?"

"Cross my heart." I made an X over my chest and gave her the biggest smile, which served the purpose of making her laugh.

"You're dangerous, Rowdy Lawrence."

"Only to your sanity, Tressy Meyers."

Another laugh, louder and with that distinctive hitch at the end.

I would know that laughter anywhere. It was so familiar. I couldn't shake the feeling that I'd heard it before. Which made me look at her more closely, trace her features and wonder why she felt so familiar.

Then she shook her head, took my hand and tugged on it.

"Oh, I already figured that out. So where are we going?"

―――

I TOOK her out the back door, so we didn't have to run the gauntlet of the entire restaurant. If we had, we'd still be trying to make it out.

It wouldn't take long for everyone to realize we were gone. This town's gossip network worked without a hitch. I liked to bitch about it, but then I'd think about how it had once saved the life of the town's grumpy widow, Mrs. Travers, when several people, whom the old woman literally hated, had realized she hadn't taken in her mail or paper that morning. They'd descended on her home and found her on the kitchen floor with a broken hip from a fall.

That's the kind of town this was. Tressy didn't have to worry about Krista spending the day with Mandy. Just like she didn't have to worry about whatever secrets she was still keeping. They'd be safe here.

"We have to make a quick stop at my place," I said, sliding her a glance. The raised eyebrows I got in return made me grin. "But don't get your hopes up. We're not staying long."

"Then why are we stopping?"

"You'll see."

When I pulled up to my house a few minutes later and shut off the car, her lips curved. "Not stopping long, huh?"

Leaning over, I kissed those grinning lips because I couldn't not kiss her. But I didn't linger, even though she tried to follow me back over the console.

"I meant it, we're not staying. And none of your womanly wiles will change my mind."

She was still laughing when I got out of the car and headed around to her side to open her door.

"So what are we doing here?"

"Switching vehicles. Your sneakers are behind my seat. Grab those before you get out."

Her nose wrinkled. "Why do I need my sneakers? And when did you get them?"

"Hey, I gotta keep some of my secrets. Come on."

She let me help her out of the truck then followed me to the garage. I'd already hit the remote to open the door and walked in to give my baby a pat.

"Hello, old girl. Ready to go play?"

"Um, you're not talking to me, are you?"

I turned to wink at Tressy then nodded for her to come closer.

"Nope. This is my first love. Tressy, meet Betty. I bought Betty when I was sixteen. She's a '73 Jeep CJ-5 Renegade. Old Mr. Dietrich left her sit in his barn for years, and it took me months of work to get her to turn over the first time. Now, she's strictly for off-roading."

Today was a perfect day to take her out. Not too hot. Not too cold. No wind. No roof.

"Off-roading?" Tressy sounded sceptical.

"Where we're going, we don't need roads."

It took her a second, but she laughed at my "Back to the Future" reference, shaking her head. "I kind of think you need roads to drive on."

"Some of the best places aren't on a street map. Come with me and I'll show you one of them."

I grabbed the ball cap I kept in the back for Rain and held it out to her.

"You're gonna need that. Just pull your hair through the hole."

Another slight hesitation, but then she smiled, set her sneakers and bag in the back seat of the Jeep, and grabbed the hat out of my hand.

I motioned for her to turn so she was facing away from me. "Give me that hairband around your wrist. I'll braid this for you so it doesn't get all messed up."

For a second, I thought she'd say no, that she'd do it herself. And again, she surprised me and handed over the elastic. Her hair felt like silk as I twisted the strands into a loose braid. I had the urge to wrap that braid around my hand and tug her head back so I could kiss her like I wanted to. But if I started, I wouldn't want to stop, and we'd end up naked in my bed. And while that was definitely on the books for later, right now I wanted to show her we could have fun outside the bedroom.

"All ready."

She turned, the look on her face hard to read.

"What? Did I do it wrong? Is it too tight?"

"No. It's fine." She drew the braid over her shoulder and looked down at it. "Perfect. Not a skill I expected you to have."

Now, she eyed me suspicion.

"If you get in the car, maybe I'll tell you all about how I acquired this amazing skill."

Her lips quirked, like she was trying to suppress a grin, then she flipped the braid over her shoulder and got into the passenger seat.

Firing up the engine, I revved it a couple of time, grinning when she gripped the oh-shit hande above the door with her right hand and the seat with her left, then shifted into first and shot out of the garage.

The rumble of the engine combined with the rush of air from the open roof made talking pretty much impossible. But I could tell from her expression that she was having fun. It was hard not to have fun with the top down on a beautiful day heading into the forest and the hills that surrounded St. David. It felt like another world out here. Town meant people, noise, work. The woods meant quiet, solitude and relaxation.

I turned off the paved road and took the first dirt track I came to. Tressy sucked in a breath as the Jeep dipped and rocked, the wheels spinning for a second until they caught. Then we bumped along for at least a mile before we got to the clearing.

Technically, we were on state game land. Most people looking to commune with nature parked at the trailhead farther along the road. This area was used mainly by hunters, but it was too late in the day for them. There were no cars in the clearing.

"Are we hiking?" She reached behind the seat to grab her sneakers and swapped out her low boots.

"Not far. It's an easy half mile or so."

"It's the 'or so' that usually comes back to bite you."

I winked, which only made her eyes narrow. "Not afraid of a little walk, are you?"

Putting her hands on her hips, she gave me another one of those looks that made my blood heat. And my cock twitch.

"Why do I have the feeling you've said that to a lot of other girls?"

I shrugged. "Never had to. St. David girls grew up in these hills, just like the guys." I nodded toward the trail. "Come on, the path is pretty tame. Can't wear myself out. Got a game tonight."

"Uh huh."

She didn't sound convinced, but I got out and walked to her side. She'd just finished tying her second sneaker when I opened the door. Her head was directly level with mine, so I leaned in and snagged a kiss. Her lips went soft against mine immediately, and her hands wrapped around my neck, like I'd try to get away. Instead, I put my hands on her hips and dragged her closer.

Heat flared in an instant, and she maneuvered herself so that her legs were around my waist, pulling me even closer, her heels on my ass. My body responded with a surge of desire that made every nerve ending feel like it was on fire. And yeah, I wanted to have her again. Hell, I'd make it work in the cab if I had to, but I didn't want her to end up with bruises or a twisted back. I could be a gentleman long enough to wait until we got back to my place.

But first…

I pulled back just as she slid her tongue across my lips, making me groan.

"Don't make me turn this Jeep around, lady."

She laughed, the sound becoming so familiar, I hated to think what I'd do without it.

"Like you don't want to?"

Hell, yes, I wanted to. "I've got plans for later, but right now, I wanna show you something."

She made a production out of her sigh and rolled her pretty eyes, but her smile was sweet.

"Okay, fine. I'm all yours."

She realized almost immediately what she'd said and how it sounded. I saw it in the way her eyes widened, and her lips parted. Lips still damp and puffy from our kiss.

I grinned. "Nice of you to acknowledge that. Come on. Let's go."

I helped her out of the truck, holding onto her hand as her feet hit the ground.

"The trail's got a gradual incline until pretty close to the end." I started walking, adjusting my gait so I didn't get too far ahead of her. "Then there's a decent uphill, but it's not long. And I promise, it'll be worth it."

She didn't look convinced, her expression skeptical as she sized up the trail ahead. But then she nodded and kept walking, though I saw her note the posted hunting signs.

"Is it safe out here?"

"At this time of day, yeah. Most hunters are here early and this part of the gamelands isn't known for having a large deer population. Sometimes, there're bears around, but they don't usually mess with people. If we're lucky, though, maybe we'll see Bigfoot."

I swear her laughter made the sun shine brighter. "Now that'd be worth the climb."

We walked in silence for the next few minutes, me watching her take everything in around her like she'd never seen so many trees in her life. But after a while, I heard her take a deep breath.

"So," she said, "I did something today I'm not very proud of."

Fuck, that didn't sound good. "I hope you're not talking about spending the night with me."

She huffed out a laugh and smacked her hand against my abs. "I'm not but keep it up and I might be."

Sighing, she paused for a few seconds while stupid relief flushed through me.

"Can I tell you something in confidence?"

"Absolutely." I was dead serious. "You can trust me."

I wanted her to trust me with everything.

"A little boy recognized me today, and I asked him to keep it a secret."

None of that sentence made any sense, so I kept my mouth shut and just nodded.

"I don't know why I did it. I mean, it's not like no one knows, or even cares, who I am anymore. But I've gotten so used to keeping that part of my life in the past, it was almost habit. But I asked a child to keep a secret for me, and, as a mother, I can't live with that."

"Are you a serial killer? Did the kid witness you kill someone?"

She rolled her eyes as she glanced up at me, her lips twisted. "No, of course not."

"I hope you know you could tell me if you had. I'd help you bury the body."

She looked up again, so quickly she nearly stumbled over a

root in the path, looking at me like she didn't know if I was telling the truth.

I shrugged, like it was no big deal. "Hey, I'm just saying. There's a lot of land out here. No one would ever know."

Shaking her head, she stared at me like I'd just turned into Bigfoot. "I've never met anyone like you."

"Probably won't. I'm one of a kind."

Sighing, she shook her head. "I just…I don't know what to do with you."

"Sure you do." I didn't mention that she'd done a pretty good job of knowing what to do last night, but I figured that would be pushing the line. "You were about to tell me all your secrets."

She paused, like she was reconsidering her confession, though what this woman would have to confess, I couldn't imagine. Maybe she was married. Maybe she had a steady boyfriend. Maybe Krista's father—

"I used to be famous."

Okay, not what I was expecting. "Um, okay?"

"I mean, not like worldwide famous. I'm not Beyonce or Taylor famous but… I was well-known as a kid."

"For what?"

"I was an actress. I was on a TV show that blew up overnight. It was a fluke, a lightning strike. But it made me—well, it made my character a household name."

I waited her out, knowing she was choosing her words. The day was beautiful, the sun shining through the leaves that were left on the branches. Oak and maple leaves littered the ground, hiding the edges of the trail. But I could walk to our destination with my eyes closed.

Finally, she said, "Did you ever hear of the show, 'Broad Street'?"

"Hasn't everyone? Isn't that where Denee Hennings got her start?"

Something blipped at the back of my brain, something important. But it was lost in the realization of who Tressy was.

"Holy *shit*." I stopped in my tracks. "You're Mabel Ann."

She nodded, staring straight ahead as she continued to walk, as if she hadn't just blown my mind. "I was. That role kept my family off the streets. It came along at a time when we were struggling and weren't sure if we were going to have a roof over our heads the next week."

Well, shit. That sounded scary as hell. And something I knew nothing about. Most people would say I'd led a charmed life, and I couldn't argue. My biggest worries growing up had been hockey and girls. And sometimes, grades, 'cause, you know, hockey and girls.

But even if my parents had had money problems, they damn sure wouldn't have used their children to make more.

"That's a hell of a lot to put on a— Wait, how old were you then?"

"Ten."

What the actual fuck? Ten years old and carrying the weight of her family's survival on her shoulders. Jesus, no wonder she had issues with her mom.

"That sounds an awful lot like child labor."

Shrugging, she shook her head, not meeting my gaze.

"My mom didn't think of it that way. And neither did I, really. I loved to act. Loved going to the set and working with different people and not having to go to school. And for a kid who maybe didn't always have cookies or chips at home, craft services was heaven."

I didn't know what to say to that. She'd said her early life had been tough. I don't think I realized just how tough.

"I'd done commercials before that," she continued. "Not a lot, but my mom kept putting me up for sitcoms. She was relentless. I think sometimes I got the show just so they wouldn't have to hear from her anymore. No one expected that show to hit as hard as it did. And it exploded after the first season. And Denee took off with it."

I thought about the little I remembered about Denee, most of it revolving around her early tragic death.

"Was she a good friend?"

Now, Tressy glanced at me with a sad smile. "The very best. The kind that only comes around once or twice in your life."

"I'm really sorry. I know she died."

Nodding, Tressy's mouth flat-lined. "She did. It was devastating. I felt like I lost my only family."

"Your relationship's that bad with your mom and sister?"

Another quick shrug. "It's better when we don't spend a lot of time together. And I have a lot of guilt about that. So," she took a deep breath, like this was the hard part, "when she asked me to appear at Tiff's concert in the city Thursday night, I agreed. I just didn't realize she wanted me to duet with my ex."

Ex-boyfriend? Ex-husband? Ex-what?

She laughed a little, probably at the look on my face.

"Ex-boyfriend," she said. "Who I hate, by the way."

"Good. I hate him, too."

Another smile. "He was a total sleaze. Of course, my mom loved him. She thought I was crazy to want to break up with him. I think she actually tried to set him up with my sister when we broke up."

Maybe I didn't want to know, but I had to ask. "Do I know this dickhead?"

She laughed and now I couldn't help but hear Mabel Ann. I couldn't believe I hadn't recognized her before. Hell, a child had figured out who she was, and I hadn't.

"I'm sure you do. It's Lucas Downs."

My mouth dropped open as my brain stuttered. "You dated Lucas Downs? The lead singer for Panda Babies?"

The five-member boy band had been a flash in the pan, but they'd made one brilliant song that had become an instant soft rock classic and was a staple on every grocery store playlist. Lucas had gone on to have a few minor hits of his own before he'd traded music videos for television and became a midlist star on a hit streaming show.

I hadn't realized I'd stopped in the middle of the trail until she grabbed my hand and tugged to get me moving again. And didn't drop it when we continued to walk. So I twined my fingers around hers, felt hers tighten around mine. I didn't plan to let go.

Then something occurred to me.

"Is he—"

"No, he's not Krista's dad."

Her tone of voice made it clear she didn't want me to ask the obvious next question. So I kept my mouth shut and let it go. I wanted her to trust me enough to tell me who it. I just had to be patient.

If she stayed.

"So what happened at the concert that made you run?"

The trail had started to become a little steeper and a little rockier, so we had to start paying more attention to our footing.

"We were backstage at the theater. I was putting my makeup on, and Lucas walked into the dressing room like he owned the place. My mom acted like he was a long-lost relative, but I'm sure all she saw were dollar signs." She shook her head, her gaze still on the trail in front of her but her mind definitely back in that theater dressing room. "Lucas and I dated for a couple of years, starting when I was seventeen. By that time, 'Broad Street' had been canceled because Denee had left in the last season and so did the original showrunner and no one else could carry the show. After that, I had trouble landing roles. I wasn't the cute little kid with the laugh that made everyone smile. I was an awkward teenager with bad skin and an attitude. My mom was making my life miserable. I just wanted to go to high school and be a normal kid, but my mom… She was never satisfied, always wanted more. I think she was afraid of everything crashing down around us again. That there wouldn't be enough money. As I got older, I realized underneath that drive of hers was fear."

"I can see where it'd be hard to believe everything'll be okay when it hadn't been before."

Sadness tinged Tressy's smile. "Yeah, but as a teenager, all you see is your mom wanting more and more. And I just kept pushing back."

I could see where this was going. "How old were you when Krista was born."

"Twenty-one. When I was twenty, I told my mom I was going to college in New York and to deal with it. I look back on that now and think how awful I'd been to her then. I had this mental image of her as my jailor, keeping me from all the things I wanted to do with my life. Now that I have Krista, I realize my mom was doing what she knew best to keep us from living on the street again."

"So when she approached you about the concert, you said yes."

She didn't answer right away, her gaze taking in the scenery around us. And it was gorgeous out here. The leaves were turning brilliant shades of orange and red and yellow. Most still hung on the branches, but there was a coating on the ground that made the trail a mosaic of color. Bird song floated through the trees, and I heard the faint rush of water ahead.

"I didn't at first. I tried to tell her Tiff would shine brighter if I wasn't there. I didn't want to take away any of the spotlight from her. And I've stayed away from any kind of performing for years and concentrated on building my agency. It's just not me anymore. But my mom thought having me there would bring in a different audience."

"What made you change your mind?"

"She promised me I wouldn't have to do anything other than make an appearance and sing one duet with Tiff."

"So you sing, too?"

Her lips curved in a lopsided grin. "I can carry a tune. Tiff has a much better voice than I do, but she's never been able to really break out. She'd rather be doing Broadway but Mom…"

"Let me guess. Your mom thinks she'll make more money singing…what? Pop? Country?"

Tressy touched her finger to her nose. "Both, of course."

"How's that working out for her?"

"About as well as you think. I keep telling Tiff that I'll help her get started on Broadway, but she's just won't take the leap."

"You know, you've never told me what you do for a living."

"I haven't?" She looked genuinely bemused. "I mean, it's not like it's a big secret."

"Like, who you actually are?"

Her nose crinkled. "That's different. I don't think of myself as that person anymore. Now I'm just Tressy Meyers, talent agent. My list is mostly children whose parents trust me to make good choices for their children, or former child actors like me, trying to transition into adult roles."

"You like being behind the scenes now?"

"Oh, yes, definitely." She lifted her hand, as if to stop me from speaking, "And before you say it, yes, I do realize that I have become my mother."

"Is your mom as hot as you are?"

Her expression when she turned to me was so comical, I had to laugh.

"I can't believe— You are— Oh, that is so not funny."

And I couldn't stop laughing as we started up the final incline to our destination.

"You're so damn beautiful, I figure it's gotta run in the family."

She went silent as she shook her head, like she didn't believe me. But she wasn't blind. She had to know how amazing she looked, even wearing one of my old hats.

The silence continued for the next few minutes, and I knew she was overthinking my comment.

"Rowdy—"

"Is your sister hot, too? You know I've got two brothers…"

"Stop!"

Now she laughed so hard she actually snorted. Throwing one hand over her mouth, she smacked my chest with the other.

"Hey, now, no damaging the hockey player before a big game."

"Is this a big game?"

My turn to snort. "None of them are big games."

Her head turned. "Why do you say that?"

"Because we're not really playing to win. We're playing to entertain."

"But you don't like to win?"

"Of course." I shrugged. "Everyone likes to win. But that's not what we're about."

"And you're okay with that?"

"Yeah."

And I was. Except… Since she'd told me her secret, I wanted to share mine.

"But?" she asked, as if she could read my mind.

"I got a call from an old buddy last week. He actually played for us for a couple months before he got picked up by an ECHL team. He played for them for a year before he got a call up from the AHL team he's playing for now. He's a couple years older than me, and he's looking at retiring and becoming a coach."

I paused, not sure I really wanted to say this out loud to anyone. It would make it too real, and I wasn't sure I wanted to have to make the decision.

"Does he want you to come play for him?"

"No. He wants me to coach with him at the ECHL level. Wants me to be his assistant."

"What does that mean?"

The ECHL is a feeder league for the AHL and the AHL feeds the NHL."

"That sounds like a great opportunity. But it would mean you couldn't play, right?"

"Yeah. I'm not sure I'm ready to leave the ice yet, plus I'm not sure I'm coach material."

"Why do you say that? I see the way your team looks up to you. They would follow you anywhere."

"That's because I'm the only one crazy enough to want to lead this bunch."

Her gaze narrowed. "Why do you do that?"

"Do what?"

"Act like what you do isn't a big deal?"

"Because it's not. This team would function just fine without me."

"I know that's not true. They depend on you to lead the way, even if what you do isn't necessarily… traditional."

I grinned at the way she paused there. "The Devils are pretty damn far from traditional."

"You make that sound like it's a bad thing. Different isn't always bad."

"No, it's not. But it can be limiting."

"And you've been given an opportunity to broaden your horizons. It sounds like you don't want to take it."

The problem was, I couldn't decide what I wanted to do. There were days I thought I did want to take it. And there were days I couldn't imagine leaving my team and my family and this town. It felt like I'd be abandoning them.

"You left everything behind and moved across the country," I said. "How'd you do it?"

She didn't hesitate. "I had a baby to care for, and I wanted to be as far from Hollywood as I could get. So I moved to New York and re-enrolled in college." She shrugged, her nose wrinkling just a little. "I was lucky. I had enough money to hire a nanny so I didn't have to worry about Krista when I went to class. I'm not saying it was easy, but the money made it less stressful. And when I graduated, I had an agency ready to hire me. I was young, but I knew the business. Plus, I was a draw. Parents like that I'd been there and done that.

"When our head agent retired a few years ago due to health issues, me and the two remaining agents made it work. Because we had to. It was scary, but we have to make money to live. And I didn't have a family to fall back on." Another pause. "I can only imagine how hard it would be for you to leave them. They're wonderful."

"They're also nosy, over-bearing, over-protective, annoying—

"And they love you."

I sighed, because…yeah. "I know. It can just get to be a little much sometimes. But I'm afraid if I'm not here…"

When I didn't finish after a couple of beats, she did. "Everything will fall apart?"

"Sounds kinda arrogant when you say it like that."

Her laughter rang off the trees and made my blood sizzle. I wanted to pull her off to the side of the trail and kiss her until I convinced her that having sex up against a tree was definitely the right thing to do.

But we only had another few hundred feet before we reached our destination. I could behave myself until then. After that, all bets were off.

"Nah," Tressy said, "I call it the Curse of the Oldest. It's programmed into our DNA to think we're the center of the universe, and that nothing and no one could function without us around."

My turn to laugh, which made her smile up at me with that grin I couldn't get enough of. I reached for her hand to tug her against me, but I heard her quiet intake of breath as we reached our destination.

"Oh, wow. This was definitely worth the walk."

I followed her gaze through the trees to the waterfall that spilled out of the hillside and into the little pond, which flowed into the stream. That stream wound down through the hills and into town. It was so damn pretty, it should be on a postcard. But people around here didn't like to advertise their secret spaces to outsiders. Of course we welcomed visitors when they happened to pass through town or showed up for a hockey game. Otherwise, we liked our town just the way it was. Ours.

"Rowdy, this is beautiful."

Yeah, she was. So damn beautiful, I couldn't take my eyes off of her. The waterfall was nice, too, but I'd seen it a million times.

"Come on." I nodded my head toward the trail. "We can access the pond down here."

She didn't move, glancing up at me. "Are you sure you have time for this?"

"I have more than enough time for you."

CHAPTER EIGHTEEN

WE WERE CUTTING it close by the time we got back to my place, but I hadn't wanted to rush her. I wanted her to fall in love with St. David. I wanted her to stay and fall in love with me.

"You hungry?" I asked as we walked in the door. "I've got meatballs and sauce on the stove. "I just need to start the water for pasta."

She bit her lip. "I really should pick up Krista. I don't want her to overstay her welcome."

I put my hands on the back of the couch and leaned forward, watching her glance at my arms for a second before reconnecting with my gaze. I'd taken off my sweatshirt and pushed up the sleeves of my t-shirt.

"Daisy already has plans to feed the kids and bring them to the game."

"I still have to check in."

"Of course. No problem." I nodded over my shoulder. "I'll be in the kitchen. Come find me when you're done."

She hesitated for a second, before returning my nod and pulling out her phone. I had the water boiling by the time she walked back into the kitchen.

"You get hold of Daisy?"

I opened the package of fresh, but store-bought, pasta – hey, I wasn't that amazing in the kitchen that I could make my own pasta – and dumped it in the water.

"What's this town's dark secret?"

I turned to look over my shoulder and gave her a confused smile. "Huh?"

She crossed her arms over her chest and gave me a look that was definitely suspicious. "I mean, are you all serial killers by night? Is the water polluted? Are you witches and you curse everyone who stops here to forget this place as soon as they leave? There has to be a reason everyone's so nice. And don't give me some song and dance about how small towns are this magical fairyland where everyone's amazing. No place is this perfect."

My smile kept growing with every word. Her almost comical confusion made my blood sizzle for some reason. She just looked so damn sexy.

"You think I'm perfect, huh?"

I wanted to get a smile out of her, and I did, but I could see she was still stewing about something. And I wasn't exactly sure what.

Her exaggerated sigh and rolled eyes made my dick harder, if that was even possible. Good thing she wasn't looking below my belt.

"No, I do *not* think you're perfect. No one's perfect." She paused. "Except maybe Jon Bon Jovi, and that's not open for discussion. Right now, we're talking about you."

"We are?"

"Well, we're talking about this town. And you're part of this town. So spill. What's the deal?"

"Can I drain the pasta while we talk?"

She waved an imperious hand toward the stove, which I took to mean I had permission. So I grabbed the pot and upended the contents into the strainer I already had in the sink.

"Well, the town's not magical and neither are the people who live here. Trust me, if we were, we'd win a hell of a lot more games."

I grabbed a dish from the counter and piled pasta on it and showed it to her. She barely glanced at it as she nodded. So I moved back to the stove to load it up with sauce and meatballs.

"The water's definitely not polluted. We draw straight from the reservoir that's fed from a spring in the hills."

I handed her the plate then made my own with twice the amount of food and waved her toward the table at the window at the back of the kitchen. The window overlooked the woods and was my favorite place to eat.

She did a double take at the view before she took a seat and glared at me. Like I'd done something to offend her.

"I mean, come on. Look at that." She pointed out the window like I'd didn't know what was out there. "That's not fair."

Since I didn't know exactly what she meant, I turned to see what she was looking at, but it was the same view I saw every morning.

"I mean, yeah, it's pretty. And no, there are no serial killers in town. At least, not that I know of."

With a huff, she started to twirl pasta around her fork. "It's too perfect here."

Still smiling, I watched her take a bite and waited for her reaction. Maybe I could seduce her with food. I liked to cook, and I liked to feed people with the food I made. I especially wanted to feed her.

"And that's a bad thing?"

She didn't answer right away, her lids lowering for a second as my red sauce hit her taste buds.

"Oh my god. Why does this taste so frickin' good?"

Grinning, I forked up a mouthful, making her wait for my answer. She looked so fucking beautiful with that scowl on her face.

"Trade secret."

It took her several seconds to respond and, when she did, it was with an "Ugh."

Laughing, I shook my head. "It's not really a secret. I add a little Worcestershire sauce with some red wine and a parmesan rind."

"So, you're like some secret gourmet chef?"

I snorted. "Hardly. This is like the only thing I do really well. When you live on your own, you either cook or you spend a lot of money on takeout. My mom made sure her kids knew how to cook."

We ate in silence for a while, but I knew she was still chewing over something.

Finally, her voice soft, she said, "I'm afraid I like it here too much."

My hand paused with the fork halfway to my mouth. "Why are you afraid of that?"

"Because we have to go home."

Yeah, that's not what I wanted to hear. "Why?"

"Because we're not really supposed to be here."

"Where are you supposed to be?"

She blinked. "I don't honestly know."

"Then maybe this is exactly where you're supposed to be."

CHAPTER NINETEEN

Tressy

I DIDN'T HAVE a response to Rowdy's statement, but I couldn't find anything wrong with it.

When Krista and I had left the city Thursday night, I didn't have a specific place in mind. I just wanted to get away. Anywhere. Didn't matter. So why was I complaining about being here?

I looked at Rowdy, my brain working overtime. Maybe he was right. Maybe I had ended up exactly where I was meant to be.

I didn't believe in fate or any of that other woo-woo stuff. Your choices determined what happened. Except I hadn't made a conscious choice to end up in St. David. My car had broken down, and I'd done what I needed to do to make sure my child didn't freeze. And then I'd fallen into Rowdy's arms.

I chewed over that while I ate my pasta with Rowdy's amazing sauce. Honestly, it was the best red sauce I'd ever had, and I'd eaten at some pretty damn-good restaurants.

"Rowdy?"

"Yeah?"

"Are you sure you're where you're supposed to be?"

His lips quirked into one of those half smiles that looked so good on him.

"Most days, yeah. Some days…" He shrugged. "My friend who wants me to coach with him, he was here for a few months, years ago, rehabbing his… well, rehabbing his career, basically. He had a lingering injury, thought his career was finished. We'd played at college together. He went into the draft. I didn't."

"Why didn't you?"

His bittersweet smile vanished almost as soon as it appeared. "Because I knew I was coming back here to play. That was always the plan. My dad built this team. It's *our* team. Our family team."

"And you never thought about playing anywhere else?"

"Sure. But I'm a realist. I'm not good enough to play at the NHL level. I never had the drive or the skill." He held up a hand before I could say anything. "And I'm okay with that. I get to do what I love every single day. And that's not a bad thing. Actually, it's a pretty damn good thing."

"But…"

That smile was back, and it stuck around a little longer this time.

"But when I got that call, I wondered if it's not time to switch things up."

"Do you want to coach?"

Another pause. "I always thought I'd coach here."

"But…?"

A tiny smile on his lips that was somehow sexier than a full-out grin. "I'm not sure I'm ready to. I'm not sure I'll be ready to coach here next year. This team can be a lot. Some of the players need a lot more help than I think I can give them. There are a few of us who've been with the team for years. But there're always one or two guys with some real serious issues."

"It doesn't all fall on your shoulders, does it?"

"No, that's why my dad hired Scotty. He played in the NHL for a few years, but he made the jump to coaching pretty quickly. Did a stint in the AHL and gained a rep for being good with the hard cases. And he's an Army vet, so the Colonel was all over that. He's also pretty young, so it's not like he's going to be retiring anytime soon."

"Then this sounds like the perfect opportunity for you to try something new. If you want to. Where's your friend's team?"

"About an hour west of Philly and an hour east of here."

That would make it not far from New York City. In fact, it was pretty damn close to New York City. My heart started to pump a little harder.

"You finished? Or do you want more?"

I looked down and realized I'd cleaned my plate while we'd talked.

"No, thank you. It was delicious."

"Thanks." That grin again, the one I was beginning to realize covered a great deal. "Glad you liked it."

I did like it. I liked him. A lot. I liked his family. I liked St. David. Maybe it was the circumstances. Maybe it was my state of mind. Hell, maybe it *was* something in the water.

I only knew I couldn't get enough of him.

He stood, reaching across the table to pick up my bowl and take it over to the sink with his. I got up and followed him, leaning against the island behind him.

"When do you have to be at the arena?"

He looked over his shoulder at me, his brows arching as his smile grew wider.

"Not for another hour." He turned and leaned back against the sink, arms crossed over that broad chest that made me want to lick him. "Why? You got something in mind?"

His voice and the look on his face made all the air in my lungs vanish. Seriously, I had to suck in a deep breath just to be able to think clearly. Because I did have something in mind. I had him on the brain. Well, him and a bed. Or maybe we didn't even need the bed.

Because it was so hard to breath when he looked at me like that, I lifted my hand and crooked an index finger at him. His smile got just a little bit more wicked, and my lungs began to demand air in large quantities.

He crossed the couple of feet separating us, bringing him almost close enough for me to rub my nose along the side of his neck. Or lick the hollow of his throat. Instead, I looked up into his eyes and smiled. It was impossible to be this close to the man and not want to smile when he looked at me like that.

"You," he put his hands on my hips, "are really short."

I huffed out a laugh that was cut short when he lifted me straight off the floor and set me on the counter. My hands found their way to his shoulders, grabbing and holding on.

"But this is much better," he said as he leaned in. We could almost look at each other directly in the eyes now, although he was still a little taller. "Now, what exactly did you have in mind, beautiful?"

I'd never had anyone call me that. Not in this situation. The guys I'd dated since moving to New York just hadn't been the kind of guys to say things like that. I would've found it disingenuous coming from one of them.

From Rowdy, it was…heart-stopping.

I had to swallow before I could make myself answer. "You."

"And what exactly do you want to do with me?"

I wound my arms around his neck, tilting my head so I could press my lips against the skin just below his ear. He sucked in a sharp breath, his hands squeezing into the soft curve of my hips before moving around to my back to press me closer.

"Devour you."

He made a sound in his chest that set my every nerve ending on fire. It lit me up from my core outward.

"Fuck, Tressy. You can have anything you want."

Then he turned his head and took my mouth in a kiss that I wouldn't have thought possible just a couple of days ago. That kiss made me lightheaded, even as every inch of my body went red-hot and heavy. I wanted to lean into him and let him wrap that big body around mine. To shut out the rest of the world for one hour and let me gorge on him.

I'm not really sure I got to do that last night. First times can be amazing, but the second time around is when you really get your groove going. When everything either aligns or falls apart.

And I had a feeling we were going to align like laser-cut edges.

The kiss seemed to last forever, with his lips and tongue working in concert to create an absolutely unbearable sense of longing. My hands slid into his hair and tugged on those waves that were messy and sexy and silky.

Sliding closer to the edge of the counter, I slid my hands down his arms then to his sides and finally back around to his ass. I coaxed him forward, feeling the bulge of his erection behind the zipper. I moaned at the lust that flooded me, making me wet and hot and almost frantic with need.

His hands slid down my back to grab my ass and crush me even tighter against him. I was running out of breath, but I couldn't get enough of him, even as I brought my hands to the button of his cargo pants and worked the button open, then zipped down the fly.

"Oh, fuck." Rowdy pulled away and put his mouth against my neck, nipping at the skin until my entire body felt electrified. "I seriously want your hands on my cock."

"I aim to please."

Sliding my hands into his pants, I rubbed him through his boxer briefs, making him groan against my skin, his breath hot. His hands moved up my back as I curled my fingers around his cock and squeezed.

"Jesus, Tressy. Do it again."

I did as he wrapped my braid around his hand then tugged on it, hard enough to make my scalp tingle.

"No, don't stop, princess. I'll tell you when I'm close because I definitely want to come inside you."

I shivered, my lips parting to suck in much-needed air, and he kissed me again, rocking his erection into my hand. I obeyed his silent command and stroked him through the cloth as his tongue slid against mine, tormenting me.

His cock burned against my palm, but I knew how much better it would feel against my skin. Using both hands, I shoved his pants and briefs down so I could get a better grip on him, could feel that silky skin against mine.

Hot and hard, his cock filled my hand as I gripped him hard and jerked him off. Rowdy liked it just a little rough, encouraging me to grip him tighter, and, when I slid my free hand between his legs, he pulled away and bit out a "Fuck, yes," when I cupped his balls and squeezed.

His hands fell to the counter as I played with him, his forehead pressed against mine.

"That feels fucking amazing."

Some undiscovered part of me preened like a wallflower finally getting her moment to shine. I'd never considered myself particularly good at making love, but Rowdy made me feel like a sex goddess.

He let me play with him for I don't know how long before he kissed me again. And this time, I tasted raw need in the way his lips crushed against mine and the strength of his hands on my hips.

"We're not gonna make it to the bedroom, princess, so just let me..."

Wrapping one arm around my waist, he lifted me off the counter and dragged my pants down with the other, working off my shoes so my legs were completely free. Setting my bare ass back on the counter, he used both hands to get them all the way off.

Then he grinned and before I knew what he planned, he went down on his knees, spreading my legs open with one hand on either knee.

I barely had time to catch my breath before he pulled me right to the edge of the counter and put his mouth over my pussy. I think I might've screamed just a little, but then I moaned when he sucked on my clit and nearly pushed me straight into an orgasm. It hovered right there, out of reach, as he licked me, his tongue a weapon of sexual devastation.

I mean, seriously, he teased me into a limp mass of desire in minutes. I couldn't catch my breath and I couldn't hold myself upright. I leaned back on my forearms and let my head drop, eyes closed.

My sex clenched, my body hanging on the edge of a climax he wouldn't let me have. He pushed right to the edge and then pulled away, just as I was about to come.

"Rowdy! Don't you dare leave me han—Oh!"

He lifted me off the counter, holding me high enough that the tip of his cock brushed against my sensitive labia.

"You know I'd never leave you high and dry, sweetheart. Just tilt your hips—Yeah, just like that."

I had no idea when he'd put on the condom. I was so slick, he slid right in. My arms curled around his neck as he stretched me. He made me feel so full, almost to the point of too much. But with Rowdy, I don't think it would ever be too much. I'm not sure it will ever be enough.

"Oh, my god. Don't move," I said, trying to breathe and absorb everything I could about the moment. "Just…stay."

He was a solid wall of strength, his arms corded with muscle, holding me against him like I weighed nothing. I wrapped my legs around his waist, changing the angle of penetration, making him groan and pushing me just that much closer to an orgasm I desperately wanted.

"Fuck, Tressy."

His words fell directly into my ear and straight into my blood stream. And my body took him literally. I rode him, moving my hips and sliding along his length like I knew what I was doing. Which I didn't. I was working on instinct. And instinct told me to move.

I loved the sounds he made, loved the way his lips clung to mine as we kissed, our breath hot, our bodies even hotter. I was naked from my waist down and I wished he'd taken the time to get rid of our shirts, too, because I wanted to feel his skin against mine. But the thought sputtered away when the tip of his cock hit that certain spot inside me and I shuddered, moaning into his mouth. I froze, everything inside me winding tight and hard until finally it broke, like a damn bursting. I held on as Rowdy took over, tearing his mouth away from mine, allowing us both to breathe.

I gasped in air, still shuddering as he pumped into me. His arms tightened, crushing me against his chest.

We stood like that for at least a minute, clinging to each other, our hearts beating furiously. I didn't want him to put me down, but he had a game to play. And I had a child currently being cared for by someone I'd just met.

What the hell had happened to me in St. David?

I wasn't sure I wanted an answer to that.

Another few seconds later, Rowdy turned his head to press his lips against my temple. My heart skipped a beat at the tenderness in that touch, and my arms tightened around his neck. I held him tight for a few seconds before I loosened them as he slid out of me and set me on my feet. And when he met my gaze, I saw that grin of his and my stomach clenched.

What the hell was I doing here?

And how the hell was I going to fix this?

CHAPTER TWENTY

owdy

"Hey, Rowdy. Can I – I need –You got a minute?"

"Sure, JJ. What's up?"

Jason Kruse motioned to me from a corner of the hall that led to the locker room. I'd just walked through the doors, so the first-year defenseman must've been waiting for me. I hadn't noticed him right away, which was almost impossible to believe because the guy's six-three and nearly two-hundred-twenty pounds.

But I'd been…distracted. Something had changed with Tressy after we'd had sex in the kitchen, which I could never walk into again without getting a hard on. She'd gotten quiet and her smile hadn't exactly reached her eyes. I'd wanted to ask if I'd done something wrong, but when she'd come out of the bathroom, whatever it was seemed to have passed.

I'd dropped her back at my parents' place so she could take a shower and get ready for the game. She'd kissed me before getting out of my truck, and it hadn't been just a little peck. There's been some tongue action and a whole lot of heat but … Something was off.

Was she thinking about leaving? I hoped to hell she was thinking more about staying.

"Hey, I need to tell you something."

JJ's voice pulled me back to the present with a jolt. My attention immediately focused on my teammate, who, I realized, was pretty damn close to having a full-on meltdown. He was sweating, his breathing heavy and labored, like he'd just spent a double shift on the ice. And I recognized that look on his face. Sheer panic.

I took a breath before asking, "What happened, JJ?"

I didn't make it accusatory or sharp, just like I was asking him what he wanted to have for dinner.

"Man, I fucked up." He shoved a hand through short, dark hair that looked like he'd done that a few times before. "And I don't know what to do."

All the hair on my arms stood on end. The misery in his voice nailed me in the gut like a sucker punch. I took a step closer, trying to see his eyes, which he kept focused on the ground.

"Did you hurt someone?"

He shook his head immediately but still didn't look up. "No, it's not like that. I…"

"Okay, then, just spit it out. It's just the two of us here. No one else. Let me ask you two questions first. Are the police involved? And do you need a lawyer?"

That made JJ look up, eyes wide. His pupils didn't look blown, and he looked genuinely shocked that I would ask those questions.

"No. No, it's nothing like that."

"That's good, then." I sighed silently and forced a smile. "Then it's not as bad as you think it is. Just breathe, dude."

JJ blinked, looking like he hadn't considered that. Then he took a deep breath and blew it out. And another. While I pulled up my mental records on the guy. He'd just turned twenty-six and had come to us from a stint in the AHL somewhere out west. Couldn't remember where and it didn't matter. What did matter was the fact that the guy had had a habit. A cocaine habit, if I remembered correctly.

"I took that hit into the boards last night." He shoved his hands through his short blond hair, making it stand straight up. "I didn't think anything about it until I got back to my apartment last night and my fucking knee started to hurt. It's the first fucking game of the season, and I can't be out already. I just thought I'd take one. I don't even know why I still have the fucking shit. Fuck, that's not even true. I know why I have them."

"JJ. Stop." I didn't want to raise my voice, but the guy was spiraling. I grabbed his shoulder and squeezed, finally getting him to meet my gaze. "How much did you take?"

"Two."

Two what? Snorts? He must have seen my confusion because he shook his head, his eyes wide. "Fuck no! I didn't do blow. I made a promise to my mom, and I'm sticking to it. But the doc I saw over the summer prescribed Tylenol with codeine for my back. I know I should've told him I couldn't take it. But my back was fucking messed up, and I knew this team was my last chance, and I couldn't fuck it up. I was real careful about it. I only took a couple until I could tolerate the pain, but I should've flushed the rest. I know I should've. But I kept them and—"

"JJ. Hey, man. Take a breath. I know you think you fucked up, but this isn't unfixable."

Okay. Not cocaine. Jesus, I thought he'd snorted a few lines. But I could tell he was torn up about this. "Where are the rest?"

"In my truck. I was afraid to bring them inside with me."

"Alright, here's what we're going to do."

Over JJ's shoulder, I saw movement. My dad, heading for the

locker room. He gave me a look that was a question. Did I need him? Did he need to get involved?

I shook my head, just enough for him to know I had this. My dad nodded back and kept going. He knew I'd fill him in later. Right now, JJ needed me.

"First, we're gonna talk to the doc about your knee." If it was bad enough for the guy to willingly take something he didn't want to, then there was something wrong. "And then we'll talk to the doc about the pills."

Sonny Morelli had seen his fair share of addicted athletes with the Devils. Dad and his soft spot for tough cases made sure of it.

"Jesus, I'm sorry, Rowdy. It's the second fucking game—"

"Wouldn't matter if it was the fifth or the twenty-fifth." I gave his shoulder a little shake, keeping that connection between us so I didn't lose his focus. "We're still going to take care of this. Together. Hey, if you'd tried to deal with it by yourself and it'd gotten worse, I might not've been able to help. But you were smart enough to know you needed help. That's all that matters, man."

The look of relief on JJ's face let me know I'd said the right thing. I could've fucked this up badly, but I hadn't so I'd take the win.

"Come on, let's go talk to Doc Morelli."

———

"Hey, Rowdy. What's up with you? You nearly let me drill you into the boards last period. Not that I wouldn't have liked it, but you're obviously not here, so it wouldn't have been fun."

I looked at Fiskers across the blue line as we lined up against each other at the start of the second period. The logic in that statement was a little twisted, but that kind of perfectly explained our league so…

"Just a lot of shit on my mind."

The ref dropped the puck, and the teams went into motion. We'd won the faceoff, which was kind of a surprise, so I skated up ice, Fiskers on my ass. I know I'd been preoccupied the first period, the conversation with JJ and the situation with Tressy battling for space in my brain, but I thought I'd kept my distraction under control.

But if Fisky, who wasn't the most observant guy, had noticed, I must've been pretty out of it. Probably why my team had been giving me some distance. They'd been way too quiet in the locker room now that I thought about it.

I had to drag my head out of my ass, or I was gonna get my ass handed to me. Maybe not by Fiskers but definitely by one of the young guns on his team. The young ones always wanted to make a statement.

Narrowing my focus back to the game, I scoped out the situation. We were in the offensive end, but we were going to lose control of the puck if I didn't do something.

I skated into the middle of the scrum in the corner, both teams fighting for possession of the puck. I checked Fiskers out of the way, which made the crowd roar, fans banging on the glass. When I got possession, I skated behind the net, trying to shake the defender. Realizing we were in scoring position, I passed to Misha, who one-timed it at the net. The goalie was ready for that one, but I skated around to the side of the net, where I picked up the rebound and shot it over the goalie's shoulder into the net.

The goal horn sounded, and the crowd screamed like we'd just won the fucking Olympics. And it felt good.

My team crowded around me knocking helmets and patting me on the back.

"Goddamn, Rowdy. Nice shot," Reid shouted to be heard over the crowd. "Nice fucking shot."

Yeah, it had been. And even though it'd been a while since I'd scored, probably sometime around the middle of last season, I still remembered my goal celebration.

First, I skated to the bench and knocked gloves with my teammates. Then I grabbed the air cannon from the equipment manager, who had a huge smile. The crowd cheered as the clip of the goal played on the screens above center ice, and I stopped to watch it along with them, my grin growing.

Last year, I'd sucked at scoring. I'd had maybe fifteen goals all season. My points total had been decent because of assists, but I'd forgotten how good it was to actually put the puck in the net and have the fans cheer.

With my goal song, "My Redemption" by Halestorm, blasting out of the speakers, I skated around the arena and shot t-shirts with my face on them into the crowd. When I got to the side with the suites, I stopped to wave to Krista, who was jumping up and down next to her mom. Tressy's smile made everything that much better.

After sending her a wink just for her, I skated back to the bench and play resumed. When I sat on the bench, Coach leaned down so I could hear him over the roar of the crowd. "Nice job, Rowdy. Another few like that, and I won't have to buy my own drinks for a while."

I nodded, confidence heating my blood. "Let's blow up some expectations tonight, Coach. Let's give them the show they deserve."

Scotty shook his head, steel-gray hair perfectly combed, a wry grin on his face. After smacking my back, he moved back up the bench to where he usually stood. "Alright, then. Let's get a few more, boys, and make hell freeze over."

As the next line headed over the boards and onto the ice, Rebel slid into the empty space on the bench next to me.

"Looks like someone got their mojo back."

I glanced at Rebel but didn't see the sarcasm I expected. I

shrugged, trying not to feel too impressed with myself. "It's the second game. I got a goal. Give me a break."

"You don't need a break. Maybe you just needed a push."

Rebel stuck his elbow in my side then jumped over the boards to take his shift.

Or maybe I just needed someone to see me in a different light.

CHAPTER TWENTY-ONE

ressy

"Ms. Meyers, this is Dana Yeh from Viewpoint Media. I would love to talk to you about an article we're doing on Denee Henning. As her closest friend, we're reaching out to get your memories of her. With the resurgence of "Broad Street" on streaming services, there's been increased interest in the cast and especially in the tragic death of Denee." A pause. "I don't know if you're aware, but there have been some rumors circulating about…aspects of her passing. We would love to get the true story and clear up inconsistencies. I hope you'll call—"

I hung up before she finished, having listened to more than enough to know what she wanted. And to guess at what rumors she was talking about. Rumors I had no intention of ever discussing.

I'd just put Krista down in the room next to the bedroom I'd slept in last night. She'd tried hard to keep her eyes open but had lost the battle on the drive home. Before we left the arena, Rowdy had asked if I wanted to join a few of the Angels and Devils at the bar for drinks or if I wanted to stay in and "take it easy."

"I'd be more than happy to keep an eye on Krista for you," Raffi had jumped in before I could say anything. "I think she's going to sleep pretty well tonight. She's had a busy day."

According to Krista, it'd been the best day *ever*. She and her new best friend had played all day and her dad had cooked on a grill, "like a hibachi outside," but he'd made hamburgers and hot dogs that tasted "delicious." She'd arrived at the arena with Daisy and her family, grinning from ear to ear, the knees of her pants scuffed and a stain on her shirt that looked like ketchup.

Daisy had asked if Mandy could sit with Krista during the game because Derek was presenting the colors during the anthem, and I'd been more than happy to keep the girls with me in the suite.

I'd noticed the voice message on my phone sometime after dinner, but I didn't recognize the number, so I hadn't bothered to listen to it earlier. But I figured I should at least check to make sure it wasn't anything I needed to deal with.

Now I wish I hadn't bothered. My stomach knotted, and I broke out in a cold chill.

I knew the reporter was fishing for information. She didn't know anything. Only a few people in the world knew what had happened the night Denee had died. And all of them were under an NDA.

So, no, I wouldn't be calling Dana Yeh back to clear up anything about the night Denee had died. But there'd been another, even more troubling message waiting for me.

From my sister.

"Hey, um, I really don't want to upset you anymore than you already are, but I wanted to give you a heads up. Lucas is being a total dick. He posted on Instagram that he was worried about you, and he hoped you were all right. I got him to take it down, but it was out there for a couple of hours. I just wanted you to know so if anyone asked you about it, you knew what was going on. I'm really sorry.

"And I got a call from some reporter, Dana something. She's poking around for info. You know she'll never get anything out of me or Mom. I hope you know that. But...I just thought you should know. Love you, sissy."

My heart clenched a little when she called me sissy. She hadn't called me that in years. The cynical Bad Girl scoffed, but I knew Tiff meant the sentiment behind it. We were sisters. First and foremost. When it came to me and Krista, Tiff would have our backs. Mom, too, when push came to shove. We had our issues, but she would never hang Krista or me out for the buzzards.

But the reporter was going to be an issue.

Checking the clock, I wondered when Rowdy would get here. I really wanted to talk to him about the situation. At least, as much as I could say about it. Because as much as I wanted to tell him everything, I just couldn't.

Walking into the living area, I made a pitstop in the kitchenette to grab a bottle of water then sank down onto the couch. Then I pulled up Instagram on my phone because I couldn't stop myself. I had to be sure there wasn't anything being said about me or Krista that I needed to get ahead of.

That was my first mistake. The second was actually scrolling through the posts. A few seemed genuinely concerned for my safety, prompted by Lucas' post, which had been screenshot, of course. Nothing was ever truly gone on the internet.

And if you didn't know Lucas like I did, you'd actually think he genuinely cared for me. I knew better. Everything he did benefited only one person. Lucas.

Many of the posts praised him for continuing to care about the woman who'd dumped him so carelessly so many years ago. Which was bullshit. Yeah, I'd dumped his ass more than seven years ago, after he'd cheated on me. Multiple times. But, of course, no one talked about what a sleaze Lucas was. And luckily, no one had questioned Krista's paternity. I'd never revealed who her father was, and I never would. He hadn't wanted her, but her mother certainly had.

I couldn't help but compare Lucas to Rowdy. Lucas wasn't even in the same league. Even in the few short days I'd known him, I knew Rowdy would never use me the way Lucas had. Continued to do.

And yet… I was going to leave. I had to leave. I couldn't just stay here.

A soft knock on the outside door made my head pop up from my phone, and I tossed it on the table in front of the couch and shot up off the couch to get to Rowdy.

All the stress that'd been building up inside me eased at the sight of his smile.

"Hi—Whoa, hey. You okay? What happened?"

I threw my arms around his shoulder and clung as soon as I'd opened the door. His arms wrapped around my back, holding me tight against him. Shoving my face in his neck, I breathed him in. He smelled like mint and lime and his still-damp hair clung to my fingers as I wound them around the strands.

With his foot, he pushed the door shut behind him, then lifted me off my feet and walked to the couch.

"Tressy. What's going on? Talk to me."

"I can't stay."

Idiot. Why the hell had I blurted that out? It wasn't even what I'd wanted to say. Not really. But it was true.

Rowdy stilled for a second before his hand on my lower back began to make small, soothing circles.

"Like, you gotta leave right this second? I thought your car wouldn't be ready until Monday. Or are you talking about forever?"

My breath caught, and I had to remember to breathe.

"And if you're talking about right now, I'd say, I'm sure you could at least wait until morning. And if you're talking about forever, well… Why not? It's not like people don't move out of New York City. I mean, smart people move out of the city all the time."

I huffed out a laugh and shook my head, rubbing my cheek against the soft cotton of his long-sleeved t-shirt.

"I think you might be biased about the city."

"You do know there's more than one city in the country, right? Like, Philadelphia's a city. Pittsburgh, Harrisburg. We've got several just in Pennsylvania."

"But none of them are where I live. Where I work. Where Krista goes to school."

His body tensed. I could tell me didn't want to talk about this. Not now. Probably not later either. But he had to know.

"We can't hide here forever."

"That's what you've been doing? Hiding?"

"That's what it feels like."

"Why? Because you didn't announce to everyone that you were on a TV show more than a decade ago? It's not like people here don't know your name."

Okay, when he put it like that, I started to feel kind of ridiculous. But that still didn't solve the underlying problem.

"I can't just pick up everything and move here on a whim."

"Why not? People do it every day."

Everything he said sounded so logical, even though I knew it wasn't. I couldn't move to another state after spending just a few nights in this small town. Could we?

I pulled back so I could look at him. "Our entire life is in New York."

Those words sounded so final. And, from the look on his face, he knew I meant them.

The muscles in his jaw clenched, but otherwise, his expression didn't change. I didn't know what I'd expected from him, but it wasn't this slow nod. "Okay. So, when are you planning to leave?"

No argument? No charm? No fight?

"The mechanic called and said he got the tires today. I guess… tomorrow sometime?"

Another nod. "Why don't you let me make you and Krista breakfast before you go? You can come over to my place."

"Sure. That'd be…um, great."

Now his smile returned in full force, and my knees literally went weak.

Girl, you are crazy to walk away from this.

Especially when he lifted his hands from around my waist to land on my shoulders. Heat spread outward from his touch, seeping into my veins, making me heat from the inside out. Then his hands slid up to cup my cheeks.

"Then I guess we better work up an appetite."

He kissed me like he wanted to inhale me.

And I held on like I wanted to let him.

CHAPTER TWENTY-TWO

"Look, I know you said you're leaving today, but if you can delay, just 'til Monday, I want to take you and Krista somewhere. I really think she'll love it."

I figured it was the best time to ask, while Tressy was still boneless in my arms after our second time, this time in an actual bed.

I didn't want to be pathetic and beg, but I was running out of options. I didn't want them to leave tomorrow. Hell, I didn't want them to leave at all. These past couple of days had shown me what it could be like with Krista and Tressy in my life. And I fucking liked it. A whole hell of a lot.

I know two days wasn't a lot of time, but honestly, how long did you have to know a person before you knew she was the right one? I mean, my parents had known each other a week before they'd decided to spend their life together. That'd worked out pretty damn well.

And I didn't want to do a long-distance relationship. They never worked. But I would if that was the only way I could stay in her life. I was smart. I'd figure out a way to make it work.

Tressy didn't answer right away, but I felt her breathing hitch, so I knew she wasn't asleep. And her hand on my chest continued to stroke across my skin. Which I really fucking liked.

"I would really like to, but…"

"But what?"

She blew out a sigh, that ruffled across my pec. "But this isn't our home. We can't just stay here indefinitely."

I wanted to tell her she could stay with me. I had more than enough room for her and Krista, but I didn't want her to get freaked out that I was asking her to move in with me when we'd only met three days ago.

But I knew what I wanted. And I wanted her and Krista here.

I had a feeling if I didn't start to make her see how I felt about her, she would walk away. But if I came on too strong, she'd run, not walk, all the way back to New York. Unless I was totally reading her wrong. I didn't think I was.

Didn't help that my brain was still scrambled from the amazing sex.

"Stay, Tressy. Just another day. Just because I want you to."

Propping herself up on one elbow, she looked into my eyes. I saw the conflict in hers and decided it was time for the Hail-Mary play.

"There'll be whoopie pies and apple cider and, if you're nice to me, we can take the hayride."

When she finally burst out laughing, the sound hit me straight in the gut. I wanted to go to sleep to that sound every night and wake up to it every morning. Tressy was the calm to my chaos. It'd only been three days, but I knew that, if she left, I'd have to follow.

"Rowdy, are you ever serious?"

"I'm always serious about whoopie pies and hayrides. You're in farm country, and Fall is our season."

"But you're not a farmer."

She looked so damn serious when she said that, but I saw the humor lurking in her eyes.

"True, but I've got a pair of overalls I can wear if that's what you're into."

I tugged her down for a kiss as her quiet laughter and the look in her eyes activated something so raw in me, I was worried I'd say the wrong thing. Her heated response gave me goosebumps. This was what had been missing from my life up until now.

She pulled back slowly, her eyes opening to look into mine. "I guess we can stay another day."

I barely restrained myself from doing a victory dance. Would've been hella awkward, but then again, she would've laughed, and I loved to make this lady laugh.

"But, Rowdy…" her gaze got somber, "we can't stay forever."

"Then I'll take what I can get for now."

And I'd figure out how to make her see that this is where she belonged.

CHAPTER TWENTY-THREE

ressy

"Hello, again, Ms. Meyers. This is Dana Yeh from Viewpoint Media. I just wanted you to know that we are running the article on Denee Henning this week. When I called you last week, I mentioned there were rumors we wanted to clear up. And since they deal directly with you, I really wanted to speak with you before we run the piece."

The reporter paused and my stomach rolled. The rushing in my ears was nearly drowned out by the noise of the busy farm, where hundreds of people picked pumpkins, petted goats, ran through a corn maze and loaded into a wagon filled with actual hay. When Rowdy had parked his truck in the lot, I'd actually looked for signs that this was a film set. I mean, seriously, it looked like it'd fit perfectly in a TV romcom.

Then my phone had buzzed with a call, but Krista was bouncing in her seat, ready to be let loose with all the other kids, and I'd let the call go to voice mail. When I'd recognized the number as being from New York, Rowdy had offered to take Krista over to the petting zoo so I could listen to the message.

Now, I wish I hadn't, because anxiety had me gripped by the throat.

"Look," Dana Yeh continued, "I didn't get into this business to be the paparazzi. I honestly don't want to ruin your life, but these rumors have the potential to be…painful for your family. Please. Give me a call back."

Looking out the front window as I erased the message, I watched Rowdy grin at Krista as she held food out to a tiny goat, who nuzzled at her hand. Krista turned to Rowdy and took his hand as if she'd been doing it forever, and they walked over to another pen with bunnies.

Panic lodged like a rock in my throat, making it hard to breathe.

She couldn't know. How would she know?

There'd never been so much as a hint of a whisper before this.

Breathe. Just breathe.

First, I had to call back the reporter and find out if she knew anything definitive, or if she was still just fishing. And I needed to do it now while Rowdy had Krista entertained.

I tapped the redial button before I could second guess my decision.

"Ms. Yeh, this is Teresa Meyers."

I heard her sigh through the line. "Thank you so much for calling me back."

"You made it sound like I didn't have much of a choice." I made sure my tone held a hard edge. "What exactly do you need to talk to me about?"

"I really don't want to do this over the phone but seeing as you're not in the city at the moment, and there really is a time-sensitive aspect to this, I thought we should speak. The rumor I was referring to has to do with your daughter."

The reporter continued to speak, laying out the story as she knew it. And she had most of it right. Of course, she was completely wrong about one piece. Denee had taken a few secrets to her grave, but she'd assured me before her death that a lawyer had taken care of everything regarding that one aspect. And that it would never be a problem.

"Do you have any comment you want to make on the record, Ms. Meyers?"

The reporter finally stopped talking, and I took a moment to think about my response.

"My only comment," I finally said, "is that, if your organization chooses to run this rumor, you'll be sued, and not just by me. You're erroneously dragging one of the most influential men in Hollywood into a pissing match because your publisher is trying to make a name for himself. And Ms. Yeh? I really hope you think twice before allowing your name to be associated with a story built on the back of a six-year-old child."

The reporter fell silent again, but I knew she was still there.

"I'll be sure to tell my editor what you said, Ms. Meyers." Dana released another audible sigh. "Off the record… and if you repeat this, I will deny it… I think you could make this go away if you approach the publisher yourself. With a lawyer. His name is Rodney Feeney. He seems to have a hard on for this story, and he's planning to run it this week, so the sooner you get here the better. Like, tomorrow."

I said thank you and cut off the call. There really was nothing else to say. I knew what I had to do.

Through the window, I saw Rowdy bend down to speak to Krista, his smile for my daughter nearly bringing tears to my eyes.

Not fair. So not fair.

I didn't want to leave. Not yet. But now I couldn't even leave on my own terms because some sleazeball thought he had a scoop. I wanted to cry and throw things, and I'm pretty sure I wanted to rip Rodney Feeney a new asshole.

And I knew exactly how to do it, because I knew him. Former actor turned entertainment blogger, he'd turned a B-list career into a profession by mining his so-called friends for gossip. Most of his posts were clickbait, with not much substance to them, but every now and then he managed a scoop.

I refused to let him have this one. All because, years ago, Denee had turned him down. He'd pursued her pretty hard, but Denee had never been interested. She'd barely even acknowledged the guy. She'd already met the love of her life. But, like every good tragedy, she couldn't have him. And then she'd died.

How about that for a Hollywood ending?

Familiar grief swamped my heart, which just made the sadness already there more intense.

I didn't want to leave Rowdy, but my daughter came first.

Taking a deep breath, and then another, I got out of the truck, plastered a smile on my face and headed toward Rowdy and Krista.

CHAPTER TWENTY-FOUR

"ARE you sure you don't want me to come with you? You look upset."

Tressy shook her head, her gaze barely glancing off me as she reached for the door handle on my truck. Krista pouted in the back seat. She hadn't wanted to leave the farm, even though we'd been there for almost three hours.

I knew something had happened when Tressy joined us after taking that phone call, but I hadn't said anything then. Tressy seemed determined to keep a smile on her face for Krista, and I'd gone along because I didn't want either of them upset.

It'd taken her an hour to finally tell me she and Krista had to return home tonight because "she had a situation to deal with." I'd been expecting it, but it'd still knocked me back a few steps. I'd tried to ask a few times if everything was okay, but she'd just given me that smile and nodded.

And now, she gave me that same smile, and I gritted my teeth.

"Thank you, but no. I don't need you to hold my hand while I do my job."

Fuck, that's not what'd I'd meant, and dammit, she knew it. But for some reason, she was pushing me away, and it fucking sucked.

"Sorry. I know you're perfectly capable of taking care of yourself, Tressy. I'm not trying to be an asshole. I'm worried about you."

Her mouth twisted into something resembling a smile and she shook her head. "I know. I'm sorry. I've just got a lot on my mind. I can't thank you and your family enough for taking us in these past few days. And our time together has been…amazing."

Now she did look at me and I saw her regret and longing and sadness so clearly. I reached for her hand resting on her thigh, but she curled her fingers into a fist.

"I can't, Rowdy." Her voice was barely above a whisper. "I have to go."

I wanted to punch Donny, the mechanic, for fixing her fucking car sooner than I'd expected. I know he'd meant well, going out of his way to get the damn thing taken care of over the weekend, but still…

"You don't have to go forever. You can come back. Take care of whatever you need to, and I'll be here."

She frowned. "You're not taking that job?"

I shook my head as she frowned. "This is home, Tressy. This is my team. These are my guys. I'm not abandoning them."

"I thought you wanted more."

"Maybe I realized I can have more. I just have to be willing to take it. You can, too. Come back."

She slid a glance over her shoulder at Krista, who was still pouting, even though she'd fallen asleep.

"It's only been three days."

I heard what she didn't say. That three days wasn't enough time to fall in love. That she didn't believe what we shared was real. Maybe she was right. Maybe I was the delusional one. Or maybe she just didn't want to see what was staring her in the face.

I wanted to lean across the console and pull her onto my lap and kiss her until she realized what she'd be giving up if she didn't come back. To remind her of the heat we generated together. That wasn't an illusion.

But she'd put up an invisible wall between us. And it was pissing me off.

"It's been three goddamn amazing days."

She dipped her head and took an audible breath. "And now I have to go back to my life."

Well, damn. I guess that told me everything I needed to know about where I fit in her life.

Nowhere.

———

"HEY, POP. YOU GOT A MINUTE?"

Monday morning, my dad sat at his desk in his office in the arena, scowling at the monitor. He looked pissed, but the Colonel didn't play well with technology. Or, more accurately, technology didn't like my dad. He was a master of spreadsheets and a whiz with financial software, but computers died on him faster than they did anyone else. No one could figure out why. Key cards for hotel rooms also gave him trouble, for someone reason. They never stayed magnetized.

Mom liked to joke that his personality was so magnetic, the key cards gave up and died on him.

My dad looked up, saw me, and his eyebrows drew together even harder.

"Of course. Guess you better close the door. This looks like that kind of conversation."

Since he wasn't wrong, I shut the door then fell into the chair in front of his desk. I only had a few minutes before I had to be in the locker room to get ready for practice, but I wasn't sure how to start.

Leaning my elbows on my knees, I looked my dad straight in the eyes. And noticed for the first time that he was starting to show his age. A few more lines around his eyes and mouth. A little less meat on his bones. He was eighteen years older than my mom, who still sometimes got mistaken for Rain's sister, so that put him in his late sixties. And I really didn't want to think about that.

But isn't that the point of your talk?

"So, I've been thinking about my future, and –"

"You gonna take that coaching position in Lancaster?"

My mouth dropped open in shock for two seconds before I leaned back into the chair and shook my head.

"How long have you known?"

He shook his head. "Doesn't matter. Hockey's a big game but a small community. I've been waiting for you to come have this talk, but you were a little, um, distracted the past few days. Heard from Tressy yet?"

Glancing away, I shook my head. "No, but that's not what I want to talk to you about. And yeah, they offered me a job, but I'm not taking it."

Pop's scowl returned. "What do you mean you're not taking it? It's a hell of an opportunity for you."

His response didn't surprise me. It's exactly what I'd expected him to say.

"Yeah, it probably is. But, Pop, *this* is my team. These are my guys. This is my home."

"And it'll always be here for you. But this is a chance to make a mark on a bigger stage. Push you out of your comfort zone. You've been getting awful comfortable here the past few years. And that's not a criticism." He held up a hand like I might try to interrupt, which I wasn't. "It's just… Maybe a challenge would be a good thing right now."

"I'm going to have enough of a challenge convincing Tressy to take me on full time, Pop. But it's time for me to take on some of your grunt work running the team."

My dad's brows rose as he leaned back in his chair, the leather creaking and groaning. It reminded me of all the times he sat behind that desk and rightfully punished me for all the stupid shit I did as a teenager, or the talks we'd have after I did something stupid my first years back from college.

Lately, though, I hadn't been in here, and I wanted to change that. I wanted to change a lot of things in my life.

"If you don't mind my asking, what are you planning to do? With Tressy, I mean."

He looked so damn nosy, I had to laugh. "You got any suggestions?"

"I just might. Tressy's got a spine. I like her. And her daughter. And your mom got pretty attached to them both. The little girl wrapped your mom around her finger pretty damn fast."

"I thought you were gonna dole out advice?"

"I'm getting there." My dad shook his head. "Always so impatient. That's part of your problem, kid. Sometimes you've got to take your time getting where you want to go."

"I seem to remember you telling me you knew in less than two days that you wanted to marry Mom."

My dad's gaze narrowed. "You going to let me talk or interrupt every couple of seconds?"

I bit back a grin and shook my head. "Floor's all yours."

"Uh huh. Like I was saying, you're too damn impatient. Sometimes, you gotta take a step back and let her come to you."

"Honestly, Pop, I'm afraid if I don't keep reminding her I'm here, she's gonna forget me."

"I saw the way that girl looked at you. I don't think she's

gonna forget you. You make a pretty damn big impression on people. But don't go blowing up her inbox."

"Did you just use an actual relevant social media reference correctly?"

"See?" He pointed a finger at me. "That right there is what's gonna get you in trouble, son. You don't know when to keep your mouth shut."

He was right. Usually, I didn't.

"Yeah, well, I did keep it shut this time. I didn't tell her how much I wanted her and Krista to stay, and she walked out the damn door, like I didn't matter."

"The woman's got a life of her own and a business to run, according to your mother. Maybe you didn't show her that you understand those things are just as important to her as you want to be."

Fuck. Had I really been that mindless?

"Shit."

"Now," my dad leaned back in his chair, looking like the cat that ate the mouse, "maybe you want to take a different approach when you contact her next time."

———

"So when are you going to fix whatever happened between you and Tressy?"

My jaw locked against the urge to say something really inappropriate to my sister. Rain didn't deserve to have my mood taken out on her. But if she continued to ask questions, I wasn't going to be responsible for what came out of my mouth.

Monday practices after a game weekend were usually optional, but most of the team was here today. I'd thought maybe I wouldn't have to deal with a lot of people, and I could skate and chew over what my dad and I had talked about. Didn't look like that was in the cards.

"Hello to you, too, Rainbow Brite." I yanked my right skate laces so hard, I heard them groan. "Don't you have somewhere else you could be?"

As I grabbed my left skate and shoved my foot in it, Rain just continued to stare down at me.

"For your information, I finalized the designs for the Christmas sweaters this morning and signed on another couple of sponsors for the wine tasting in February." She crossed her arms over her chest and continued to stare down at me. "What did you do this morning? Besides mope?"

I huffed out a laugh at her bratty sass and looked up. "Since when do you care?"

"Since I've never seen you like this. I don't like it. It's weird. Snap out of it."

I stood, towering over her, the skates giving me an extra couple of inches of height.

"I'm fine, Rainy."

Her brows rose as she stared up at me. "But are you really?

Taking the few steps to close the distance between us, she wrapped her arms around my waist and hugged me. Tight. Like she wanted to squeeze the bad mood out of me. With a sigh, I hugged her back, dropping a kiss on her head and ruffling her hair, because I knew she hated it.

"I love you, too, big brother," she muttered into my practice sweater. "But you're a big damn idiot if you don't track her down and tell her how you feel."

Sighing, I let my head fall back so I was looking at the ceiling. "Rain—"

"She ain't wrong, man."

My eyes closed. "Jesus Christ."

Kane had somehow managed to creep up on me, the first of my teammates to even attempt to talk to me today. My face had scared them all off, I guess. Probably the smart choice because my first instinct was to tell Kane to go fuck himself. I managed to keep my mouth shut, but only barely.

"Just hear me out, man. Then you can tell me to fuck off. I ain't seen you happy like you were with her in years. Man, she literally fell into your lap. If that ain't fate giving you a massive slap upside the head, I don't know what is."

"Kane—"

"As much as I hate to admit it," Rebel added his two cents, "I think she really liked you. No idea why, but if you don't figure your shit out, she's not gonna wait. Hell, I wouldn't wait for you."

I heard a rumble of voices behind me and turned to find the entire team gathered behind Kane and Rebel.

"Oh, for fuck's sake." I scowled at them all. "When did everyone become so damn interested in my fucking love life?"

The guys exchanged looks with each other like I was speaking another language.

Finally, Reid, looked at me with those puppy-dog eyes. "'Cause you're our captain."

The other guys shrugged and nodded, like it was the most natural thing in the world. And like I was delusional if I didn't know what they were talking about.

Well, shit, what the hell was I supposed to say to that?

"Look, I appreciate your concern, but..."

But what? They weren't wrong.

Rain took a step back, crossed her arms over her chest and smirked up at me, like she'd won. I don't know what the hell she thought she'd won, but I sure as hell wasn't going to ask.

"Look, I planned to text her later and ask how's she's doing."

"You should probably call," goalie Kaden Felix chimed in, shoving a hand through his mop of brown hair and pushing it off his face. "Girls—uh," he flashed Rain a look when she glared at him, "women like when you call them. You know, make an effort."

Like a bunch of robots, all the other guys nodded their heads like they knew what they were talking about.

"How the hell would you—would any of you know what women like, considering most of you aren't even in a relationship with one. Only KooKoo's got an actual girlfriend, and she's not even in the country."

Pontus "KooKoo" Kokkenen grinned like a loon. "She is coming for visit in two weeks. Just got notice."

"Aw, KooKoo, that's great." Rain skirted around me to give the brawny forward a hug. "I can't wait to meet her. She seems like such a sweetheart online."

"She is amazing. Smart and funny and—"

"So why's she with you?" Rebel snarked, earning him a smack from Rain on the chest and one from Kane on the back of his head.

Just when I thought maybe I'd been let off the hook, Kane just couldn't keep his mouth shut.

"So when you gonna call her?"

Fuck me. "When I'm damn good and ready? Now are we gonna practice or not?"

I didn't wait to hear anything else. Just took my ass down the tunnel to the ice and tried to figure out what the hell to say when I called Tressy after practice.

CHAPTER TWENTY-FIVE

Tressy

"Mom." I blinked at the woman standing outside my door Monday morning, shock holding me in place. "I didn't— I wasn't expecting you."

Bebe Meyers looked like she was headed to a meeting. She'd scraped her perfectly tinted blonde hair into a twist on the back of her head and wore a black pantsuit with a white silk shirt. She looked ready to do battle. Oh god, I wasn't ready to deal with this now. I had something more pressing to handle.

"Hello, Teresa. Can I come in?"

Shock stuck my tongue to the roof of my mouth and my feet to the floor for a few long seconds before I shook it off and said, "Of course. Sorry. You just…took me by surprise."

My mom didn't respond, just walked through the door then turned to look at me as I closed the door.

"Is Krista at school?"

I gestured for her to sit as I sank into a chair in the living area.

Our home in Chelsea wasn't a three-story townhouse, but it wasn't a one-room studio, either.

Of course, it couldn't rival Rowdy's home.

And nope, not going there.

"No, she's with Mrs. Santiago. They missed their brunch this weekend."

Mom nodded. "Good. We need to talk."

I took a deep breath and held it, readying myself for the confrontation I was sure was coming.

"I assume you heard from that reporter? What's our strategy? Have you contacted your lawyer? Do you need me to take care of it?"

Okay, that's not what I'd been expecting. I sat there and stared at her, my mouth hanging open a little until I remembered to close it.

"Mom, how—"

"They called me for comment. No idea why they think I'd ever tell them anything about my family. Scumsuckers."

Finally, I shook my head, trying to get my thoughts in order. "I'm going to confront him. Make it clear to him that if he says anything about my daughter in his rag, I'll sue him."

My mom nodded. "Good start, but I think you should let me come with you. I think he needs a little more than the threat of legal action. I did a little digging—"

I held up my hand. "I don't want to know."

She smiled. "Not a problem. You don't need to know."

At that moment, I wondered just how much she hadn't told me growing up. Maybe I'd been too young or too naïve to think about what she'd been doing behind the scenes. And when I'd gotten older, I just hadn't wanted to know. I'd let her do her thing and told myself it wasn't anything I needed to worry about. That I didn't want any part of what she was doing.

"Just know that I can have that story squashed in a few hours. All I need is your OK."

I'd been dreading talking to my mom since we got home last night. It'd been late and Krista had been sleepy and weepy when I'd finally tucked her in. I'd hoped she'd wake up this morning, happy to have slept in her own bed in her own room with all of her things all around her.

Of course, she'd immediately wanted to know when we were going back to visit Rowdy and Raffi and Mandy. She didn't want to go back to school. She didn't want me to go back to work. Only the thought of seeing our neighbor got any kind of positive response.

Mrs. Santiago was more than happy to visit with Krista this morning, since they'd missed their Saturday brunch this week. She'd offered to take Krista to lunch, if it was okay with me. I'd thanked her so profusely, she laughed and said, "You must have had an interesting weekend."

You have no idea.

But then I'd been alone, and I still didn't know how I was going to deal with the asshole threatening to expose my secrets.

"Mom, look, about last week—"

"Actually, Teresa," my mom cut in, "I have a few things I need to say first."

Shit, I'm pretty sure I don't want to hear this, but she looked so uncomfortable, I bit my tongue.

"I realize now that the situation I created was…not the best."

Good thing I was sitting down, because I think that might've taken my knees out. My mom never apologized. It just wasn't in my nature. But now, she actually looked contrite. Something I never thought I'd see. Or even believed she was capable of.

"I know we haven't seen eye to eye on, well," she grimaced, "much of anything lately. And that's okay. I just hope you know that everything I've ever done has been to make sure you and your sister, and now Krista, are taken care of. My technique isn't always polished, but I will always fight for my babies."

My stomach clenched a little. "I know that, Mom. I do. And I appreciate everything you've done for us. It's just—"

"I realize I broke your trust Thursday night, and I apologize for that. I was out of line, and I should've known that." She took a deep breath, then she nodded, like she'd shut the door on that whole deal. "So, what are we going to do about this scumbag?"

Tears welled, but I blinked them back. It was exactly what I'd needed to hear from her and had never expected. "Thanks, Mom, I appreciate that."

"I know I should say it more, but I'm proud of you, Teresa. I hope you know that."

Honestly, I didn't. I've never doubted her love, but I'd never considered the fact that she was proud of me.

"You put yourself through college while raising a baby." She held up one finger then two. "You manage your own business." Another finger. "You created a life for you and Krista."

"I didn't do it alone."

"But you didn't do it with my help, did you?"

I couldn't deny that. But… "You had Tiff." When I became a parent, I understood what that meant, the commitment and the fear and joy. "And you showed me how to be strong mom."

"Well, I'm glad you got something from me." Her expression softened for a second as her lips curved in a little smile. It softened the lines of her face and made her look younger somehow. "You're a better mom than I ever was, Tressy. But I've got a hard streak that you don't. Let me help you handle this. I can't help but feel some responsibility for this. I put you in a horrible position, then I tried to shine a spotlight on it. You felt you had to run to escape me, and that makes me a horrible mother."

"I didn't run because you were a horrible mother. I ran because…" I sighed, "I don't know. I guess I just needed some time to get my head straight."

"And did you?"

I didn't even have to think about my answer to that. "Actually, I did. And…I met someone who helped me do that."

Mom's brows arched so high, they disappeared beneath her bangs, which she pulled off amazingly well. "Really? Like a male someone? Do you want to talk about it?"

I realized I did want to talk about it. About him. Rowdy.

"I think I screwed everything up, though."

Mom rolled her eyes. "Anything can be fixed. You just have to be willing to do the hard things, sometimes."

"And if I'm not sure I'm able to do the hard thing?"

"You've been doing the hardest thing for years. You're raising a daughter on your own. What could be harder than that?"

"Well, I met this guy…"

Shaking her head, Mom sighed. "Men aren't hard, Tressy. Actually, they're pretty damn easy to figure out. They either want to get you in bed then forget about you, or they want you to take care of them."

"Rowdy isn't like that." I knew that to my bones. "I think…he wants to take care of us." I held up my hand before my mom could open her mouth. "And not in a bad way. He's sweet and sexy and he cares about us—

"And you're not used to that."

"I don't trust myself to know that he's not playing us. I want to trust him, and when I'm with him, I do. I trust him more than anyone, but…"

"Honey, your dad was a miserable SOB who deserves to rot in hell. He's a piece of shit, but he gave me you and your sister, which is the only reason I didn't murder him in his sleep. But not all men are like that."

"I know. Rowdy's nothing like that."

"Then trust your instincts. You've been doing pretty damn well up to now. Though it does seem kind of sudden."

I nodded, worrying my bottom lip between my teeth until it hurt. "It was. Maybe too fast. How fast is too fast?"

"No one can answer that for you, hon. You have to trust your instincts. Mine are shit, especially about men, so I can't help you there. Are you getting *any* red flags?"

"No, and his family's amazing. I think… he's too good to be true."

"Well, in my experience, that's usually the case. I mean, if he seems perfect, that's probably a signal to run. Because no one's perfect."

"He's not perfect. He's a little cocky, but he's not a dick. He's confident but not too much. He's kind and funny and Krista thinks he's the best."

"Then what's the problem?"

"He lives in the middle of Pennsylvania, and I don't see that ever changing."

"And that's a dealbreaker?" Mom's brows rose again. "When you can basically work from anywhere now? And the middle of Pennsylvania is only about three hours from the city. You know that, right?"

Yes, I knew it, and I'd been thinking more about that. Krista and I didn't have to stay in the city. I would still be close enough to drive in for meetings and auditions.

"But Krista loves the city."

"Krista would love living anywhere you are. You're her home, hon, not a city or a building."

I stared at my mom like I'd never seen her before, my lips parted as if I was going to say something, but nothing came out, which made my mom laugh.

"You know, sometimes your mom actually knows her shit."

Shaking my head, I huffed out a laugh. "I never doubted that. You were always the smartest person in the room. And you showed me how to be strong. I want to be strong for Krista."

"I wasn't always the smartest or the strongest. But it's nice to know you think that. And that old saying, with age comes wisdom, that's pretty much true. Which is why you need to have me with you when you go to meet this asshole."

And we were back to the problem I'd been avoiding. "I can't screw this up."

I'd been planning to walk into Rodney Feeney's office with my lawyer and tell him if he mentions my daughter's name in print in any way, shape or form, I'd slap him with a lawsuit so fast, his head would spin. But now I was doubting everything.

My mom smiled again, but, this time, it held a bite. And I pitied anyone who was the recipient of that bite.

"We won't. Now, here's what we're going to do."

CHAPTER TWENTY-SIX

It didn't take me as long as I thought it would to get to New York City, but it still left me with a lot of time to think as I drove.

Traffic along I-78 moved pretty fast and, yeah, I had a lead foot. I also had a reason to get where I was going as fast as possible. I needed to be there for whatever Tressy was dealing with. Show her I'd stand by her side no matter what.

"You did take a shower before you left, right? I mean—"

"Rainy, I know you're just trying to distract me right now, but I still need that address."

Her long-suffering sigh streamed through the car speakers, making me grin even as tension continued to bite at my ass. "All right, I got it. Geez, you're grumpy. I don't know why you just didn't ask Mom for it before you left."

Because I didn't think about it. Hell, I'd almost been to the state line before I realized I didn't know where Tressy lived, except somewhere in Chelsea. But I didn't tell my perfect sister that. She would've had a plan and a backup plan before she left to do what I was going to do.

"I texted you the address."

"Thanks, brat. I appreciate it."

"I'd tell you not to do anything stupid, but you already did that. You let her go without telling her how much you care about her."

"I don't need you to rattle off my faults. And since when did you become an expert in relationships? Last time I checked, you're not in one."

"I'm not ready."

I heard the ache in her voice and my hands clenched the steering wheel until it groaned. "Rain, you just say the word and I will hammer that man into the boards so fucking hard, he won't wake up for a week."

Another sigh. "And you'll be suspended for the season, even in our league. I don't need you to fight my battles, Rowdy." A pause. "But I appreciate the sentiment."

We'd all wondered why Rain had dated Mo Zelinsky, the captain of the Deer Run Stags. The guy was grade-A dick, on and off the ice, and not at all good enough for my baby sister, but she'd told us all to keep the hell out of her business because she was a fucking adult and could do what she wanted.

So we had. And that bastard had broken her heart. Coach was careful to keep me off the ice when he was on, because he knew I'd flatten the guy. And not in any way that would be good for our team.

"But I suggest when you get to Tressy's place, you don't immediately tell her you're gonna fix everything for her."

"I didn't—"

"Rowdy. I know you. Dad's the bull in the china shop, but you're the golden retriever whose tail wags all over the damn place, knocking shit around. You mean well, but you're a fucking hurricane."

"Did you seriously just compare me to a dog?"

"Ugh. Stop. Just listen to me, okay? Don't try to take over. Just be chill."

"Do you know me?"

She snorted, which wasn't as adorable as when Tressy did it. But I was a smart man and kept that to myself.

"You're right. I do. Just be yourself, Rowdy. That's the man she fell for."

I mulled that over after I hung up with Rain, blasting the stereo as I cruised through Jersey and finally into New York through the Lincoln Tunnel. I fucking hated the traffic. All the cars, the buses, the taxis. All the fucking people and none of them looking where they're going or giving a shit if they walk into the street against the lights. I swear it took me longer to drive to the parking garage I found near her address than it did to get here.

But as I walked to her home, I realized that this part of the city wasn't as hectic. Yeah, there were more people on the streets than I think our entire arena held, but most of them looked like they lived here. Not like tourists. They talked and laughed, holding their kids' hands while they hustled to wherever they were going. Little old ladies wheeled shopping baskets down the sidewalks. People dressed for business carried briefcases, weaving around everyone.

It only took a few minutes to walk to her building and, when I found it, I took a few seconds to take it in. It looked like money. Three stories, all brick. Decorative wrought-iron grates over the windows and a wrought-iron fence around a small courtyard in front of the building. The front doors looked intimidating. The building looked pretty as a picture, but no one was getting through those doors without a key or a battering ram.

I'd planned to call her when I got here, ask to see her. Or maybe ask to take her and Krista to dinner. Standing here now, I realized I'd leaped without first looking to see if there was anything to land on.

"Shit."

I stood there for a few minutes, trying not to look like I was stalking the place so someone didn't call the cops on me. I pulled out my phone and opened my texts and was just about to message her when I heard someone shout my name.

"Rowdy! Rowdy! Rowdy! You're here!"

Turning, I grinned when I saw Krista come flying down the sidewalk, an older lady trying her best to keep up.

"Hey, Krista, did you miss me?"

The little girl held out her arms, and I scooped her up so she could hug me tight. Okay, maybe I held her just as tight.

"I'm so happy to see you!" She pulled back so she could pat my cheeks with her pudgy little hands. "*I* didn't want to leave you, but Mamma said she had something she had to do, and Mrs. Santiago took me for brunch, even though it's not Saturday. I'm so glad you're here. Do you want to come in and wait for Mamma to get home?"

"Krista! You can't run off like that. I'm so sorry. She got away from me. You can put her down now. Please."

I understood the fear in Mrs. Santiago's eyes. I was big, and I probably looked like one of the homeless guys on the corner with the too-long hair. At least my clothes were clean.

Krista came to my rescue, her arm around my neck. "It's okay, Mrs. S. He's my new best friend, Rowdy. I told you we stayed with his mom this weekend."

Mrs. Santiago looked like she wasn't buying it, but she didn't look ready to call the police just yet. So I gave her my most charming smile and watched her consider it for a second, before maybe giving me the benefit of the doubt. But probably only because Krista looked absolutely thrilled to see me. At least someone was happy. I really hoped her mom would be too.

"Hello, ma'am. I'm Rowdy Lawrence. I met Krista and Tressy last Thursday, and yes, they stayed with my parents over the weekend." I considered my next words carefully. "And to be honest, as soon as they left, I missed them. And I knew I needed to see them again."

I put every ounce of sincerity into my voice that I possessed. Maybe the fact that every word was true helped because I could see Mrs. Santiago softening. "I really appreciate the fact that you're looking out for Tressy and Krista, and I will be happy to wait at a coffeeshop until Tressy comes home. Or I could take you and Krista for ice cream? I saw a shop just down the block."

Krista immediately began to do a happy wiggle for ice cream, and Mrs. Santiago finally succumbed.

"I suppose we can do that. Just let me text Tressy and let her know what's going on."

"Yes, ma'am. We'll wait right here."

As Mrs. Santiago got out her phone and texted Tressy, Krista told me about her day, how she missed everyone back in St. David, especially Miss Raffi and Rainbow and her new best friend, Mandy. Her rambling conversation soothed something in my chest that I hadn't known was causing the ache until now.

I'd happily let this little girl wrap me around every one of her fingers if her mom gave me another chance.

"Well, you've been vetted." Mrs. Santiago stowed her phone in her purse and finally smiled. "And apparently, she's looking forward to seeing you. You must have made a good impression on her. It usually takes Tressy a few weeks to trust anyone into her little circle."

I offered my arm to Mrs. Santiago—my mom did not raise a heathen, contrary to popular belief—who took it with a knowing grin.

"Let me tell you how I met Tressy and Krista."

TRESSY

. . .

ROWDY WAS HERE. In the city. Apparently, taking my daughter and neighbor for ice cream.

Good thing we'd left Feeney's office, which had turned out to be his apartment in a rundown building in Hell's Kitchen. Feeney was still an asshole, but he'd gotten even sleazier the past few years, if that was possible. He was a few years older than me, which made him early thirties, but he came off with the cynical bite of a seasoned pro.

Until my mom started in on him. I had to admit, she'd had the right approach. I would've come at him differently. I would've attempted to reason with him. Mom went straight for the jugular. Told him flat out she had the contacts to ruin him if he so much as intimated on his site that I had a child, much less mentioned her name. But, if he played nice, she'd be more than happy to help a struggling entrepreneur grow his business. The gossip sites thrived on clickbait headlines, a lot of which were given to them by media relations for the so-called stars. It was a tight ecosystem that thrived on mutual support. And my mom played the game so well.

She impressed the hell out of me. It'd been a while since I'd seen her work, but I don't think I'd ever seen her work like this. She took names and got shit done. I know I'd never given her enough credit for being the badass she was when it came to doing the dirty work behind the scenes.

"Tressy, everything okay? You look a little flushed. I don't want you to worry about anything with that guy. If he even dares to look in your direction again, I'll handle it."

"I'm fine." I motioned to my phone. "Mrs. Santiago just texted. Rowdy's here."

My mom's brows rose. "Huh. Guess you gotta give the guy props for being persistent. He's not a stalker, is he?"

A week ago, that question would've pissed me off. Now I

laughed because I understood my mom a little better. She always thought the worst of people. And sometimes, she was right. Most people in the business were only out for themselves. Friendships were rare, like the friendship Denee and I had had.

Laughing and shaking my head, I said, "No, Mom. He's not a stalker. He's actually a really nice guy. Like, one of the nicest people I've ever known in my life."

"Sounds like he's in the friend zone."

"He's also one of the sexiest men I've ever slept with."

Her mouth pinched like she'd just sucked a lemon. "I'm still your mother, and I don't need to know all the details of your sex life, but I'm glad you found someone. So what are you gonna do about him?"

He was here. He'd come for them. "I think I want to keep him."

"Well, he did come to the big city to track you down and all."

My eyes rolled. "He's not a mountain man, Mom. It's not like he's never been to a city."

"I think I'd like to meet this guy."

"I think I'd like you to."

———

I KNEW EXACTLY where he'd taken Krista and Mrs. Santiago. It was one of Krista's favorite places. Their huge and unusual topping bar had drawn national attention a few years ago, along with their strange flavors, like dill pickle, rosemary and chives, and my favorite, barbeque chips and dip.

The taxi dropped us off a few doors down from the shop, and I slid out of the car, heart racing and a knot in the pit of my stomach. I couldn't tell if it was from nerves or excitement. Probably both.

"Tressy? You okay?"

I looked up and caught sight of myself in the window of a flower shop.

"I look like I got cast as the virgin librarian in a slasher movie. Do I always dress like this?"

"I guess the question should be why do you dress like this?" Mom waved a hand at my reflection. "You're young and beautiful. It's beyond me why you don't flaunt it."

Because I hadn't wanted anyone *to* notice me. Not in the past few years. I'd worried about someone recognizing me and then noticing Krista and maybe taking too close a look at her. At her features. She was practically a replica of her mother, except for the nose. That she must have gotten from her father, whoever he was. Denee had never told me. And it'd been better that way.

"I have to tell him about Krista."

"Do you think it'll make a difference to him? Honestly, at this point, I don't know that I'd bother. You just never know with some people. It could all go bad at some point and blow up in your face."

That was the thing, though. "I trust him. I've never trusted anyone like I trust him."

Mom shrugged. "I'll back your play, but if he gets out of line, I'll be waiting to cut him off at the balls."

I laughed so hard I started to snort, which made my mom laugh, too.

And that's when Rowdy walked out of the shop.

That knot in my gut loosened and all my muscles felt like goo. And I couldn't stop smiling.

I think my mom might've rolled her eyes and huffed out a laugh, but honestly, I wasn't sure of anything but Rowdy.

His smile was all I saw, his eyes crinkled at the corners. He lifted one hand to shove back the thick waves as he walked closer.

"Hi."

I had to unstick my tongue from the top of my mouth before I could answer.

"Hi."

"I'm sorry to show up like this but—"

"I'm glad you did. I'm glad you're here. I…"

…didn't know what else to say. *I missed you. I want you. I'm so glad you're here. Please don't go. Please take us home with you.*

My mom elbowed me discreetly then stuck out her hand.

"Hi, I'm Bebe Meyers. Tressy's mom. It's nice to meet you. And now I'm going to go see my granddaughter while you two… do…whatever."

My mom disappeared, leaving Rowdy and I alone. On a busy Chelsea sidewalk. I realized now that people had to walk around us, and we were getting a few dirty looks.

"Why don't we walk back to my condo, and we can talk there."

"Can we talk while we walk?"

Rowdy gave me another one of those smiles that made my core clench. I think at that moment, I might have agreed to anything just to have him here with me.

"Of course."

We turned and headed back toward my apartment. I expected him to start talking right away, but he stayed silent for those first seconds, and I couldn't take it.

"I'm sorry I left the way I did. I owe you an explanation and –"

"Tressy, you don't *owe* me anything. Would I like to know why you hustled out of town like you did? Yeah, but I hope it wasn't because of anything I did. I know it seems fast, but you fell into my life and my arms, and I'm not ready to let you go. I love you. I know you probably need a little more time but I –"

"I don't need more time. I had a whole night to think about it." I smiled, but I wasn't joking. I was *so* not joking, and I needed him to know that. I grabbed his hand and squeezed, and his smile widened as his hand engulfed mine. It felt right. This felt right. Us. Together.

And trusting him with my biggest secret felt right.

"I love you, too, Rowdy. And yeah, it's way too fast, but it also feels right and—"

He turned on his heel, put his hands on my cheeks and kissed me. And not just a closed mouth, public kiss. This was full tongue and meant to make a statement. I rose up on my toes to put my arms around his neck and clung to him, my lips parting for his tongue to slide along mine. He kissed me with a hunger that was so familiar and so exciting and so wild that I wanted to have him pin me up against a wall and kiss me even harder.

I heard a few whistles from down the street, but I didn't care who saw us. I just wanted to devour him. Or have him devour me.

My hands moved into his hair, rough silk against my skin. I tugged him closer, kissed him deeper and forget where I was.

Until he pulled back, both of us breathing hard and fast.

We didn't speak, but we smiled. Then I grabbed his hand and pulled him back to my home.

———

I HURRIED to open the door to my condo, with his hands on my hips and his mouth kissing a trail from my shoulder to just below my ear. Shivering with heat, my core clenching and needy, I finally got us through the door and locked it behind us.

His head popped up to look around, but we didn't have all day. My mom would keep Krista entertained for at least another half hour, but it was close to dinner and my daughter would need to eat.

And I wanted him.

Crooking my finger at him, I led him to my room. Not bothering to turn on the lights or close the shades, I started to strip, kicking off my sensible pumps and throwing my boring professional clothes all over the floor.

Grinning, he watched me with heat in his eyes while I got naked and sprawled on my bed. I propped myself on my elbows as he pulled his henley over his head and dropped it then unbuttoned his pants and shoved them down his legs with his underwear.

The next thing I knew he was naked and on top of me, his lips on mine, his hands stroking my body anywhere and everywhere he could reach. And mine were doing the same. His skin felt hot to the touch, sleek and muscled. Every place he put his hands, my body arched to give him more access.

But I needed him to give me what I wanted. He didn't make me wait long. He rolled onto his back, handed me a condom. I rolled it on as fast as I could then swung one leg over his hips and took him.

He groaned and reached for my hips, his fingers pressing into my flesh, helping me, though I was doing pretty well on my own.

We moved together, like we'd been doing this forever, like we were made for each other. And maybe we were.

I rode him hard and fast and made him groan out my name as he came, while I convulsed around him and fell forward onto his heaving chest.

"Come back with me, Tressy. To stay."

"I thought you'd never ask."

CHAPTER TWENTY-SEVEN

"DOES IT HURT?"

"Yeah, like a motherfucker. Damn, that kid had a wicked right hook."

I stood naked in front of the mirror in my bathroom after a game against the Anderstown Animals, poking at the bruise on my jaw that was gonna leave a hell of a mark. Tressy leaned against the vanity to my right, her expression sympathetic, but I saw the humor lurking in her eyes.

"He's only twenty years old. And he's bigger than you. Why exactly did you think it was a good idea to try to beat the shit out of each other?"

"The boys needed something to wake them up."

"Well, the crowd certainly loved it."

"Yeah, they're bloodthirsty, but they pay the bills."

I turned then and caught Tressy around the waist, pulling her close and kissing her hard, even though my jaw ached. But it was all worth it when she wrapped her arms around my waist and pressed her body against mine.

"Krista asleep?" I asked when Tressy rested her head on my chest.

"Yep. Practically the second her head hit the pillow. She's becoming quite the little heathen here in St. David."

"Good. She'll fit right in."

Tressy paused for a second, and I knew she was working herself up to say something. She and Krista had fully moved in about a month ago, November second to be exact. My family had gone a little crazy with the holiday decorations for her, but every time I saw her smile when she looked at the advent calendar my dad had made for me three decades ago or wrapped herself in the red and green quilt my mom made for her, it was all worth it.

I probably should worry that Tressy was going to tell me she was leaving, that it wasn't working out here for her, but I knew that wasn't true. We were happy. Hell, I was fucking ecstatic most of the damn time.

"Her mother was like that, before she died."

It took me a second to work out what she was talking about and, when I did, it didn't really surprise me.

"Denee Henning?"

"Yeah." Tressy's voice went soft, but I could hear the love and the loss so clearly. "Denee was a force of nature. But when she got pregnant, she knew there were going to be complications. She already had high blood pressure and she developed preeclampsia, but she was determined to carry to term. I think… she knew she wasn't going to survive."

"No dad in the picture?"

"When she told him, he wanted her to have an abortion. He's married. Has a few kids of his own. I didn't know she was seeing him, and it hurt that she never shared that part of her life with me. Denee had him sign his rights away legally when it was clear he didn't want to be a part of her life. I was in college when she called and asked me to come to India, where she'd spent most of her pregnancy. Of course, I went. She was family and I would've done anything for her. When she died the day after Krista was born, I legally became Krista's mom.

"That's why I couldn't let that sleazebag Feeney anywhere near Krista. I can't even let him say her name. If people found out about Krista and Denee's relationship, it would dig up all kinds of shit that no one needs to know. Someday, I'll tell Krista about Denee, but only when I think she's ready to hear it. Not when someone else forces my hand."

This woman constantly amazed me with her huge heart and her steel spine.

I pulled back and tilted her chin up, to be sure she saw my face when I said, "I'll be by your side to make sure that never happens. And if they don't take the hint after I punch the crap out of them, we'll sic your mom on them. She scares the shit out of me sometimes."

Her laughter made my bones turn to jelly. "I can't say she's all bark and no bite, but I won't let her take a bite out of you. Besides, she seems to like you. And thank you."

"For what?"

"For being you. For being here for me. And for her."

Krista would always have a home with me. Didn't matter who had brought her into the world, she was Tressy's daughter. And if Krista wanted me, she'd be mine, too.

"I love that little girl. I will never do anything to hurt her. And I love you, Tressy. With all my heart."

Tressy's smile widened and softened. "Good, because I love you too. So damn much. I don't plan on going anywhere. Except to bed with you."

I swept her off her feet and took her exactly where she wanted to go.

EPILOGUE

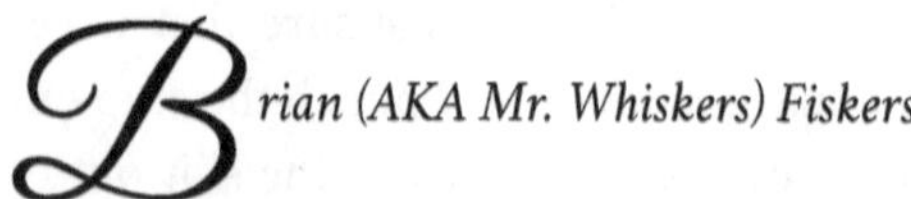

rian (AKA Mr. Whiskers) Fiskers

"I'M NOT HAVING this conversation with you. I told you I don't want to see you again, and I mean it."

"Come on, Rain. I just want to talk. It's not like I'm asking you to go on a date or anything. Of course, you didn't say no the first time."

"Well, I'm not going anywhere with you ever again. And I'm leaving now. Go back to the locker room, Zelinsky. I'm done."

"Hey, don't be like that. I said I was sorry. Do you want me to grovel?"

"Honestly, I don't want anything from you. I just want you to leave me the hell alone."

I'd been heading for the restroom outside the locker room at the St. David arena when I heard Rain Lawrence's voice coming from the shadows farther down the hall.

I stopped, even before I heard the response from Mo. The bastard was the captain of my team, a position he held only because he was the longest-tenured player. I certainly would never vote for the shithead, but I knew him better than most of the other players because I'd been playing with him the longest.

"Damn, no wonder you're single, Rain. Who the hell would want to date a pissy woman like you?"

Yep, that's it. That was the final straw.

I stalked down the hall, not even hearing Rain's response. And I know she had one. But the buzzing in my ears was so fucking loud, I couldn't hear her.

It takes a lot to piss me off, but where Mo's concerned, it takes nothing at all. And the way he just spoke to Rain…

"You need to go now, Zelinsky. And don't ever—"

"Hey, asshole."

Zelinsky turned, a pissed-off snarl on his face.

"Go back to the locker room, Fiskers. This doesn't concern you."

I was a pretty easy-going person most of the time. Everyone knew that. Mo thought it meant he could walk all over me. The fucker had never realized I didn't give a shit what he thought or how he thought about me.

What I did care about was how he treated Rain.

Ignoring him, I looked at Rain. Her jaw looked ready to crack, she held it so tightly, and her wide, midnight-dark eyes sparked with fury.

She was so damn pretty, she tied my tongue in knots. Always had. And gave me a fucking hard whenever she looked my way. Which had never been all that often.

"Rain." I made sure she looked at me before I said, "You okay?"

Zelinsky's eyes narrowed, and his nose wrinkled. I know most women thought he was good-looking. At least, he got laid enough that I figured they had to seduced by the looks because once you got to know him, he was a pig. Which was appropriate because, right now, he kind of looked like a pig.

"What the *fuck*? Why wouldn't she be okay? What the hell are you implying?"

Rain's eyes met mine, and I saw pure feminine rage and an intense frustration.

"Rain?"

"I'm fine." She sounded like she was speaking through clenched teeth.

Zelinsky sneered at me. "See. She's fine. You don't need to play hero. You can—"

I cold-cocked him. He never saw it coming. Probably never expected it, especially not from me.

My fist swung out and connected with his jaw hard enough that he went down, landing on his side, his arms only just preventing his head from hitting the cement floor.

I didn't care if the coach benched me. Hell, at that moment, I didn't care if the team cut me and black-balled me. I only cared about the fact that he'd tried to intimidate Rain. To coerce her into doing something she obviously didn't want to do.

Most people thought Zelinsky was cocky but toothless. I'd never trusted the bastard, and he'd just shown I was right not to.

"Are you okay?" I asked Rain again.

Her gaze dropped to Zelinsky on the floor, her jaw slowly unclenching as Zelinsky shook his head, like I might've rattled his brains a little. Served him fucking right.

Then her gaze lifted back to me. The anger was still there, and the frustration. But she looked at me like she was seeing me for the first time. Or maybe just seeing me in a different light.

Stepping around Zelinsky, she stopped by my side, close enough that the light flowery scent she wore drifted into my nose and, yep, my cock started to harden.

"I'm fine," she said. "I appreciate your concern, but I could've handled him."

Maybe, maybe not. Seemed prudent not to say that. Instead, I nodded.

"Yes, ma'am."

Then she looked into my eyes and smiled.

And I knew something so surely, I could feel it in my bones.

I had it bad for Rain Lawrence.

And her brother, Rebel, would pummel me if I so much as touched her.

It'd be so worth it…

RAIN AND BRIAN's story will be here soon.

Rock My Heart

WICKED & CHARMING
Seducing Whitney
Claiming Ellie
Sharing Brianna

INDECENT
An Indecent Proposition
An Indecent Affair
An Indecent Arrangement
An Indecent Longing
An Indecent Desire

LOVERS UNDERCOVER
Lovers & Lies
Sinners & Secrets
Beauty & Brains

DIVINE DESIRES
Dark Desires at Dawn
Rough Caress of Midnight
Double Fantasies at Twilight
Enchanting Temptations in Shadow

DARKLY ENCHANTED
Spell Bound
Moon Bound
Twice Bound

MAGICAL SEDUCTION
Seduced by Magic

Seduced in Shadow

Seduced & Ensnared

Seduced & Enchanted

Seduced by Chaos

Seduced by Danger

Moonlight Seduction

LUCANI LOVERS

Kiss of Moonlight

Visions of Moonlight

Edge of Moonlight

Temptation in Moonlight

Grace in Moonlight

Shades of Moonlight

ABOUT THE AUTHOR

Stephanie Julian is a USA Today and New York Times best-selling author of contemporary and paranormal romance.

Visit her website at www.stephaniejulian.com for more information.